## Abigail Did Not Expect The Involuntary Jolt That Her Heart Took as She Saw Jeremy, Standing Tall and Strong . . .

He pulled her into his arms despite her struggles against him. Before she had time to protest, his mouth clasped her own as tightly as his body held hers to him. Soon her head spun from the heat of his body and insistent soft lips. She responded despite herself and allowed her lips to answer his in a way she'd never known.

Her breath came strangely heavy as he pulled away and looked down upon her, still holding her. "Almost as good as my dead brother? Better, perhaps?" he whispered.

*Dear Reader,*

*We, the editors of Tapestry Romances, are committed to bringing you two outstanding original romantic historical novels each and every month.*

*From Kentucky in the 1850s to the court of Louis XIII, from the deck of a pirate ship within sight of Gibraltar to a mining camp high in the Sierra Nevadas, our heroines experience life and love, romance and adventure.*

*Our aim is to give you the kind of historical romances that you want to read. We would enjoy hearing your thoughts about this book and all future Tapestry Romances. Please write to us at the address below.*

The Editors
Tapestry Romances
POCKET BOOKS
1230 Avenue of the Americas
Box TAP
New York, N.Y. 10020

# Daughter
## of
## Liberty

*Johanna Hill*

**A TAPESTRY BOOK**
PUBLISHED BY POCKET BOOKS NEW YORK

An *Original* publication of TAPESTRY BOOKS

A Tapestry Book published by
POCKET BOOKS, a division of Simon & Schuster, Inc.
1230 Avenue of the Americas, New York, N.Y. 10020

ISBN 978-1-4516-8802-3

First Tapestry Books printing June, 1984

10 9 8 7 6 5 4 3 2 1

For Lanny Aldrich, Ann Vigliotti, Dana Bryan and my mother, who know why; For Linda Marrow and Patrick O'Connor for making it possible; And always for Joey Willens Widzer and John Hill, who were there *before* I was, waiting for me to become.

Thank you all.

## ACKNOWLEDGMENTS

The following works were especially helpful to me in my researching of colonial Boston and I thank the authors of these works:

*Colonial America;* second edition; by Oscar Theodore Barack, Jr. Macmillan Publishing Co., Inc. 1968
*Cities in Revolt: Urban Life in America 1743–1776;* by Carl Bridenbaugh, Knopf, Inc. 1955
*A New Age Begins: A People's History of the American Revolution;* Volume I; by Page Smith, McGraw-Hill Book Co. 1976

Of special value in its chronicling of the Stamp Act and the mob action which I wove into *Daughter of Liberty* was:

*The Stamp Act Crisis: Prologue to Revolution;* by Edmund S. and Helen M. Morgan, Macmillan Publishing Co., Inc. 1962

# TO MY DEAR AND LOVING HUSBAND

## by
## ANNE BRADSTREET

If ever two were one, then surely we,
If ever man were loved by wife, then thee.
If ever wife was happy in a man,
Compare with me, ye women, if you can.
I prize thy love more than whole mines of gold,
Or all the riches that the East doth hold.
My love is such that rivers cannot quench,
Nor ought but love from thee give recompense.
Thy love is such I can no way repay;
The heavens reward thee manifold, I pray.
Then while we will, in love let's so persevere,
That when we live no more we may live ever.

# Daughter
# of
# Liberty

# Chapter One

## Boston—May, 1765

"JANE, I HARDLY UNDERSTAND THE NECESSITY OF SUB-jecting my hands to this harsh lye soap when they will be concealed in white gloves all afternoon," Abigail complained.

"They will not be concealed when you are at your spinning wheel on the Common, amongst friends and neighbors," Jane countered tartly, then looked to Abigail's hands covered with thick suds. "Rinse them, if you please," Jane ordered.

Dressed in her muslin stays and hoop petticoat, Abigail stood at the washbasin and swirled her hands in the heated well water. When the last of the suds was washed away, she removed her hands and examined her slender fingers. The printer's ink stains were barely visible and she secretly admired the fresh whiteness of her hands. During the course of the week as she wrote and assisted her brother, Levi, in setting

1

the type and inking the large press for Friday's issue of the *Boston Word*, she had neither the time nor inclination to think of such vanities. However, still disgruntled at having to leave her commentary but midway composed in order to attend the Spinning Celebration, she refused to reveal her pleasure to Mrs. Jane Stewart, who at the moment was scrutinizing Abigail's hands. Jane's kindly face was set in a stubborn expression that matched her own displeasure, Abigail had no doubts.

With a shake of her head, Jane turned her stout back to Abigail and walked to the bed. As she began to ready Abigail's apple green homespun dress and matching bonnet, laid out beside her stockings and gloves, Jane was able to relax her face from its forced sternness which she had assumed to match Abigail's own obstinacy. For despite Abigail's headstrong and stubborn nature, no one knew better than Jane how kind and sensitive Abigail was and how deeply she pained when her stubbornness or flair of temper injured the feelings of someone she loved. Cajoling Abigail would have little effect. Jane knew she had to meet Abigail's will with her own when it came to matters of principle or obligation—especially since Abigail had assumed the printing business and newspaper after her father, John's, tragic death.

Jane knew that Abigail hated spinning as she hated most domestic chores. Moreover, Abigail saw her attendance at the Celebration as frivolous, despite its patriotic nature, compared to those essays she wrote expressing alarm and displeasure with the Parliament's latest acts to bring the colonies to their knees. It was useless to tell Abigail that an afternoon among good company in the warm May sun would not alter the fate of Boston. She was her father's daughter, most certainly, in a way that Levi had never been his father's son. Yet Jane was certain that if John Peabody were still alive, he would be equally adamant about getting his lovely Abigail to the Common this afternoon, especially if he had learned, as Jane had at the market this morn, that Jeremy Blackburn had returned from England. As certain as she was that God watched over them, was Jane that Jeremy would present himself at the Celebration. Once he again set his eyes upon Abigail's shining red hair and lovely large green eyes . . .

"I do wish you would go along with Katie instead and leave me to my work," Abigail complained once more, as she lathered and scrubbed her hands again. She knew better than to voice further complaints when she had already tried Jane's large reserve of patience, but her obstinacy pushed her on. "I know that it's the fifteenth year since the formation of the Spinning Society, but I have last year's column. All I need do is change the names to those who shall win this year, though I doubt if the names will *ever* change. The same can not be said about my report on the latest outrages of Governor Bernard. That man's audacity to urge the Assembly to humbly accept the advent of the scurrilous Stamp Act! So why should I while away the afternoon spinning, for which I have little talent and less inclination—"

Jane turned swiftly, despite her bulk. Her doe-like hazel eyes darkened with anger, causing Abigail to instantly regret her words, as heartfelt as they were. "Enough, *Mistress Peabody*," Jane declared. "Kindly

3

close your mouth and apply your wrath onto those hands." With one long scathing look, Jane then turned away again.

Abigail refrained from releasing the laughter that bubbled in her throat whenever Jane sardonically addressed her by proper title. For in truth, Mrs. Jane Stewart was far more than housekeeper, and had been most of Abigail's life. Mrs. Stewart was a widow who had arrived from Ulster, in Northern Ireland, as an indentured servant for the Peabodys when Abigail was five, fifteen years before. That was the same year that Abigail's mother, Mary, had died in childbirth, the boychild stillborn as well. Levi was ten at the time. Jane Stewart became as much a mother to them, especially to little Abigail, as if she had borne Abigail herself. When Jane's years of indenture passed, she stayed on as a hired housekeeper, but was actually a member of the family, for by then none of them, least of all Abigail's father, could have done without her ministerings and love.

It had often puzzled Abigail as to why her father had not married this strong, kind-faced, and caring woman. She knew that most widowers married within a year. Many of their neighbors had taken two or three new wives after each died in childbirth or illness. Once, Abigail had broached the subject with her father. He had treated her question with the dignity and respect that was always the hallmark of their close relationship. He had explained that his love for her mother was so special and rare that it would be unfair to offer any other woman merely the shadow of that love.

4

Unconsciously, Abigail scrubbed more ferociously as she fought back the tears that welled behind her eyes. Even two years later, it was difficult for her to endure the grief of her loss, or to remember the nightmarish circumstances of his death in that terrible fire that had destroyed their house as well on that cold winter evening. She had done the only thing she knew—thrown herself into her work and hoped that she could carry on the pride of her father's life, his *Boston Word*, with the dignity and respect that his paper had engendered in Boston during the ten years he had published it. It had been a constant struggle, but she hoped that her father looked down upon her earnest attempt from his place in heaven and smiled at her.

Abigail rinsed her hands again. Finally they were immaculate. When she looked up, Jane was staring at her with a softness in her eyes that belied her impatient stance, with strong, stubby hands on broad hips. As usual, Jane knew what pained her without words having to cross between them. Abigail dried her hands and then walked to Jane and planted a kiss on her cheek.

"You are a sweet girl, even if you are enough to shake the calmest soul at times," Jane said in her lilting Northern Irish accent that had not changed from the day she landed in the Boston Harbor. "It is just that I worry about you, shouldering your dear father's work, may he rest in peace, while Levi spends far too much time in the harbor taverns, filling his head with stories of the sea. Though I don't say that he isn't as loyal a brother to you as one could hope for. It's just that he's as much a dreamer as you are a doer. You should be thinking about things besides politics. About finding a fine husband and having little ones of your own, like sweet Katie."

"Oh Jane, I think that the babies you will see will be Katie's. I am already an old maid, or haven't you heard so? In fact there is a new word they have begun to use—spinster, from those ladies whose training at the spinning school have led them to lives of fruitful work when the fates didn't bring them a pledge of marriage—"

"Nonsense! Do not speak such foolishness in this house. I will not hear it and I will certainly live to see many babies from you over the years!"

Abigail wiggled her long, tapered fingers before Jane's face to break the conversation. "Are these not the hands of a fine lady, Mrs. Stewart?" she teased, and broke into a broad smile.

"Aye, a lady to be sure, Mistress Peabody," Jane replied in kind. "Why I do believe that you could sashay into the governor's house up on the hill with those lily-white hands. I am certain he would be most happy to receive you after having read your latest diatribe against the mother country," she stated with a sniff, but her eyes twinkled. "Now, my fine lady, if you would honor me by allowing me to aid you with your fine silken gown?"

"The one with the French laced sleeves and bodice, of course?"

"Certainly, for I dare say it is too warm for the flowered brocade," Jane added with a playfully pretentious air.

With a laugh, Abigail stepped into her homespun dress and Jane began to fasten the backhooks as Abigail stood before the looking glass.

"Did I hear words of silk and brocade gowns?" a smiling Katie called as she edged through the doorway, protectively covering her mound of belly with one hand and carrying one-year-old baby, Sarah, with the other against her shoulder. She rested herself heavily in the rocker chair. By summer's end, she and Levi would have a new babe.

"We were just sporting, as you could guess," Abigail spoke to her smiling, sweet sister-in-law. Through the looking glass, Abigail noted that Katie looked paler than usual. Already her delicate blondeness, bright blue eyes, and girl's pink-cheeked coloring had begun to fade, though Katie was not yet turned seventeen. But she was a good wife to Levi. In the past two years since their marriage, Levi's green eyes, so much like Abigail's own, had lost a bit of their wanderlust, though he still spent what pleasure time he had by the wharf where the largest masted vessels brought their cargoes from the farthest ports. Abigail thought of Katie as a sister-in-blood rather than as marrying kin.

"Levi and Nathan have taken our spinning wheels to the Common," Katie announced, her pale eyes brightening with excitement. "Oh, I do so love the Spinning holiday!" she exclaimed as she rocked the sleeping Sarah in her arms. "I asked Levi to place the wheel 'neath the oak tree where we have agreed to meet Polly Smithers and Elizabeth and Penelope Osborn." Katie watched as Abigail turned from the looking glass and impatiently shuffled her feet as Mrs. Jane stretched to afix her bonnet to her thick hair that shone crimson in the sunlight streaming through the small bedroom window. It was a shame, thought Katie, that Abigail's glorious locks had to be tied away from her face for propriety. In the evenings she had often brushed her sister-in-law's waist-long hair before they retired to bed, although recently, with the babe inside of her, it had become too wearying to raise her arms at length.

"Now, if you'll place your stockings and shoes on those bare feet, the two of you might still reach the Common before the contest begins," Jane said. "I did try to hurry her along, Mistress Katie, but I found Abigail tarrying with her hands blackened with ink—"

"I was trying to continue upon my essay—" Abigail started to defend, but then became contrite. How selfish of her. She knew how Katie so anticipated the Spinning Celebration. "I shall hurry, Katie, and we shall arrive in plenty of time for you to win first prize this year that should have been yours, by all rights, last spring!"

"I was honored to have taken second place," Katie demurred.

"Aye, but if Gwendolyn Corey had not the advantage of such a fine London-made wheel, there is no one in Boston who could have even matched your facility! See, I am wearing the dress and bonnet created by your fine hand." Abigail preened a bit, for modest Katie's pleasure. "Do I not look as well as the finest lady?" she asked, her green eyes sparkling.

"Oh yes, sister, you look so very beautiful!"

"Beautiful, I don't know, but it is a rare pleasure to see your sister-in-law in a frock that is not dull and ink-stained, that much I'll say," Jane sniffed. Then she turned from Abigail to give Katie a wink.

Katie watched Abigail quickly roll on her stockings and fix her feet into her fine buckled shoes usually worn for church. Beautiful indeed was Abigail. The soft, green, square-necked dress flattered not only her vivid coloring, but set off her graceful white neck as well. The bonnet likewise framed Abby's delicate heart-shaped face, large sea-green eyes, and high cheekbones. Ezra's cruel words of the other evening stung at Katie once more. For Levi's friend to call Abigail a "cold-blooded old virgin" was more than hard-hearted, even if she were past twenty. But then, Katie remembered that Ezra had tried to court Abigail years before to no avail. They were drunken words, spoken from a spurned suitor, Katie reminded herself. For she could not bear an unkind word about her wonderful Abigail. Without Abigail to see her through the thirty-six-hour torturous birthing of baby Sarah, Katie was convinced that she would have given in to the calling of heaven.

"Let me take the babe," Jane said as she lifted Sarah from Katie's arms, bringing Katie back to the moment. "Be sure to fetch the basket with luncheon in the kitchen. Then the two of you be off!" Jane ordered. "And do try to keep Abigail at her wheel, as arduous a task as that might be, if you might, Katie. For knowing this one as we do, we can be certain that she will otherwise manage to be nosying about among the gentlemen busying themselves at their lawn games and whatnot, for more political notions to write in her newspaper."

Abigail opened her mouth to protest, for surely Jane knew that she would conduct herself as a lady. Instead she broke into rich laughter. Once again, Jane had pronounced the simple truth.

# Chapter Two

ABIGAIL FELT MORE LIGHTHEARTED THAN SHE HAD IN some time. The sky, which she seldom had time to gaze at during daylight, was a bright blue with a few puffed white clouds that complemented the yellow sun high in the sky. Abigail glanced about her with an admiring smile. The girls and women, dressed in their prettiest homespun dresses as they sat at their wheels, painted a pretty picture: awash in sky blue, lemon, scarlet, green, dove, and lilac. Homespun dresses and leather working pants for the men were the order of the day, part of the colonial expression of protest against England, as was the boycotting of other English goods besides wool. Even those women who had some fine silk daydresses had packed them into their pine trunks, not to be worn until England ceased to harass its loyal but overburdened colonial subjects.

Of course, the loyalists, most of the richest aristocrats and merchants in Boston, continued to wear their finest silks, velvets, and laces imported from England and drink their Madeira and other imported wines, as they did now, sitting together across the Common under another clump of fine trees. Already neighbor had been turned against neighbor, and Abigail knew that anger against the colonial loyalists grew each day. Thus far it had been expressed in words and barbs, but she feared that unless the Stamp Act was repealed before it was to become effective in November, the anger would ignite sooner than later into explosions with tragic effects. Levi, who sat among the sailors and manual laborers each night in the taverns by the wharf had already reported a growing anger amongst the men without suffrage or means, who listened hard to the words of patriots like James Otis and Sam Adams when they spoke of the rights of Englishmen and the natural rights of men.

Everyone listened, even the Tories—perhaps they most of all, she suspected. Since the winter of '64 there had been nothing but foreboding talk about the odious Parliamentary acts that would bring further hardships to the colonies, already suffering from hard times since the Treaty of '63 that ended the French and Indian Wars. For despite the threat of Indian attacks to those who ventured to the frontiers, the war had been a boon to Boston's merchants and shipbuilders. Then, last April, the worst fears had been realized with the passage of the Sugar Act and the introduction of the vice-admiralty court in Halifax, where innocent merchants and shipowners would be forced to travel to defend themselves against charges of smuggling or failing to declare their full cargo— charges corrupt customs officials could make with apparent impunity since they would be exempt from the jurisdiction of the colonial courts. Moreover, those accused would not have an opportunity to be judged by a jury of their peers since the admiralty courts functioned under the principles of Roman rather than common law. As if there were not already enough hardship and lack of work in the Massachusetts Bay Colony, especially in Boston, now there would be the Stamp Act that would be not a tariff but an illegal tax placed upon the colonists by the Parliament that didn't represent their interests—

"Abigail," said Penelope Osborn, who nudged her from her seat at the wheel beside Abigail's. "Did you hear tell that Mary Carter and Adam Willis bundled, but then Adam reneged until it was said that Mary was with child?" Penelope giggled. "Naturally they have issued a bann announcing their marriage. Did you not print it in Friday's paper yourself?"

"Yes, I did. However I did not know the circumstances. I wish them the best, as I'm sure you do," Abigail answered. Penelope was a notorious gossip, as was her mother. Abigail disdained such trivia, but on the other hand, after an hour she was already bored by the spinning which she found tedious. Yet she dared not interrupt Katie, who worked industriously with quiet concentration. Just as Jane had warned, Abigail was ready to rise and wander about. Sitting for too long a time made her disquiet. In fact, the walk from their house and shop, in the bright noonday sun of this pleasing May day, through the twisting streets of town to the green lawns of the vast Common had exhilarated her. Abigail remembered how, as a girl, she would explore the cobblestoned streets of Boston, climb the hills, and inevitably wind up on the quiet marsh by the river. There she would lie in the grass and read or imagine all sorts of adventures, the cool breeze of the river blowing through her hair as she would remove her cap with little fear of being discovered. For it was only her brother Levi who knew of her hiding place. And thank the Good Lord that Levi did. For it was Levi who had saved her almost five years before. But she would not think about that terrifying afternoon and all the horrific events that ensued because of it.

"Mistress Abigail." Again a nudge, this time from the small hand of Nathan Smith, brought her back. "May I have a piece of meat? I am so hungry," Nathan asked as politely as his hunger would allow.

"Certainly, Nathan," she said and smiled at the orphan boy they had taken into their home as an apprentice only months before her father died. "Allow me to prepare it for you," she offered, as much to help the ten-year-old, black-eyed boy who was like a young brother to her as to have a reason to stretch. "Are you thirsty as well, Nathan?" she inquired, and smiled as he nodded. "Then come sit upon the blanket and eat and drink," she said as she rose and tousled his thick dark hair. "Katie, would you care to stop for a moment and eat or drink?" Abigail asked, already knowing that Katie, intent on her work, would decline.

"Thank you, sister, but no," Katie replied with a quick smile, and returned her eyes to her work.

Abigail fixed the boy a plate of dried beef and boiled yams. She herself felt little hunger yet. Then she returned to her wheel.

"Did you hear tell that Sir Bentley Blackburn was appointed to the vice-admiralty court in Halifax?"

Penelope continued as soon as Abigail was seated. "My father says good riddance to him! But he heard tell that Jeremy Blackburn has returned from London—" Penelope's brown eyes widened. "Oh, I am so terribly sorry, Abigail. It has been so long—I mean I'd quite forgotten—I truly didn't mean," she continued to fluster.

"Pay it no mind, Penelope," Abigail tried to assure the girl who was sincerely distraught. Abigail was determined that her countenance would not give away the disquietude she felt at hearing Jeremy's name. Abigail had assumed that he was in London to stay. Why had Jeremy returned to Boston? She could not bring herself to ask, for her hands on the wheel shook too hard for her to rely upon the power of an even voice.

When she met Penelope's face again she saw that the girl had turned ashen. "Penelope, truly, it is no offense—"

"I certainly hope not, because Jeremy Blackburn is walking our way with Mistress Belinda Wattington, in her fine silk gown, on his arm. I say it is much nerve for the Tories to show forth their face at this Spinning Celebration that stands for all they so disdain in Boston," she whispered.

"I doubt muchly that Mr. Blackburn will actually approach us," Abigail whispered back, forcing herself to refrain from looking in the direction of Penelope's vision. Curiously, Penelope returned her eyes to her spinning and was mute.

"Good afternoon, Mistress Peabody," the unmistakable voice spoke, producing quivers up her spine despite the warmth of the afternoon.

Abigail turned her face to his direction and forced her hands to continue their work on the wheel. "Good afternoon, Mr. Blackburn," Abigail answered with all the formality she could summon, for the first time grateful for the demands of the spinning wheel upon her feet that were moving more swiftly than they had all afternoon. She hoped that her smile was polite but did not betray the tremors that continued to course through her.

He offered his hand which propriety forced her to accept. The touch of his flesh burned her and she feared that her own was moist from nervousness. Nevertheless, Jeremy held her hand in his own for a moment longer than fashion dictated, until he pulled his away with a deft motion of raising it to his brow and brushing away some unseen particle. Abigail's lips began to quiver so apparently that they moved her to conversation she hadn't intended to make. "You are looking well, Mr. Blackburn. Obviously London has been most hospitable to you these past years." She did her best to merely skim his face rather than to look into his eyes while he deemed not to reply to her comment.

Her first perusal proclaimed it the same face of the man she had loved so deeply five years before, but a face made stronger and more manly with the deepening lines around his mouth and the furrow of his forehead. At thirty-one he had reached his prime, and she would have noticed him as a fine, aristocratic gentleman had she never laid eyes on him before. Finally she found the courage to look him directly in the eye. Her stomach lurched. For the man who stared back at her with a steely, cold gaze was not the Jeremy she had known and had secretly dreamed of these past five years. The man who stood before her, his golden-brown eyes darkened with contempt, could have been Damon, his twin, risen from the dead. Abigail's head began to spin. Quickly she turned away, under the pretext of adjusting the flax on her wheel. With a peripheral glance, she noted that he had turned his back to her and seemed to be searching the small groups across the Common. That was when it occurred to her for the first time that Belinda, daughter of Lord Wattington, himself a member of the Royal Governor's council, as Sir Bentley Blackburn was, was not at his side. Abigail followed Jeremy's gaze until she too spotted pretty Belinda, in her scarlet silken daydress, many yards away, obviously chatting with the Rivington sisters, whose father was a colonial official partial to the Crown.

Jeremy turned back to Abigail, apparently satisfied. "I apologize, but I did want to be certain that Lady Wattington was happily preoccupied. We are about to announce our engagement," he said with a smile she knew was meant to knife her—and it did, though she hoped her face showed no reflection of her heart.

"I had heard you were betrothed to a fine lady in London a year or so ago. I presume that you did not marry after all."

"No, I didn't," he answered curtly, his proprietary smile vanishing for a moment. "I have just returned this past Thursday, Mistress Peabody, so time has not allowed me to pay a proper courtesy call to your father, Goodman Peabody," he stated respectfully, although his eyes once again spoke to the contrary, gleaming more coldly than she'd believed possible.

Abigail quickly remembered the close relationship Jeremy had shared with her father when she was still a young girl. But before she could reply he continued, "You see, I have been appointed by the Crown to review the colonial papers for libelous and seditious material, and I have been apprised that the *Boston Word* should be summarily reviewed. So I will stop by on Monday morn and make an appointment with your father to discuss the matter."

So he didn't know, Abigail realized. She forced herself to speak with a quiet dignity, holding back the tears that might be interpreted as a plea for compassion she did not want from this man who was now truly a stranger to her. "I'm afraid that you will have to take up your discord with me, then. For my father died in a fire two winters ago last."

For a moment the frost that filled his eyes and froze her, melted, and she watched them turn the golden brown she remembered, watched them soften with genuine surprise and what she read as true sadness. In that moment, he was the Jeremy she had loved, the sensitive, gentle, and caring man, as different from his identical twin, Damon, who was all cunning and evil, as two beings could be.

"I am truly sorry, Abigail," he said softly. "I did not know."

His kind words and warm eyes brought the sorrow to her afresh, and although she tried with all her might to blink back the tears, her eyes filled and blurred her vision until he was awash of color in his blue velvet

18

coat and silken shirt. She swallowed hard and when she saw him clearly again, the Jeremy who had reappeared for a moment was as dead and buried as his brother, Damon.

"I too know what it is like to have lost a loved one," he said with a bitter note in his voice second only to the scorching bitterness in his eyes.

"Aye . . . I know that."

"Who better than you should know?" he replied with a sardonic grin that pierced her as it had five years before when she listened to his accusations in silent shock. "In any case," he continued, "I shall have to then arrange an appointment with your brother, Levi, I presume, which is all the more to my liking." He chuckled malevolently.

So that was it! A bitterness struck her heart and darkened her green eyes to the color of a stormy sea. He intended to seek the revenge he still believed was his due against Levi. That was why her paper, the smallest in Boston, would be the first to fall under Royal attack.

"Your business, I believe, is solely with me, Mr. Blackburn," she said, anger leveling her voice and giving it resonance for the first time since they had begun to speak. "Levi is master printer, but it is I who write the words. I am the legal and rightful publisher of the *Boston Word*, sir. So should you label the truth I print as libelous, you will have to refer your complaints to me alone."

"Libelous and seditious," he answered shortly, seemingly taken aback but quickly recovering. "But far be it for me to spoil your Saturday Spinning

Celebration with such matters. Then Monday morning at half-past the hour of nine would meet with your approval?"

"That will be fine, sir."

"Good, then . . ." He glanced again to Belinda Wattington, who now stood staring at them, hands on hip and face set in obvious annoyance. "I believe my lady awaits me, Mistress Peabody. Good day." He bowed, but even his bow was ripe with sarcasm. Then he turned on his heels and strode away.

Abigail watched him, barely noting the blue of his fine velvet coat and the ruffle of lace flowing from his wrists, or the tight satin breeches and sashed garters above his stockinged calves that strode quickly away from her. For in her mind's eye she saw his face—his thick, gold-flecked chestnut hair, broad forehead, and straight brow that framed his russet eyes, dark with mistrust and anger. The eyes that had once filled her with such happiness as they shone golden and full of tenderness. She saw his full mouth tightened into a thin smile that was belied by the pulsating muscle at his jaw. The mouth that but once she had kissed, the chin whose cleft her fingers had timidly traced, but once. Just once and yet forever in her dreams. Now his presence evoked a quivering inside that felt like fear but which she sensed was different, although she couldn't name it.

Five years before, she, shy of sixteen but a most proper age to be courted and wed, and Jeremy, already a fine man at twenty-five, had spoken of vows of love. Jeremy had been the man she intended to love and honor as she had loved and honored none but her father—until that afternoon in her hiding place at the river. There, her girlish dreams had died, as did Damon, two nights later.

Now, Jeremy Blackburn had returned to Boston and all the memories, all the shame and horror washed over her anew. Jeremy had returned, perhaps more her enemy than when he'd left. But she feared more for Levi than herself. Better Jeremy should seek his imagined retribution by attacking her through the legal weapons of the Crown. That she would handle, somehow. But if he and Levi were to confront one another with their shared and festering hatred, the consequences might be too dire to contemplate with less than terror.

"Abigail . . . Damn you, Abigail!" Jeremy swore beneath his breath as he strode in Belinda's direction. For years her face had haunted his dreams. How many ladies had lain in his arms, their bodies bursting with ripe passion, while he tried to vanquish her face, her voice, her silken thick crimson hair from his memory? And he had, or so he had thought. For his love had been a conjured vision of a girl as pure and innocent as her beauty was arousing—but that had been no more than the spell she had cast over him. For Damon had proved her otherwise. Damon had sworn to it upon the Holy Bible.

Even then, Jeremy had accused his twin of blasphemy, finally forcing Damon to crush him with all the weight of the hideous truth until Jeremy could no longer clutch at his brother's throat. Until he could no longer fight back the tears that wracked his broad frame as he listened to Damon prove to him that all he had believed was lie and pretense. For had Abigail not

21

lain with Damon the many times he claimed, how could Damon know of the small, heart-shaped birth-spot beneath her round white breast? How could he have even spoken of how Abigail would run her tapered finger down the cleft of his chin and sigh with pleasure, as she had done but once with Jeremy himself, that one moment he had never spoken of to Damon?

Damon had met Abigail repeatedly at their secret lovemaking spot beneath the oak tree by the river. The same spot she had so innocently brought him to but once, and where he was to have met her that same afternoon until she apparently decided that she preferred to spend those hours with Damon in wanton lovemaking rather than with himself in pretended chastity and innocence.

So Damon had met her. But this time there was to be no joining of the flesh. Damon had told her that since Jeremy had announced their impending marriage in secret to him, that he could allow the deception to continue no further. If Abigail were to break off her intended marriage to his brother, Damon would allow her to preserve her pretense of virginity and spare her the shame of exposure. Otherwise, he would be forced to tell his brother the truth, as hurtful to both of them as that would be.

At this ultimatum, Damon said, her green eyes grew as evil as the devil's brew and she leaped upon him like a wildcat, ripping at Damon's eyes. This is how Levi came upon them. Levi pulled her off of him with labored difficulty.

Then the brother and sister concocted their tale in a

vain attempt to save her from the shame she'd reaped upon herself and to keep Jeremy within her web.

"I will have my fine, rich husband and live in that glorious house! I shall be a lady and you will not stop me, Damon Blackburn!" she had sworn, as Damon recounted. Even now, these words repeated in Jeremy's head, burning his brain as they had the first time he had heard them.

Two nights after Jeremy lost his heart and soul, he lost his flesh and blood, his best friend, his twin, Damon—by Levi Peabody's hand. The venal colonial jury had proclaimed Levi innocent.

Jeremy had told himself that he had reluctantly returned to Boston upon his father's bidding. But from the moment he set eyes upon Abigail he knew the truth. He would have her once, then discard her. He would see to it that her paper was closed by order of the Royal Council. And Levi. After he took Levi's sister and made sure that Levi learned of it, he would avenge his brother's murder. The time for retribution had been delayed far too long.

Jeremy laughed as he approached Belinda, his future wife. He had almost allowed himself to be taken in by the tears that had filled Abigail's eyes. But she could fool him no more.

# Chapter Three

JOHN DAVIS, THE SMITHY, ARRIVED BACK FROM NEW York today," Levi said, then forked another bite of his giblet pie, relishing his Saturday dinner. Baby Sarah lay between Katie and himself in the crib he had built for her. Nathan sat on Katie's other side and ate with the speed of a boy readying to grow into a man. Levi looked from Abigail, whose keen eyes waited for him to finish chewing and tell her what he had learned, to Jane, who then rose to ready the next bowl of food. "He told us that folks there are as outraged as here. He heard tell that Virginia's House of Burgesses was already meeting and intended to tell King 'Georgie Three' and the Parliament that taxation without representation denies us our rights as Englishmen. John inquired as to whether we would shut down the newspaper in protest, or whether the cost of the stamped paper after November would be our damnation—"

"And you answered nay to both inquiries I may rest

assured?" Abigail interjected, her green eyes bright with indignation.

"Aye, I did. Though the truth be that I don't know how we'll manage to meet the cost of the stamps, especially with the restraint on bills of tender since last fall. We will have to pay the tax in gold or silver, and unless you've hidden a cache somewhere in this house—"

"I do not wish to hear of it, Levi. The Stamp Act will be repealed, for Parliament will be forced to recognize that they do not have the power to tax us internally. William Pitt and Isaac Barre have stated such themselves in Parliament, have they not? For these wise and just English gentlemen know that they cannot bleed these loyal colonies to the bone and expect us to accept tyranny on humbled knees, which is more than our *esteemed* Governor Bernard and Lieutenant Governor 'Stingy Tommy' Hutchinson can say for themselves."

"I'll drink to that," Levi said, and raised his glass of ale in a toast. "You know of the town meeting to be called next week on the second of June. I expect we'll be hearing some fine talk from the likes of James Otis and Sam Adams."

"Humph," Jane growled and began to clear the cobalt blue stoneware plates. She set down the steaming gravy soup and chicken. "Talk is facile. But will talk feed the stomachs of those who are in need of charity? To me it appears that there's much talk and all that occurs is that times grow harder and the Mother Country grows more greedy." She ladled the gravy atop Abigail's chicken and greens. "You hardly touched your giblets, missy. Eat up."

"I've been talking with some men in the taverns, Jane. They are more than angry and unwilling to sit on their breeches like chastised children for much longer, believe you me. There will be more than talk soon." Levi's eyes shone with some secret knowledge deeper than what he had stated.

Katie looked from brother to sister. Her husband was five and twenty, but looked no older than his sister, perhaps because of the freckles that crossed his turned-up nose. With so light a beard he might look almost girlish were it not for his thin-lipped wide mouth, the mouth of his father. But it was the glint in Levi's sea-green eyes which she sometimes glimpsed, as she did now, that frightened Katie in a way she did not comprehend. Yet she knew that Levi's passion for the latest news from England or from the other colonies, which he learned from seamen and travelers in the taverns, was different from Abigail's. It was connected to his less frequent dreams of adventure on the high seas, although she knew he tried to harness this sense of restlessness for her sake.

Katie had known Levi since she had been a girl of ten, but she would never comprehend this aspect of his soul. She had addressed her concern to Abigail forthrightly, but Abigail did not share her concern. Of course, Levi inhabited a special place in Abigail's heart. Abigail, usually so keen-sighted, could see not the slightest shortcoming in her brother. The events five or six years before, which Katie knew little of in specific detail, had tied sister and brother uncommonly close, even before the death of their dear father. Katie had never requested full disclosure nor had it been offered, so she had kept her peace about the matter, though it puzzled her from time to time as it did tonight.

Levi caught the eye of his wife, and once again her tender beauty moved him. He recognized the almost hidden, troubled look in her eyes and knew that it was he who had engendered it. Resting his spoon and fork, Levi reached across the table and patted the small, white hand of his wife. Embarrassed by his public act of affection, he looked down into baby Sarah's cradle. As if she knew it was her father watching her, she opened her big blue eyes and smiled at him. Smiling back proudly, he realized again that the talk he was recounting from the men at the tavern was right. For he had a wife and family to provide for as did the others. If their rights as Englishmen weren't upheld, then by God, they would be forced to seize them as proud men. But this was not discussion for the womenfolks' ears. And furthermore, he as well as the others who were weary of those who called themselves citizens of the colony but lived as if they were royalty in London. They would see their come-uppance sooner than they might dream—

"Levi," Jane asked, "would you like more chicken before I bring out the pie?"

"No, sweet Lady Jane," he called her, his favorite name when he was in a funning mood. "Is the pie my favorite butter apple?"

"Aye. I made it in honor of Katie's second-prize award today!"

Levi beamed at his wife. "Can you imagine one so small in size and large with child winning for the second year!" he proudly declared.

Abigail smiled at her sister-in-law and then at Levi,

but her mind was on other matters. She had been considering how to arrange things so that Levi would not be at the shop when Jeremy arrived Monday morning. She toyed with her potatoes but didn't have the heart to eat.

"What's wrong, sister?" Levi asked, noticing that Abigail's plate was full when she, such a hearty eater for one so slender, should be reaching for seconds. "You have hardly eaten."

"Do you have a pain in your stomach again, Abigail?" Jane asked, her brow knit with concern.

Abigail forced a smile and a bite of chicken down. "No. I am fine. Just tired and preoccupied. I must finish my essay tonight, what with church tomorrow."

"Spinning always puts Abigail in a cross mood," Nathan added and took a large spoonful of pie into his mouth.

"Are you a wee bit jealous that Katie won second prize while you did not finish your cloth again this year?" Levi asked, teasing.

"That's a terrible thing to suggest, Levi!" Abigail's flare of genuine anger when he had only been teasing surprised them all. "You know that I am the one who states that by all rights first place should have been dear Katie's again."

"Abigail," Katie said softly. "Do not let him tease you to anger. For I above all know how happy you were for me. I think something else clutches at your mind. Perhaps your essay."

"Yes," Abigail quickly agreed, as surprised by her unprovoked burst of temper as the others. "I do apologize for speaking so rudely." She looked at her brother's forgiving grin and smiled in gratitude.

"Levi, I am also preoccupied with all that we need done on Monday morn. I had neglected to inform you that both Goodman Manning, the cobbler, and Good-wife Greene, the baker's wife, wish to place advertisements in next week's paper. And I promised you would cross to Cambridge to see them early Monday. Can you see to that?"

"Most assuredly, sister. I always enjoy the ride across the river and my old nag could use some air and exercise. I shall be happy to see to it first thing Monday."

"Good, then." Lying was so difficult for Abigail that she felt impelled to remove herself from the table and retreat to her upstairs dormer bedroom, despite the fact that the evening had turned cool enough for need of the toasty fire blazing in the kitchen hearth. In truth, she had not specified when Levi would visit the merchants, so they should not be surprised by his early arrival. "If I might excuse myself from the table, I do feel a bit peaked . . ."

"And I think you are a mite pale," Katie said with concern.

"And I should be starting for the tavern if I am to meet Thomas and Charles," Levi spoke. "I shall eat Abby's untouched pie tomorrow unless she creeps down in the night to devour it!"

At last alone in her bedroom, Abigail sat at her desk and began to write in the flickering candlelight. This nightly routine of reviewing her attitudes, successes, and shortcomings had been imbued in her since she first held a quill. As her father had, she faithfully spoke to herself and with herself in her diaries. But tonight she could not find the words she sought, for so many feelings fought one another for her attention. Instead of words she viewed the image of Jeremy's face. First, she would conjure his face brimming with love, but then, as if in a frightful dream, his face would remold itself. His full, captivating mouth would curl tightly into a sneer. His golden sun-flecked eyes would darken and narrow with cold contempt until she could bear the image no more.

The tears fell from her eyes onto the paper of the leather-bound book. She must not cry, she ordered herself. For what had been, was long over. He had not loved her enough then to trust her. Neither her love nor devotion had been able to save them from Damon's lies. Now she was no longer a lovesick child. She was a woman and her family's survival rested most heavily on her slight shoulders. She would fight Jeremy by will and intelligence. For as much as she'd once adored him, he would not succeed in destroying the *Boston Word* or in harming Levi—just as the Crown itself would never succeed in plundering Boston or the rest of America. With her eyes pinched tightly closed, she swore so to her father in heaven.

Abigail recognized the soft rapping at her door as Katie's. "Please enter," she called out and quickly wiped her eyes.

Katie in gown and stocking cap shuffled into the room. "If I am keeping you from your work, please tell me and I shall excuse myself," she said.

"No, please sit upon my bed," Abigail replied. So often, when Levi was out with his friends, Katie and she would talk late into the night. Abigail found Katie a comfort at most times, but didn't expect that even Katie could be that now.

"I think that it is not your belly that ails you, sister," Katie said in almost a whisper. "I overheard bits of your conversation with Jeremy Blackburn, I am afraid," she confessed, color rushing into her pale cheeks. "Should you wish for me to leave the subject, I will do so most humbly . . ."

"No . . . you are correct, I am afraid."

"And somehow that is why you have decided to send Levi to Cambridge, so that he will not be present when Sir Jeremy arrives?"

"Yes . . ." Abigail felt the tears caught behind her throat.

"You know, sister, that I have heard but bits of what happened years before I came to your house as Levi's wife. I have never inquired further and Levi has never offered to speak of it, although I suspect his mind returns to those days quite often. So I am asking now. . . . Should you remind me of my place I would not be offended—"

"Place, what place? Do not speak as if our affection for one another was less than sisters-in-blood. It is a terrible story, but I fear that I can think of little else since I saw him. It would be a relief to speak of the pain if it will not upset you too much to hear of it." Abigail studied Katie's face.

"What upsets me is to see you so sorrowful. Come, sit by me," she gestured to the bed, "and talk."

Abigail rose but she was too agitated to sit as yet. She walked to the looking glass and stared at herself. For a moment she could see the girl with green eyes brimming with excitement, and a full mouth in perpetual shy smile . . . "I was not yet sixteen," she began, as much to herself as to Katie. "Jeremy had been coming to the shop to talk with Father for as long as I remember. You see, while Sir Bentley was—and remains—very wealthy, and their house was always the height of luxury and decorum, he was not one to speak with his only two sons. Jeremy's and Damon's mother had died at their birth and Sir Bentley had married twice hence, but both poor women died in childbirth. Jeremy and Damon had only one another —that is, until the day Jeremy first came to Father to borrow a book about mixing inks. Jeremy had his paints then and Father said he was quite sensitive and talented."

"Did his twin, Damon, visit as well?"

"Nay. Damon had no inclination to books, paints, or the like. By the time I was old enough to make their acquaintance, Damon had long been a rogue and scoundrel, although somehow Jeremy never saw him as such. I believe it was because he saw them to be as much the same inside as they appeared outwardly identical."

"And so when you were not quite sixteen you fell in love with Jeremy?"

Abigail felt herself blush in remembrance. "Aye . . . though we kissed, most chastely, but once. With some impropriety, Jeremy asked me to be his wife before he asked Father's permission. He said . . ." Abigail's voice drifted off as she saw them together, that afternoon that she had taken him to her hiding place by the river. It had been a sun-drenched, glorious summer day. "He said that he had to know for certain of my love before he could ask Father. . . ."

"How endearing," Katie said, and sighed.

"Yes . . . that was the Jeremy I loved then. So gentle and sensitive. So tender, as if the world had somehow wounded him and he could not stand being wounded further. I told him that I would think about it."

"Think about it? But you knew you loved him!"

Abigail laughed despite herself at the prideful, foolish young girl she had been. "Of course. But somehow I had gotten the notion that I should make him wait and wonder. I was too foolish and obstinate to openly declare my love . . . and too afraid, I believe, in retrospect."

"Yes? So then?"

Abigail, suddenly weary, sat herself beside Katie. "So then I told him to meet me at the hour before supper, at the same place 'neath the tree, and I would tell him whether to speak to Father or not. He accepted my foolishness with such heartfelt joy that I thought I should burst out and speak my true feelings. That was when I leaned against him and we kissed. Then we laughed and romped like two puppies. I lay beside him on my belly and looked up at the tree. It was then I believed that my giddiness had caused me to see double. For I thought, for one brief moment, that I saw Jeremy himself hidden in the tree above us. I was about to tell him, when he leaned toward me and caressed my cheek. He told me that I was God's perfect creation. He said it so very earnestly that I lost all modesty and told him that I was far from perfect. That God had even placed a mark to remind me of such."

"A mark? What do you mean?"

"Oh, it was all so silly. I was chattering on with no discretion. I meant that I had a birthmole," Abigail pointed to beneath her small, rounded breast, "right here."

Katie's cheeks flushed. "You mean you showed him?"

"Certainly not. I pointed and told him it was heart-shaped. Then he looked at me with such loving tenderness that I boldly touched the indentation that ran down his chin. And I felt a remarkable tremor pass through me . . ." Abigail continued in a mere whisper, never having told another soul this part. "And I sighed in a manner I had never thought of or heard before."

"And then?"

"And then I put back my white cap and raced home."

Katie watched as Abigail's eyes darkened with whatever followed. Surely it had to have been quite awful. Katie could not bring herself to speak. She reached out and took Abigail's hands into her own. Abigail's hands were as cold as winter.

"The following afternoon, I waited for Jeremy to arrive . . ."

"And he did?"

"I thought so at first, but as soon as he was upon me, I knew it wasn't he!" She clutched Katie's warm hands tightly.

"I don't understand."

"Jeremy and Damon were identical twins. Few could tell them apart by face or voice, except for Father and myself. To me they never looked alike. To me Damon was as cruel as Jeremy was tender. Damon's eyes always frightened me, while Jeremy's warmed me. So I knew instantly as I looked up, my hand cupped to shade the sharp sun from my eyes, I knew that he was Damon. At first I feared that something terrible had befallen Jeremy and that Damon had come to fetch me. But as he stood above me and grinned like the Devil himself would, I knew it was something worse."

"What did he do? I'm afraid to hear, I fear."

"I can not repeat his words for they are words that no proper woman should hear." Abigail swallowed hard and then the tears flowed as the memory came back to her as if it were happening again at that very moment. "He fell upon me, filthy utterances spitting from his mouth as he ran his hands over my body, and then his words stopped as he forced his mouth upon mine. I fought at him but he was stronger. I remember little after I heard the ripping sound of my chemise and knew my breast was exposed. . . . Then suddenly I saw a flash of red." Abigail began to laugh and cry.

"Red?" Katie asked, her own eyes blurred with tears.

"Aye, carrot red. For it was Levi's hair I saw through my tears. He had come to fetch me for dinner. He pulled Damon away and beat him to a bloodied state although Damon was older and half a head taller. Then Levi took me home. The next thing I remember was being in my bed and Jane feeding me some broth as Father sat and held my hand."

"Did Levi tell—I mean?"

"Yes. He told Father everything, I quickly gathered. I looked at my dear father and was suddenly afraid that he was ashamed of me. That was worse than anything, and I sobbed. Finally, as he comforted me, I said, 'Father, I am a good girl.' That was all I could utter through my choking sobs. Then Father placed his strong hands on each of my cheeks and said, 'You are more than a good girl, my Abby. The sun shines on you and within you. I love you. Never again lower your eyes in shame before me, my daughter.'"

Abigail and Katie hugged and cried together until the pain inside Abigail began to subside.

"The next day, when Father was in the shop, Jeremy stormed into my downstairs bedroom in the old house. Jane was in the kitchen and did not hear him at first. I don't know which was worse—yes, I do. This moment was the worst. For he looked at me with such hatred and claimed in the vilest terms that I had been intimate with Damon. I denied it of course, but he ranted on about how else would Damon have known about my birthmole. Then he pulled back my gown and exposing my mole declared that it was heart-shaped, just as Damon had claimed. I fell mute. I realized as I listened to his ranting that it had been Damon I had glimpsed in the tree two days before. That was how he knew of my sigh and my touch upon Jeremy's chin, which Damon said was applied by me to his own. But I could not speak of it, for I knew then that Jeremy had never trusted my word at all. Therefore he had never truly loved me. Thus, there was no more to say. Do you see?"

"Aye . . . but he was distraught at his brother's lies—"

"Still . . . that night, Damon was said to have been carousing at a tavern by the wharf. He was robbed and murdered by some ruffians."

"That was why Sir Bentley accused Levi, who stood trial and was acquitted by the colonial courts? Of that I knew, but never understood why the finger had been pointed his way. Now I understand. My poor Levi . . . And Jeremy?"

"Never did I see him again until this day. A fortnight after Damon's murder, he sailed off to London and stayed to attend the Inn of Court."

"The school for barristers in London?"

"Aye."

"Then why has he returned?"

"To serve on the Governor's Council and tend to his father's affairs, I would guess, with Sir Bentley in Halifax as vice-admiralty judge. As a lawyer, he's been appointed, I presume, to suppress the Boston press. But I fear there is more—" Abigail halted abruptly. How could she dream of afflicting Katie, heavy with child, with her terrible premonition? "Pay me no mind. Jeremy Blackburn cannot harm us. For I print the truth and therefore am neither libelous nor seditious, unless we will be truly denied our rights as Englishmen. Jeremy, with his fine legal training, will see that. And his personal animosity I shall endure until our business is finished with him. I am no longer the tender girl he last encountered," Abigail insisted, as much to buoy her own spirits as Katie's, who stared at her with wide, worried eyes.

# Chapter Four

GILES'S TAVERN, ON THE ALLEY ACROSS FROM THE STATE House, had become a gathering place for those patriotic Boston citizens whose sentiments daily grew more antagonistic toward the Crown, Parliament and fellow Bostonian Tories. It was this mutual bond that tied those of differing social classes and economic conditions more closely than they had ever been. One had to merely gaze about the taproom to see the richest of merchants standing beside the common laborer, both downing their tankards of flip or other homegrown brews as they heatedly condemned the recent news of the passage of the Stamp Act.

Therefore, more than one set of disapproving eyes fell upon the finely dressed, aristocratic party of young Tories seated at the center table of the cheerfully decorated room, drinking costly, heavily taxed Spanish Madeira wine. "Tories, be like that," John Lee, the cooper, whose kegs stood in the corner of the tobacco-hazed room, said to Mr. Isaac Hall.

"Aye," stout and powdered-wigged Mr. Hall,

owner of one of the leading shipbuilding companies in the Bay Colony, heartily agreed. "They have no shame about them. Flaunting their sympathies to the hardhearts who bleed us."

"I'll drink to that. To your health, Mr. Hall," John Lee proclaimed as they raised their tankards.

"Aye, and to yours, Goodman Lee," Mr. Hall said to the tall, wiry man dressed in leather breeches and gauze shirt. Mr. Hall eyed Jeremy and the rest of his group. He belched and raised his tankard again. "And to the end of tyranny and all those who take their stand alongside the oppressors in England and in Boston!"

Jeremy noticed the gaze of the two men but thought little of it. For, so soon after his return from London he was not yet fully cognizant of the depth of colonial feelings. His mind was already replete with conflicting thoughts and emotions as he and his friends finished off the second bottle of Madeira in his favorite Boston tavern.

Pretty, black-haired, black-eyed Belinda engaged Jeremy's thoughts, or at least his loins, for the moment, as he studied the creamy mounds of her full breasts that rose above her scarlet silk-and-ribboned gown. Belinda was in the midst of an arch, laughing conversation with Rebecca. For William Harris' wife, who sat across from Belinda, had just remarked about some lady of their acquaintance who attended the last governor's reception in a strikingly unfashionable gown. Jeremy was bored by the foolishness of their conversation. He would have preferred to spend the evening alone with Michael Harrington, his oldest and best friend who sat beside him, and William, a fellow lawyer and drunkard of greater substance than his corpulence and tipsy air might indicate. But since he wished to—no, *needed* to—bed Belinda tonight, he tried his best to hold his patience with the frivolous chatter in which she happily engaged. For what more could one expect from well-bred girls? Serious and worldly discussions were conducted man to man. Women were to be pampered and lustily enjoyed, then protected once a man chose one for his wife.

Only with Abigail had he ever had discussions of consequence that challenged his intellect. More than challenged, were he to be candid, as he remembered how boldly Abigail would disagree with him on matters of philosophy, history, art, or anything else that struck her ardor— Good God! He was doing it again! For the fourth time in less than one hour she had come to his mind.

Why should he be thinking of that woman in the plain, homespun green dress, all modesty in cap and artless eyes, when he had a full-bodied, fine girl of his class at his side who openly adored him and therefore privately allowed him the liberties usually taken only with a pretty buxom barmaid in his very own bed. Ah, but Abigail had grown from a delicate pretty girl into a deceptively fragile-looking china doll with vivid, burnished, thick red hair and deep green eyes that he could dream into forever— Damn! Again! He would not think of her again. Not until he was ready to take her and have her out of his system once and for all. Discreetly, he reached for Belinda's hand beneath the table.

"Another bottle of Madeira, if you please, miss," William demanded of the saucy barmaid who appeared at their table. "Michael, are you going to join us in this bottle?" William asked, baiting an uncharacteristically quiet Michael.

"Thank you, no. I shall have another flip. My stomach seems to have lost its taste for fine wine," he answered in attempted good humor.

Jeremy noted the smile that the lusty blonde barmaid gave to Michael in unspoken approval, which brought a flush to Michael's fair complexion. Jeremy had heard that the colonists had been boycotting imported wines and even English teas since last winter. He thought that a man should be able to drink his preference without petty inferences as to his politics. Never had he cared for flip, but if Michael chose to imbibe his polished tankards full of home brew, it did not imply that he was less the gentleman for it. Jeremy wondered if the matter at hand was that Michael fancied the buxom blonde barmaid with the wide-mouthed, charming, if impertinent, smile.

Since his return to Boston, Jeremy had found little time for anything more than superficial conversation with Michael. He resolved that he would have supper alone with Michael this coming week. He, for one, needed the kind of interchange that his letters to Michael had by nature prohibited. Yet, despite his need to confide some of his confusion to his closest friend, Jeremy wondered if he would be able to allow himself to do so. To speak matters of the heart and soul had always been an arduous task. Through most of his life, Damon had been his sole confidant. For nearly five years now, even during his moments of greatest torment, Jeremy had held his own counsel.

Unconsciously, Jeremy traced his strong, tapered

fingers the length of Belinda's thin, cold hand. She turned and smiled for an instant but then returned to her conversation, her hand remaining cool to his own. Despite the liberties she allowed him in his canopied bed, Jeremy did not delude himself into believing that Belinda enjoyed their lovemaking, for she was by nature as bloodless a lady as she was beautiful. He had noted the expression of relief on her face that she did not know he glimpsed moments after consummation. Still, from a future wife he had learned to expect no more. Shared passion was to be found in the arms of a barmaid or servant girl. Wives were an investment to be made as wisely as the purchase of an estate or business.

Belinda was Lord Wattington's only daughter. Lord Wattington was a powerful gentleman on the governor's council with friends and relations in the House of Lords in London. Jeremy's father had arranged for his introduction to Belinda last Christmas in London. Weary of his rakish behavior and the same kind of women in different beds, Jeremy had agreed with his father that it was high time that he married and bore children who would benefit in the world from a well-arranged marriage.

Jeremy swallowed the last of his wine as the barmaid set the bottle of Madeira on the table, while trying to avoid having her bottom pinched by William's fat, drunken hand. "Sir, if you please!" the girl pleaded to little avail. It was Rebecca's stern expression that brought the barmaid her most desired relief from William's fleshy fingers. His father had been correct, Jeremy thought once again. Only poets or foolish young men, like he had been, believed in the possibility of true love, passion, and communion of souls with a woman. Abigail had seemed the epitome of every romantic notion ever invented and she had turned out to be more devious than the most common of—

"Jeremy!" William's clap on his shoulder and words mercifully brought him from his thoughts. "I wish to make another toast!"

"Here, here," Michael added, his tankard raised.

"Oh yes, another toast!" Belinda said, removing her hand from his to clap hers together as Rebecca did. "Is this not the fourth or third? I daresay I have long lost track!" she said as she and Rebecca broke into a flourish of tipsy giggles.

William's small eyes in his fat face glanced from one to the other as he raised his glass. "A toast to Jeremy Blackburn's return to Boston. London's loss and our gain! And . . ." William winked at Belinda. "To the lady who shall soon be his wife! Cheers, I say!"

With a hearty laugh, Jeremy clinked his glass to the others. For this was the third time that William had made the same toast. William's inability to handle alcohol had changed little in the time he had been away, Jeremy realized. He wondered why he, himself, was still cold sober and resolved to change this condition as rapidly as possible.

"And I should like to make another toast as well," Michael said as he again raised his tankard.

"What kind of proper toast may you make with that dreadful flip?" William chided. "To Mister Samuel Adams, James Otis and their hothead followers?"

Jeremy laughed good-naturedly until he saw the uneasy look in Michael's slate-blue eyes. In that instant he realized that he'd been so preoccupied with his own affairs that he'd overlooked obvious signs that something was amiss with Michael. So much like himself, Michael was not one to reveal his innermost feelings easily. As Jeremy reflectively met Michael's sober eyes, he realized that his friend was as much in need of a confidant as he. At the moment, however, all he could offer to Michael and himself was the comfort of alcoholic haze, although they had a far road to travel to meet up with William. "I for one wish to hear my dear friend, Dr. Harrington, make his toast. Then I wish to make a few of my own!"

By the time Levi and his friends Adam Taylor and Charles Osborn arrived at Giles's Tavern from Blue's Tavern near the Long Wharf three-quarters of an hour later, they had enjoyed more than a few tankards of flip themselves. Levi's green eyes gleamed more with exhilaration than inebriation, induced by the talk they'd heard down in the waterfront tavern.

From the time he was a boy, the masted sailing ships, the salty seamen with their tales of exotic lands and languages had excited the dreamer in Levi's soul. Out of respect for his father's wishes, Levi had bound his wanderlust and learned his trade, first as a "devil" —an apprentice to his father—eventually advancing to master printer. All the while he had spent what little free evenings he had vicariously living the adventures of the sea through the tales of many a shipmaster, captain, or mate who came and went from the large Boston Harbor. After his father's death and the birth of Sarah, there was less time than ever and therefore it was all the more precious.

But now, adventure was about to come into the city of Boston itself. He had no doubts that the talk he had heard tonight at Blue's Tavern, from McIntosh himself, the leader of the South End Mob, was not idle boasting. The talk was about secret meetings with upstanding, politically influential citizens where plans were being drawn for action against the colonial governor and his toady officials. Levi knew that McIntosh was considered to be a ruffian of sorts. Levi's own father had disdained the commonplace battles that had taken place for the past few years between McIntosh's South End Mob and the North End Mob. His father had not lived to learn that McIntosh had prevailed, nor would he have cared. But Levi had spoken with the beefy, strong cobbler a time or two and had heard much about him which he admired. With prudence, Levi kept his high opinion of McIntosh to himself. Tonight, Levi had found no need to publicly deny the soundness of McIntosh's logic.

How could anyone but a Tory deny that there had been far too much polite talk and supplication to the Crown and Parliament? And what had it brought to Boston or the rest of the colonies? New restrictions and now an internal tax, an abridgment of their rights as Englishmen and an insult to their natural rights as men. McIntosh and his followers were no longer satisfied to be begging, woebegotten, second-class Englishmen. Nor apparently were many of the wealthiest and most influential leaders of the colony, although they sought to cloak their truest feelings behind the broad back of McIntosh and his common followers. But the sentiments McIntosh boasted were obviously not limited to Boston or the Bay Colony, not if the seaman from New York, who toasted his fellow Americans—a brave new people, Americans—was an indication of a growing sense of identity throughout the colonies. While a few of the more cautious men in the tavern had gasped in response to this outspoken toast of treason, most of the men, Levi among them, had raised their tankards high. Americans . . .

Adam Taylor, the cabinetmaker, had been almost as excited as Levi, but Charles Osborn, the master carpenter, had expressed skepticism as the three friends wended their way through the cobblestoned streets and alleyways to Giles's Tavern on this cool May night. Their debate, lively and frank, continued through their first round of homebrew in the crowded, smoky taproom.

"I still believe McIntosh to be a hooligan," Charles declared again. "I cannot believe his insinuations that the likes of Sam Adams and other respected gentlemen would have any congress with him or his South Side gang."

"I think you do McIntosh an injustice," Levi said as he glanced about the taproom. "The man is not a common ruffian. He is an artisan, like we are. A fine cobbler, I've been—" Levi halted in mid-sentence. Damon! No, that was impossible—Damon was dead, may the Lord have mercy on his wretched soul—Jeremy!— But he was a barrister in London—

"What is it, Levi?" Adam asked, his eyes tracing the path of Levi's own until they fell upon Jeremy Blackburn at the front table before the leaded window.

Levi's throat grew dry. He downed his tankard of brew, then wiped his mouth with his sleeve. "What the devil is *he* doing here?"

"Who—oh, Jeremy? Do you mean that you did not know? Why, at dinner Polly spoke that as she sat spinning this afternoon with Katie and Abigail—" Charles became flustered. "Do you mean that Abigail did not tell you of her conversation with Jeremy?"

Levi's wide mouth was drawn into a tight line. "She did not . . . tell me . . ."

Already Levi's eyes were as turbulent as the stormy sea. Charles hesitated. "Polly only overheard bits and pieces . . ."

"Come now, Charles," Levi demanded. "Your sister Polly is a fine girl but we all know that she is not one to turn her ear from private conversations."

Charles chuckled despite the tension he felt. "You are most tactful. My sister is a hawk-eyed gossip who recounts every and any conversation. She is as loose-mouthed as Abigail is tight-lipped."

Adam's thin, sharp-nosed, honest face grew indignant. "I find Polly most charming and I don't believe—"

Charles laughed again. "We know that you find many of Polly's charms irresistible," Charles teased. "And as soon as you have attained the courage you intend to ask Father for permission to marry. I love my sister dearly, but she is an incurable gossip."

Levi grew more impatient as he listened, his eyes focused on a laughing Jeremy seated with his aristocratic Tory friends. "Just what did Polly tell?" he demanded.

As Charles recounted the conversation between

Jeremy and Abigail, Levi's green eyes darkened and blazed. The muscle in his jaw pulsated. When Charles had told him all that had been said, Levi's face paled, but his voice remained firm as he spoke. "Libel and sedition! Damn the Blackburns to hell!" he declared and bolted toward the table, but Adam's strong large hands finally restrained him with some difficulty.

Jeremy, pacified finally by the warm and sleepy glow of the Madeira, laughed as William mimicked the strange manner of James Otis in oration. Belinda laughed so heartily that the exposed mounds of her satiny white breasts quivered. Jeremy felt the heat rise within him, despite the retarding effects of the alcohol. It was time to take leave and he felt better than he had all day. How pleasant to be amongst old and cherished friends in his favorite Boston tavern—

Jeremy's veil of alcoholic pleasure slipped away as he gazed about the taproom and saw first the shock of red hair and then the hate-filled eyes of Levi Peabody glaring at him. He had no intention of allowing Levi to spoil the mood he'd fought so hard to garner. He would avenge his brother's murder in his own way in his own good time. Still, Jeremy could not resist the temptation of defying Levi's malevolent stare. Jeremy gave a slight nod of his head and then allowed a sardonic smirk to issue across the room.

Levi lurched from the grasp of Adam's hand. Jeremy felt the muscles in his body ripple and grow taut as he rose from the table, determined to meet Levi halfway across the room. He did not wish to embarrass Belinda with this seemingly inevitable confrontation.

"Now, now, young man," an elderly man admonished, as Levi pushed his way across the crowded room until he stood inches from Jeremy—older, stronger and a half-head taller. Levi's hands were tightly fisted.

"Stay away from my sister," Levi hissed through almost clenched teeth. "Any business you have with the *Boston Word* shall be conducted with me, *Mr.* Blackburn!"

"That would be my preference. But Mistress Peabody insisted that I indeed conduct my business—the Crown's business to be accurate—with none but her. I am sorry. For as much as I despise you, Goodman Peabody, I have *less* use for your sister."

Without knowing exactly how, Levi was able to contain himself and refrain from smashing the handsome face with his fists. Adam and Charles stood at his side once again. "I warn you but once more. Keep away from Abigail or you shall live to regret the consequences!" Levi glanced in Belinda's direction. This time it was he who grinned spitefully. "I see you have found a *fine lady* to keep you occupied. A proper *Tory* lady in her silk and lace gown." He spat the words as if they were poison.

"Yes, Belinda is a lady," Jeremy answered with a disarming smile, as if he had not heard the slur. "Therefore . . ." Jeremy continued so softly that the three had to listen hard to hear his words. "I have no need for used colonial goods. Be they cloth, furniture, or whores—"

"Why you bloody bastard! Tory bastard!" Levi cried and lurched at him. Jeremy raised his fists as Adam and Charles yanked Levi away.

"Fighting words, Goodman Peabody. Why I almost

have a mind to challenge you to a proper duel to defend my honor," Jeremy said with a deceptively easy air and matching smile.

Michael Harrington, who had appeared at that moment by Jeremy's side, discreetly pulled him a step back. "Good evening, Levi, Charles, Adam," he said as properly as if they had met in church. "Fine evening, is it not? Levi, do send my respects to Mistress Abigail. It's been a time since I've had the pleasure of greeting her."

Levi found himself disarmed, despite his best intentions. "Michael Harrington, you are a fine man," Levi said. "How you choose to associate with such finely dressed scum—"

"Michael, please tell your father that his highboy shall be ready on Tuesday," Adam quickly interjected as he and Charles held Levi firmly. "We have all had a bit too much brew I fear. Good evening to you, gentlemen."

"Are you daft, Levi!" Charles declared as they stood in the sobering night air. "Do you not realize that Jeremy was attempting to provoke you into accepting a duel?"

"He is a master swordsman I hear," Adam added.

"Then I will meet his challenge at his call!"

"You are a fool," said Charles. "Do you think that your fists are a match for his sword?"

Levi began to punch his own fist. "He insulted my sister's honor," he insisted.

"And you insulted his lady's before that. I thought you wished to be alive for the important fight against the Crown's tyranny," Adam stated innocently enough, fully knowing that Levi's political passion would bring him back to his senses.

Levi visibly lost his bluster as he lay his hands at his sides. "He has the audacity to believe that I murdered his brother. I'm only sorry I wasn't the one to stick the knife into Damon's heart, I tell you!"

"I understand," Charles said. "For were not Adam and myself there with you that night?"

Levi fought back the tears for it would be unseemly to cry. He hadn't cried since his father's death two years ago. He linked his arms over the shoulders of his friends. "Aye . . . it is time we headed home, I think."

Jeremy straightened his brown velvet coat and smoothed his linen cuffs. Then he bowed to the ladies. "I apologize for any embarrassment that ruffian may have caused."

"Oh, but there is no need," Rebecca answered.

"It was quite exciting!" Belinda exclaimed, her eyes glowing.

"One more drink then?" William asked.

Jeremy joined in the last round of Madeira, but he forced his pose of joviality. He should have remained in London, despite his father's strongest exhortations, he thought. Belinda's hand came to rest on his thigh but he felt no ardor now, only the old familiar sorrow entrenched in the depth of his heart. The only living person who could soothe him was the red-haired, green-eyed girl who was the cause of the pain itself.

# Chapter Five

THE COCKS HAD JUST BEGUN TO CROW AND THE HENS scratch in the small yards behind the shops and houses off Dassett Alley. From her third-story dormer window, Abigail gazed across the city to the glorious sunrise that was breaking through the haze of the harbor. She could smell the salty, invigorating sea air in this earliest hour of the day. In the quiet before the daily clatter and clamor of the bustling city commenced, she could almost hear the squawking of the gulls in flight. She watched them as they circled the schooners, clippers, and great sailing ships quietly lulling in the gentle, lapping waters of the Inner Harbor. In stolen moments such as this, her deep, abiding love for Boston filled her heart. Truly, there could be no more beautiful nor exciting city in the world. Though she'd heard tales of the wonders of London and fancied the idea of one day seeing its sights with her own eyes, should she live and die without leaving Boston and its environs she would not feel her life less than full and wonderful.

Six bells tolled from South Church, reminding Abigail that she could linger but a minute longer. The day was new and long; much serious business awaited her. Thinking of Jeremy's visit and her argument with Levi had kept her awake most of the night. Now she forced herself to suppress a weary yawn.

As she washed with the well water she'd drawn earlier, her mind returned to her worries. Since their angry words upon returning from Sunday church, she and Levi had barely spoken.

She heard him downstairs, readying himself for his trip to the village of Cambridge. She had not seen him when she'd slipped downstairs to fill her bowl with water. Now she knew that part of her slowness this morning was hesitation at having to confront his disapproving eyes. And she feared that her own anxiety and guilt, that no doubt wove itself in her face, would give her away.

Throughout the night her conscience had pained her. For when Levi angrily recounted the story Polly told Charles, Abigail soon realized that either Charles had forgotten or Polly had not overheard her agreement to conduct a meeting with Jeremy this morning at half-past nine. She did not wish to lie to or evade the truth with her dear brother. But she still believed that alone she could most judiciously expedite their business with Jeremy in his position as agent for the Royal government. She would most easily prove to him, in the very type they published, that the *Boston Word* printed neither libelous nor seditious statements —just the truth.

It was more than Levi's uncharacteristic anger that plagued her. She was certain that Levi had deleted something in his telling of seeing Jeremy in the tavern Saturday evening. She was unsure as to what had transpired, but despite his vehement denial, Abigail suspected that bitter words had passed between the two men. Levi, as stubborn as herself when he chose to be, remained implacable. Despite how much she abhorred lies and falsities, she was still convinced that no good could be derived from an encounter between her brother and Jeremy this morning. Still, Levi's questions before dinner nagged at her.

"Did Jeremy say when he wished to examine our past papers?" Levi had asked.

"No," she said with false quickness, for to hesitate would give her away. "He did not."

"Abigail . . . when Jeremy sends a message for an appointment, I wish to set the time with you so that I may be present. Is that a promise, sister?"

She chose her words carefully. "When I receive a communication from Jeremy or his office I shall show it to you immediately." Since no message would be forthcoming, she told herself, she could promise with impunity.

The creak of the door and subsequent clatter of the nag's hoofs upon the cobblestone road told her that Levi was on his way. She hurried to the window again and saw him riding down the street. Then she caught a glimpse of Katie with Sarah in her arms, watching Levi ride off as well.

After breakfast, Katie would accompany Jane to market. Nathan would be in school until midday. Jeremy would have come and gone before anyone knew the better of it, and it would be his first and only visit. For despite his personal hostilities against her and his hatred of Levi, Jeremy would not have the time to harass them, she'd realized last night. The *Boston Word* was the smallest paper in the city, with a minimal circulation. Were it not for whatever printing orders they received they would have had to declare bankruptcy years before. Since 1763, the continual failure of businesses, a result of the deepening depression in Boston and the other colonies, had affected the amount of business Peabody Printers received as well, and they were barely holding their own the past two years.

If Governor Bernard were seeking to suppress outraged colonial protest, Jeremy would be spending long hours in battle with Ben Edes, the publisher of the *Gazette* down the way on Dassett Alley. For not only was the *Gazette* the most vociferous in its attacks upon the injustices being heaped upon the colony, but it was the most influential Boston paper, with the widest circulation. Mr. Edes, who was a member of a group of patriotic leading citizens calling themselves "The Loyal Nine," would be a most formidable adversary for Jeremy, despite the power of the Crown behind him. Of that she had no doubts.

Abigail reached for her working dress hanging in her small closet. As she stood in her nightclothes, her eyes drifted to her blue and white gingham petticoat. It was one of her favorites of the few presentable dresses she owned and did flatter her coloring, she thought, as her hand brushed its soft cotton-laced edge. Why was she indulging herself in such idle vanities, she sharply admonished herself. Her brown cloth petticoat, muslin shift and apron were clean, pressed, and proper for any business activities. Jeremy's call was a potential attack on their livelihood, not a social visit!

Quickly she dressed and then undid the plaited hair that fell to her waist. As she brushed her thick red hair she couldn't refrain from remembering how often Jeremy had admired it and asked her permission to run his hands down its length. Foolish thought! For that time was in another life. She pulled her hair behind her head and bound it in a loose knot. Only a few crimson tendrils escaped from her firm hand.

At breakfast, Nathan was quieter than usual and ate little. Yet he declared that he felt fine. Jane talked to him and touched his head. "He shows no trace of fever," she said in a cheerful voice, though a worried look lingered in her eyes.

"I have oiled the flat press, Abigail," Nathan informed her with a smile that appeared less lively than usual. "The church pamphlets are ready for printing and I have stacked the broadsides for Mr. Howard in the corner of the front office."

"Very good, Nathan," Abigail answered. "Need I know more?"

"Aye. I almost forgot. Levi told me to inform you that Mistress Pomegrant wants to check the handbills announcing her new dancing school once more before we print them. She will be in later this morning."

"Has she not checked them three times before?" asked Katie, who looked more rested and flush than usual.

"Such foolishness! A dance school when people go without work and with little enough food! What is this city coming to!" Jane declared. "I think the days when the church banned dancing were better for all. But now with those fancy Anglicans. Why I sometimes have difficulty in recalling how virtuous this city used to be!" Jane walked to the hearth and withdrew the loaves of fragrant baked bread.

"Times change, Jane," Abigail began to tease out of habit. Quickly she realized that she was not in the mood to start Jane on her tirade about all the changes in Boston since the older woman had arrived. "But you are probably right. However, as frivolous as a dancing school may be, we most certainly can use the shillings Mistress Pomegrant will pay for the work."

"Aye to that, I say," Jane acquiesced. She gave Abigail a second glance. "Is there something wrong with the gruel and sausages?" she asked.

"No, of course not," Abigail answered. She looked down at her plate and realized that she'd barely taken a bite. She had little appetite, but forced herself to begin eating in order to allay any suspicions that something was amiss with her.

The jingling of the bell above the outer shop door startled Abigail, who was in concentration, proofing the galleys of the Congregational Church's pamphlet speaking out against the rise of the Episcopalians and their plans to bring an Anglican bishop to America. She rose from the large wooden desk in the cramped office antechamber and gazed at the grandfather clock that had once belonged to her father's mother in England. It was only quarter past nine. Already the day had grown bright and warm, she noticed, as she quickly wiped the trace of perspiration from her brow and walked into the front room of the shop.

Abigail did not expect the involuntary jolt that her heart took as she saw Jeremy, standing tall and strong, dressed in a long golden-brown frock coat of fine broadcloth over black silk breeches and silk stockings of a complementary beige shade. For a moment, the sight of this aristocratic gentleman, one of the "better sort" as those of his class proclaimed themselves, with his three-cornered hat in hand and his sunlit golden-brown hair pulled into a tail behind his neck, took her breath away. He was so beautiful. Instantly, Abigail felt drab and common in her plain muslin clothes. Self-consciously she adjusted her white day cap, then smoothed her apron. Finally she met his eyes.

"Good morning, Mr. Blackburn," she said with as much dignity as she could muster. "I see that you are more than prompt."

"Good morning, Mistress Peabody," he said with a slight bow. "I do hope my early arrival has not inconvenienced you. But I did not realize until I was on my way that you no longer lived and worked on Primrose Street, until I passed your shop and saw the sign."

Abigail had forgotten again that he did not know of the fire or the circumstances of her father's death. But it was not a subject she wished to pursue. They must conduct this unpleasant business and let that be the end of it, she knew as she fought the desire to touch his hand. "Yes. I should have informed you. We have been relocated for little more than two years. Please, will you not take a seat?" she asked and motioned to the two sturdy chairs flanking the pine table.

"Certainly. May I ask your permission to light my

pipe?" he asked as he settled his broad-shouldered, lean-hipped frame into the chair.

"Of course," she answered and watched Jeremy busy himself with filling his long, slender clay pipe with tobacco. She couldn't help but remember that he'd once confided in her that he chose to smoke it when he was nervous and wanted to busy his hands. Then at least, in this they were on equal par, she thought, somehow pleased.

"I must tell you that one of the reasons for my early arrival is that since my return to Boston last week I have been amazed at the clang and clatter of the congested streets. I was nearly run over by a chaise darting down State Street last week. Without sidewalks, as in London, there is no guarantee of safety in the muddled streets. And such distractions. Never have I seen such a conglomeration of chimney sweepers, sawyers of wood, merchants, ladies, clergy, carts, horses, oxen, coaches, marketmen and women . . ." he had to stop to catch his breath. "And my ears filled with the rattle-gabble of them all! I do not remember it as such!"

Abigail, so disarmed by his honest astonishment and displeasure that sounded a note so close to Jane's own, began to laugh. For a moment Jeremy's glowing large brown eyes narrowed and his natural relaxed expression hardened, and he appeared to think she was laughing at him. Suddenly he grinned and began to laugh himself. The sound was like a favorite but forgotten tune to Abigail's ears. How she had loved his rich, melodic laugh and wide smile that dimpled at his cheeks and around his eyes, and deepened the strong cleft of his chin. It was as if the Jeremy she'd loved had risen from the dead and returned to her— Abruptly her own laughter stopped. She could not indulge herself in wishful fancies.

His laughter halted and he looked at her for a moment with an expression she could not discern. "Tell me about your father," he asked so softly and with such tender eyes that she lost her resolve.

Abigail sighed and wasn't sure she could find her voice. For how many times had she pictured his face composed exactly as dearly as it now was, his voice as tender, in her dreams when she needed him to help ease the sharp pains from the wounds deep within her heart? She pulled at her rope belt, which held her keys, and her fingers rounded the edges of the keys as she readied to speak. She looked up into his eyes, expecting his countenance to be changed again, but he looked at her with the same gentle concern that lit a hope that had no right to exist in her heart. "It was the third of January in '63," she began. She swallowed hard. "We do not know how the fire began for certain. But it was late in the night when I felt Father's sturdy hands pull me from the smoke-filled bedroom. Levi, Katie, his wife—do you remember young Katie Wentworth, her father, the smithy?"

"Yes, I believe I do. The pretty petite blonde girl who was at your side at the Spinning Celebration. Am I not correct?"

"Aye. They married but six months before, after her mother died and her father moved to the village of Cambridge. Katie, Levi, Jane, we were all in night-clothes and shivering in the snowy night but un-harmed. Then Katie cried that Nathan, who had been at her side when they fled the house, was nowhere in sight. Jane suspected that he had returned into his back room in the house to find his treasured satchel of letters that rarely left his side. Letters that—"

"Pardon me, but I am confused. Who is Nathan?"

"That's right. You had left years before—" Abigail felt her face flush at having spoken the words that meant so much sadness to her. She felt the morning heat forming beads of perspiration on her upper lip. Her throat was so dry.

"Abigail," Jeremy said with alarm on his face. "I fear that I have brought up a matter that too deeply disturbs you—"

"No . . . yes it does but I need . . . I mean, I would like to tell you. But I could use a cup of water. The sun in this room is suddenly too much. Would you care to come into the kitchen? I could offer you a cup of punch," Abigail said as she rose, suddenly very tired.

"I would be most pleased, but some cool water will be fine if you please." He rose and placed his hand lightly on her shoulder but then quickly removed it as he followed her from the shop into the cool large kitchen-living area. "Allow me," he offered and gratefully she sat down at the table and watched as he poured her a cup of water and handed it to her. As she sipped at its sweet coolness that helped to calm her lightheaded feeling, she watched him pour and sip at his own cup.

"Nathan was not quite eight years of age at the time. His mother was a cook for the Hutchinson family. His father a seaman who had been lost at sea but months before. Then his mother died from the small pox. Our minister brought him to church one

Sunday and spoke with Father. That night Nathan came to live with us, officially as an apprentice, and although he was no more than the size of a six-year-old, he was so sweet that we took him into our hearts as he took us. Jane and he had a special affinity, for she said he was the spitting image of her own long grown and dead son, Tom. The same black eyes. And Father soon saw him as much a son as Levi. That's why when Jane insisted that he must have raced back into the house to find his leather satchel of letters—"

"Letters from his father, the seaman?" Jeremy correctly surmised.

"Yes, for he had loved his father dearly. By this time the house was in a total blaze. Already part of the second story had collapsed although the fire brigade was on its way—we heard the horses galloping down the cobblestones, but streets away. Levi began to run back into the house but Father forbade him and ran in himself . . ." In the telling, Abigail could see that night again as vividly as if it were yesterday. She forced herself to continue although her eyes focused not on Jeremy's face, but on the pewter mug that had been her father's that hung beside Levi's on the lintel above the hearth.

"And both your father and the boy died?" Jeremy asked quietly.

"No. Nathan is alive and well, may the Lord bless him. He suffered bad burns on his forearms as he lay under the small beam clutching his satchel. The gentlemen of the fire company were able to bring him out safely. For a time, the physician feared that he would lose movement in his arms permanently, but he did not and the burns healed although his arms remained badly scarred. But otherwise he recovered completely."

"And Goodman Peabody?"

"A large beam had fallen across his body. The fire roared so badly that the firemen were unable to bring him out. The heat was too severe and he was trapped . . ." Abigail's tears blurred her vision of the pewter mug causing it to become a silver glare.

"Abigail . . . I am sorry . . ."

She felt Jeremy's strong tapered fingers touch her hand tightly gripping the earthenware cup. Abigail looked into his face and saw that tears filled his own eyes as well.

"I was very fond of your father. For a long time he was more of a father to me than my own—" Jeremy's voice choked and his other hand took her hand that rested on the table into his own.

"Thank you. I know," she smiled gently. "Father loved your talks, for they were something he never shared with his own son. He loved your curiosity and thirst for learning. He always said that it was so remarkable that you were twins when you were the one who was so sensitive and—" Dear Lord, why was she speaking talk as inflammatory as the fire that took her father itself? She stopped herself but it was too late. Jeremy's hands tightened on her own and his face became so distorted that it made her heart beat with sudden fear.

"I was the *sensitive* one," he sneered. "And you agreed, I am sure. I the almost girlish dreamer and Damon the man of *passion!* Is that not so? Admit the truth, for it was in his arms that you lay—"

Abigail pulled her hands from his despite his greater strength, and bolted to the middle of the room. "That is not so! That was never so—" she yelled, but then he was upon her.

He pulled her into his arms, despite her struggles against him. They were so close that she could feel his pounding heart against her face, as his one hand held her own behind her back and his other arm pulled her closer yet. "But I have learned a thing or two about passion," he said in a soft, mocking tone.

Before she had time to protest he lowered his face to hers and his mouth clasped her own as tightly as his body held hers to him. At first she clamped her mouth shut, but soon her head spun from the heat of his body and insistent soft full lips. She responded despite herself and allowed her lips to answer his in a way she'd never known. She couldn't breathe but she didn't care. Nothing mattered as she gave her mouth to his, as she felt the heat that emanated from his groin as his hips danced into hers, melting her insides, making her dizzy and mindless.

Her breath came strangely heavy as he pulled away and looked down upon her, still holding her. "Almost as good as my dead brother? Better perhaps?" he whispered with a cruelness that made her stomach turn. Then he released her and laughed a mocking, loud laugh that echoed in the room.

Abigail was stunned speechless; then the rage came upon her. Never had she felt such fury and before she knew it she had swung her arm and slapped his face with more power than she knew she possessed. Even as the slap reverberated and stunned him into silence she went at him again with her hands, but he caught her by the wrists this time.

"The kiss was worthy of one slap, but not another," he taunted with a sardonic grin.

"Let me go!" she demanded.

"I will when I have finished with you. Speaking that is. For one kiss has satisfied my curiosity, you see—"

"Let her go! Let her go!" Nathan, who neither had heard enter the kitchen, yelled in his child's voice as he kicked and beat his fists against Jeremy's body.

Jeremy looked down at the boy and blanched. For in the boy's struggle against Jeremy, his cuffs had risen above his brown, scarred forearms.

Instantly Jeremy released Abigail. He bent down and gently held Nathan by his shoulders. "Young man . . . Nathan. It was not what you believed. I would never hurt your mistress. But you are a brave fellow and her protector, as you well should be. Will you accept my sincerest apologies for frightening you so with no cause? Our game was perhaps too vigorous. Is that not correct, Abigail?"

Abigail was dizzy with confusion and concern. "Yes, Nathan. Mr. Blackburn was a friend when I was but a girl . . ." She kneeled and opened her arms. "Come to me, dear Nathan," she asked softly and the boy ran into her arms. She hugged Nathan who began to cry. "You are truly my protector and I love you. Do not tell Levi or the others, or I am afraid Levi will become jealous. It shall be our special secret, aye?"

"Aye," black-eyed Nathan said as he clung to her. "I did not know it was a game. I thought the man was hurting you. I am sorry if I misbehaved," he said as he hugged her tightly.

Abigail looked up but Jeremy was gone. She would sort it out later. Right now she had to tend to the boy whose forehead felt hot to her touch. "And why are you at home? Are you ill?" she asked gently. Nathan nodded. "Aye, you have a fever and are quite pale. I think we must put you in bed. Would you like to rest in my bed where you can still smell the air of the sea?"

"Yes," he said with a weary smile and they both rose.

"Good. Then up with you. I shall bring you some broth and a cool cloth for your head once you've climbed into bed. Off with you now."

As Nathan climbed the stairs, Abigail arranged her clothes and walked into the shop, closing the kitchen door behind her. She was surprised to find that Jeremy sat upon the same chair, smoking his pipe. Except for the pale of his complexion he looked quite composed and rose as she entered.

"I believe that it would be best if we conducted our business on another day," he said in a quiet voice but one devoid of apology.

"I believe that would be a good idea."

"And it would also be best if your brother, Goodman Peabody, were present."

"As I told you before, I am the publisher of the words you claim to be libelous. Your business is with me alone. Despite your behavior of the most common sort, I do not believe I need my brother to defend me from you as he did once before from your brother!"

Rage filled Jeremy's strong face and he stamped out his pipe.

"I assure you that my breach of manners will never recur, for there is nothing but business that I wish to engage in with you."

"I would hope so. Now that you've humiliated me

the way you intended to, although I am not a lady of your 'better sort' as Miss Wattington is, I would hope you will conduct yourself with the courtesy one is to expect from a gentleman of your station. Perform your role as the governor's mouthpiece and leave us to our work and lives!''

She watched as his mouth opened, but not a word came out as Jeremy spun on his heels, threw open the door and stormed into the street. Abigail gently closed the door and wearily walked back into the living quarters of the house.

As Jeremy sharply turned the corner he nearly collided with Levi, who was leading the nag into the backyard.

Levi was about to tell the Tory scum a thing or two, but the look of fury on Jeremy's face silenced him unexpectedly. Better he should hurry into the house and ask Abigail what brought Jeremy to the shop today without announcement.

Jeremy wove his way through the crowded streets as fast as he could, but still his heart beat fiercely. He was furious and ashamed of himself. Yet his lips against Abigail's soft lips, his body pressed against hers so strongly that he could feel her nipples as they hardened instinctively and the heat from beneath her skirt as he pressed against her tender thighs, replayed in his mind. God how he loved her! How he had always loved her and never another! He had been lying to himself when he said he wanted to take her but once. He didn't want to take her like some streetwalker in London. He wanted to rejoice with her. Even if she had done the same with Damon. He had to forgive her because she was all he ever wanted.

But he had so humiliated her, mocking her sweet response. How would he make her forgive him—

"Young man! How dare you be so rude as to cause an old woman to lose her step and almost her bundles—"

"Jane!" he exclaimed, glad to see the stout, sweet-faced lady who used to feed him home-baked cakes. "I am so sorry. I did not see you because I was so far—please," he pleaded and touched her shoulder, "forgive me for my bad manners."

"Jeremy Blackburn!" Jane exclaimed. "You are a fine sight! Pray tell what has riled you so that you are crossing these treacherous streets so blindly?"

He wanted to tell her but couldn't bring himself. For what if Abigail recounted his brutishness? "Matters on my mind . . ."

"Matters of commerce?" Jane asked innocently.

"Yes, that's it."

"Jeremy. You never were good at fabrication. Even when you were a boy! Forgive a gossipy old woman. You have seen Abigail, have you not?"

"Yes. But on business matters. Nothing more," he strongly insisted.

"I see . . . I understand . . . business matters. Of course, for you are soon to be wed, are you not?" she asked with a bewildering smile in her eyes.

"Yes, I am." He'd actually forgotten, and the reminder just made him the more miserable. "It was good seeing you, Mrs. Stewart. I do hope I shall see you again sometime." Jeremy smiled as politely as he could.

"Yes, dear boy. Somehow I think that you will. Good day to you now. And watch your way so that you do not knock down some genuinely *old* lady who cannot steady herself from your attack!" Jane said and laughed.

Jeremy bowed, allowed her to pass, then walked on. Jane turned behind her once and was reassured to see that the speed of Jeremy's long gait had considerably slowed. If she hadn't seen him coming toward her he might have actually knocked her down rather than bumping into the bag of potatoes she'd swung in his way, she thought to herself with a laugh. Yes, she had learned what she wanted to. Definitely he had seen Abigail. With God's help and a little push on the part of Mrs. Jane Stewart when needed, it wouldn't be long before they were reunited, finally.

# Chapter Six

"YOU HAVE NO RIGHT TO SPEAK TO ME AS IF I AM SOME mere child who cannot conduct herself in—" Abigail shouted, no longer certain at whom she was most angry—Jeremy, Levi, or herself.

"Used colonial goods!" Levi sputtered.

"What is that you say?" Abigail asked, confused. She stood shoulders erect, arms crossed against her chest, as if to strengthen herself.

"He called you used colonial goods," Levi repeated more softly, yet the fury raged in his eyes. "He said he had no need for such, your fine *Tory gentleman*. He said it before Adam and Charles, in the tavern."

Abigail was stunned into silence. Even as she studied her brother's face she knew that Levi would never fabricate so hateful and humiliating a statement. What a fool she had been. For a moment, when Jeremy had kissed her, she'd actually believed . . .

Sorrowfully, Levi watched the sag of his sister's strong, straight shoulders. Her complexion turned so ashen that her eyes, filmed in tears, shone like green stones set in alabaster. He desired so to take her pain away, but the truth had to have been spoken. Even now, he knew it useless to interrogate her further. Something beyond odious business had transpired during Jeremy's visit. Not only was Abigail's hair in disarray, but the stormy expression on her face when he'd entered the kitchen had matched the previous stony rage of Jeremy's countenance.

There was nothing more to be said, Abigail decided. Only then did it occur to her that Levi had returned from Cambridge earlier than she'd expected. "Did you get the orders from Goodman Manning and Goodwife Greene?" she asked as she walked to the table and sat at the high-backed chair.

In the heat of what had transpired during the past fifteen minutes, Levi had quite forgotten the news. He walked across the room, reached for a mug, and poured himself a bit of cool punch. Then he sat across from Abigail at the long, chestnut wood table. "Goodman Manning is closing his shop."

"But why?" Abigail asked. "He is said to be a fine cobbler. . . . Is it this insidious depression?"

"Yes. He is filing for bankruptcy. Another fine artisan ruined by the Currency Act. Without paper money, he has not been able to pay his creditors. And he has not been receiving payment from the farmers and villagers because of their own plight—as we well know, do we not?" he said and sighed.

"Yes. And beyond those whose accounts to us are overdue, how many bankruptcies have we listed in the paper this past year alone? Too many to contemplate without feeling sickened by the malaise."

"And we are hanging by our own thumbs this

month, sister, are we not? I need not keep the books to know how our business has dwindled this past year. We all suffer, all but the 'better sort' who feed on our troubles like worms on a corpse. *Mr.* Blackburn may not gain the satisfaction of closing us down should we continue to lose accounts and orders." Levi downed his punch and rose.

Abigail silently regarded her brother, acknowledging all he said. Why had Jeremy returned to sow more misery when they already had their fair share of burdens? She rose and crossed the room to Levi. It was not often that either showed their affection with hugs or kisses, but she much needed to hug her brother and she did. Even as she held him, the tightness of his frame did not lessen. She knew it was not anger at her but worry. "We will survive these difficult times as we have survived greater troubles in the past, Levi."

"Aye, I know. You are so much like Father was . . . so much more than myself." His eyes softened. "It is you that I fret for. Promise me, Abigail. A true promise. That you will not be in the presence of Jeremy again without informing me of his appointment. He is dangerous. More dangerous to you than to me or our paper."

"I promise," she answered with genuine sincerity as they separated.

"Jeremy was once a fine man. Now it appears that all the evil that consumed Damon has passed into his brother. He is no longer the man you once loved. That Jeremy is as dead and buried as Damon."

"That is not so!" Abigail retorted so sharply that she startled herself. Why was she pleading his case after his abominable behavior this morning and his assumption of the detestable position as censor for the Crown? But she had seen the old Jeremy—or was that a sham he'd conjured to entrap her and thus humiliate her? Before he departed he had said that he had no use for her, and apparently he had said worse yet about her to Levi. She had no cause to remember what was long dead. For surely she could never forget his derisive laugh after he'd kissed her and evoked before-unknown sensations aroused by that kiss and the fire of his lean, strong body against her own.

". . . how you can defend him?" Levi was lecturing at her, his anger exploding once again. "You force me to tell you what I'd believed was unnecessary to speak. Jeremy wished to challenge me to a duel, as he is an expert swordsman I am told. He wishes to kill me. To avenge his brother's murder although I was proven innocent. This is the man you are so quick to defend."

Abigail's fingers played at her keys. So, her worst apprehensions had been justified. "But you were not in the vicinity of the waterfront when Damon was beaten, robbed, and stabbed to death. Witnesses testified to such. You were acquitted."

Levi smiled sadly. "That matters not to Jeremy. Gentry like himself are accustomed to having their due, law be damned. What kind of man would otherwise work as one of Governor Bernard's henchmen? Jeremy Blackburn is an infernal Tory who lived the lascivious life of the 'better sort' in London. I have heard such stories already, of vice, women, such matters that are not for your ears. Trust me, sister. Do you doubt my intentions?"

Levi looked, for the moment, as he had as a boy, his face so open with doubt. "Of course I do not doubt your intentions!" she declared in a soft, chiding voice. "But you worry needlessly. Do you not have faith in my discernment? Or virtue?"

"I have implied no question of that sort. It is curious that you should be thinking such notions."

"Levi Peabody! How dare you—"

"Good day to you both!" Jane called out as she entered the kitchen from the back door, her hands heavy with bundles. Levi immediately turned to Jane and helped her carry them to the table. Neither Abigail nor Levi spoke. "Lovely day 'tis, at that. Almost like summer. The city is as bustling as I've seen it for a time, on such a fair day as this!" Jane continued as she busied herself with the large sack of potatoes.

Only the jingling of the shop door ceased her chatter. "It is probably Mistress Pomegrant. I shall attend to her," Abigail said.

"No, I shall," Levi insisted. "I suggest you straighten your day cap and falling hair before you present yourself in the shop. Better still that you and Jane attend to Nathan."

Abigail reached to her head. She blushed as she discovered that not only was her cap in disarray, but that her hair had slipped from its pins. No wonder Levi had been so convinced that more than she'd admitted had transpired! Abigail turned from the small looking glass to Jane, who stood with a silly smile on her face. "Pray tell, why are you grinning at me!" she snapped.

"Grinning you say?" Jane inquired with a mask of

puzzlement. "I did not realize. It is just that I had a most pleasant encounter after I left Katie to wait for the fresh chickens. Whom should I pass on the way home? Mr. Jeremy Blackburn. My, he looks more elegant and handsome than ever! I did not know he had returned to Boston," Jane said, her lie not evident on her face.

"How could you have not heard after the row with Levi yesterday?" Abigail accused, not taken in. "I do not want to hear his name spoken in this house, Mrs. Stewart!"

"Why certainly, *Mistress* Peabody. I had no idea that his name could excite such emotion from—"

"It is *not emotion*. . . . It's . . ."

"Yes, I see." Jane turned her back to Abigail with the pretext of bellowing the fire. "Surely. I do apologize."

"Nathan has been sent home with a fever," Abigail informed Jane, as much to evade the subject at hand.

Jane turned to her. Her thinly disguised twinkling smile had disappeared. "A strong fever?" she asked with alarm. "Where is he?"

Abigail softened. "No, do not worry. A mild one. He is asleep in my bed. I should already be attending to him."

"Aye, I shall prepare a cool cloth you may take and some broth."

As Abigail sat beside him, Nathan slept fitfully. She changed his compress and felt his head. Already his fever had lowered. She yawned, wishing that she could crawl into bed beside the boy, for she was so weary and her eyes so heavy. She gazed about her small bedroom replete with canopied bed, dresser, washstand and small pine desk. Perhaps she should take a few moments and write in her diary . . . Abigail's eyes caught her reflection in the looking glass above the dresser. For a moment she thought she saw a stranger. For the woman who appeared before her, lips parted and red against her white teeth, and an unaccustomed expression in her eyes, did not seem to be herself.

Fascinated, despite her guard against vanity, she slowly stared at this woman and traced her finger over her mouth as she remembered Jeremy's lips upon her own. She pulled off her day cap and slowly unpinned her hair. Eyes staring in the looking glass, she watched her hair fall full down her shoulders, over her breasts and to her waist. She traced her hand from the crown of her head down the crimson silky length of her hair.

Nathan stirred. Quickly she returned to her senses. Fortunately the boy remained asleep. Efficiently, she repinned her hair and afixed her cap. Turning back to the looking glass, it was herself who returned her stare—except for the strange glimmer that lingered in her lambent green eyes. Abigail turned from her reflection and changed the compress on Nathan's forehead.

As she departed the bedroom, Abigail assiduously avoided the looking glass.

# Chapter Seven

JEREMY DINED ALONE AT THE ELEGANT MAHOGANY table. He took a bite of the duckling and continued to read a letter to the editor in the latest issue of the *Boston Evening Post,* dated June 2, 1765. He shook his head and laughed aloud at this nasty but witty letter that brutally caricatured the easy target of Governor Bernard's petty pomposity. Glancing down the column to the signature, Jeremy was not surprised to see that it was protectively signed, "An outraged Boston citizen." Jeremy could already visualize the governor's rage at tomorrow's council meeting and his order that Jeremy investigate until he discover the identity of the signer. Despite Governor Bernard's character deficiencies, he was not a stupid man and understood that the editor would not disclose that information. He'd already twice in the past week spoken to Benjamin Edes, the editor and publisher of the *Gazette,* about such inflammatory, anonymously-written essays that had appeared in his paper. While everyone knew for certain that the author of one essay was none other than James Otis and of the other Edes himself, no confirmation was in the offing. Nor had Jeremy expected any. He knew, as well, that he would be lectured about the Peter Zenger case in '35, which upheld freedom of the colonial press.

Jeremy read on and laughed aloud again.

"Have you finished with your duckling, sir?" Mrs. Latham was his father's housekeeper, who, along with her sixteen-year-old daughter, Prissy, and Tom, the coachman, had stayed behind in Boston to attend to Jeremy's needs while his father remained in Halifax.

Jeremy was almost tempted to read the letter to the bony, sour-faced, middle-aged woman. Last week, when the governor had paid a courtesy tea call, it had been one of the few times in Jeremy's memory that Mrs. Latham had demonstrated any display of emotion. That she fawned and supplicated was not a particular surprise to Jeremy, who had always disliked this woman.

How different was her daughter, Prissy, a ripe, pretty brunette who was as saucy and impudent as her mother was taciturn. And so Prissy had been since before Jeremy left for London. His only surprise was that the girl was not yet the mother of a bastard child. Since his return, Prissy had taunted him with her abundant physical charms, but thus far he had resisted her attempts, which were so artless that they were as comical as they were tantalizing. Jeremy wished he could pride himself on his morality, but he knew it to be that he was too ensnared by his conflicting emotions to be tempted by a carefree romp with the girl—who was probably as succulent as the fine duckling he had just distractedly enjoyed.

"Yes, thank you, Mrs. Latham. It was most succulent and tasty," he said, so heartily that he engendered a rare smile from the unpleasant woman. He realized that he'd been referring as much to Prissy as to the duck, and had to tighten his jaw to keep from laughing. He was becoming giddy from too little sleep, too much wine and work, he realized. He did wish Michael Harrington would arrive so they could be off to Faneuil Hall where the town meeting this evening was being held.

"Would you care for your plum pudding presently?" Mrs. Latham inquired.

Jeremy decided that he had eaten quite enough. "No, I think not," he answered politely. "I believe that I will retire to the study and continue with my work. When Doctor Harrington arrives," Jeremy said as he rose from the formal table, "please show him in."

Jeremy was again engrossed in an issue of the *Gazette,* as he sat in his father's richly wainscoted and paneled study. He lit his clay pipe and puffed until the aroma of the sweet tobacco filled the room. Jeremy glanced at the fireplace with its two flanking pilastered motifs. The one to his right contained a china closet with an intricately carved shelf upon which his father displayed many of the family heirlooms, such as the silver tea service. It was far too warm an evening for the fire to be lit, which disappointed Jeremy, for it was the fire that lent warmth to this otherwise well-appointed but cold room. How are you, old boy, Jeremy thought rather disrespectfully, as he gazed upon the portrait of his great-grandfather, Sir Henry

79

Blackburn, that hung above the mantel. The chimes of the Willard clock indicated that it was already half-past the hour of six.

Jeremy tried to read but found his mind wandering from the repetitive diatribes against the Crown, Royal government, and Tories. Ostensibly, Jeremy was attending the town meeting in his role as barrister for the governor; he would bring to court those publishers who printed libelous or seditious statements against the government. But he was more than curious to see the charismatic James Otis in action. He'd been told that the man was brilliant but also of rather an unstable temperament. Some called him daft. Samuel Adams was thought to be of sounder mind, but just as inflammatory and shrewd.

Word was that a few of the "middling sort" had formed a secret group, calling themselves "The Loyal Nine." Ben Edes, the publisher of the *Gazette,* was a member, as well as his partner, John Gill. Most surprising was the name of John Avery, a wealthy merchant, who lent an unfortunate respectability to the otherwise unprominent group. Jeremy had learned that the names of Sam Adams and his cousin John, and James Otis, were conspicuously absent from the list. However, this ruse did not fool Bernard or the council, who were aware that these gentlemen were the driving force behind the group's formation. Still, unfortunately, no conclusive alliance could be proved between "The Loyal Nine" and the radical leaders of the Assembly. His years in London had led Jeremy to think that these radicals were making much ado about little—

"Sir?" called the sweet-voiced Prissy. She was dressed in a chemise of such thin gauze that against the backlighting of the whale-oil lamps, it offered the shape of her round breasts and full buttocks as she stood in profile to him.

"Yes, Prissy," he said, smiling at this pleasant diversion. "Has Dr. Harrington arrived?"

"No, sir," she answered with a pretty smile. "He sent word that he was detained and that he would be here shortly."

"Ah, I see. Thank you." As a physician Michael was often detained, and Jeremy had suspected this was the cause of his friend's tardiness.

"Would you care for a brandy, sir?" Prissy asked as she crossed the room and deprived him of the pleasure of the show of her ripeness.

"Yes. That would be good, if you please," he answered to Prissy, who was already at the sideboard preparing his drink. Jeremy puffed on his pipe and began to read the paper again, in part to distract himself from the girl.

Prissy brought his brandy to him with a mock curtsy that offered to his eyes her curvaceous breasts and a hint of pretty brown aureoles. "What's that you're reading?" she asked, as she leaned further over him as he sat on the brocaded chair. Her face was so close to his that he could smell the scent of some sweet soap as he took in the full view of her charms.

"It's the *Gazette*. Have you learned to read, Prissy?" he inquired, playing her game with her for awhile.

"No sir, I have not *quite*, yet. But I can make out a

word here and there! Let me show you—wait, I can't see very well from this position." With that, she rested her bottom on the arm of the chair and teetered in against him, her arm over his shoulder, her breasts and middle pressing against his arm and chest as she pretended to be diligently searching for a word she could read. "The!" she exclaimed, then pointed with her stubby finger to the word, thereby transferring the weight of her body further against his until Jeremy could feel the hardness of her nipple through his shirt.

A real coquette, he thought to himself. With a little training she could probably match some ladies of notoriety in London, he mused. But it was not he who would be her teacher, he knew with just a trace of disappointment. Prissy continued to call out words, as her hand played at his neck in a seemingly innocent manner, which felt too fine for him to stop it.

"I'm weary," she declared petulantly. "You must teach me to read, now that you're home again, so that it is not such a difficult task. Right now, read to me, will you, Jeremy? Please!" she pleaded and threw herself into his lap, causing the pipe to fly from his hand to the floor. Prissy pretended not to notice. "Damon used to read to me as I rested in his lap," she insisted, with such a willful, open face, as girlish as it was wanton, that it caused him to laugh. "Why are you laughing?" she demanded with mock indignation as she shifted about, as playful as a child upon his lap.

"Prissy, if that were so, you were but a girl at the time. Now you are a grown woman. A very grown woman," he declared, trying to appear stern and unmoved, even as he felt himself becoming aroused from the squirming of her full buns agitating against him.

"Oh, poo," she insisted. "Read to me, please," she insisted. "I shall lie very still, I promise." She fitted her head into the crook of his arm and threw her legs over his other arm.

"How can I read to you when you have both of my arms captured?" he asked with pretended innocence. He knew that he would have to remove the girl from his lap, but although he had bedded Belinda just last evening, silly Prissy was more full of warmth, affection, and unadulterated lust than his future wife could ever be, even during the most intimate moments of lovemaking. In fact, in the week since he had created the terrible scene with Abigail, when he had acted more reprehensibly than the worst rake, he had found little comfort in Belinda's arms. In truth, just to fulfill his manly role, he had had to pretend that it was Abigail, his emerald-eyed, crimson-haired, slender beauty in his arms. As she came to mind, his ardor for comely and available Prissy physically diminished. Gently, but firmly, he pushed Prissy from his lap.

"Oh, please, Jeremy," she pleaded in vain. "I'll be good and allow you to read—"

"Prissy," he admonished. "It is not seemly for a fine lass like yourself to be in such close proximity with a gentleman whose intentions are spoken for another."

"Oh, Damon was right about you," she said as she stood before him and arranged her chemise and petticoat. "You are so proper and serious!" Then she grinned mysteriously to herself. Suddenly she blanched and reached into her pocket, from which she withdrew a letter. Her demeanor returned to servant as her brown eyes widened with fear of reproach. "I was to give you this letter from your father earlier. I forgot. I am very sorry, sir," she said so earnestly that Jeremy could not find it in his heart to chastise her.

Jeremy was about to ask why Mrs. Latham had not delivered his letter herself. But he knew that the dour Mrs. Latham had sent Prissy to him with full knowledge and tacit approval of her subsequent flirtatious behavior. It was not uncommon for a woman of Mrs. Latham's position to throw a comely daughter at a gentleman of his station, in the hopes of ensnaring him through a pregnancy to marry the daughter, thereby ensuring their rise to the ranks of the "better sort."

The doorbell chimed. "Do you wish me to answer it, sir?" Prissy said, hoping to work herself out of the chastisement she expected.

"Yes. Please do. I am certain it is Dr. Harrington. Please show him in, Prissy. And do try to remember such things as letters in the future, will you, girl?"

"Aye! I swear to it!" She started to the door, then turned and whispered. "Please, do not tell my mother of my error, sir?" she beseeched.

"Which error is that, Prissy?" he teased, and winked at her.

With a full smile, all the more lovely because of its sincerity, she thanked him silently and ran for the door as the chimes rang again. Upon hearing the bells a second time, Jeremy's suspicions about Mrs. Latham were confirmed. For otherwise, she would have been at the door of the study to announce Michael.

Obviously, aware that he and her daughter might be in a compromising position, she dared not interrupt.

As Jeremy and Michael briskly walked the half-dozen streets from Jeremy's home on fashionable Hanover Street, the street of mansions built by the wealthiest of Boston's aristocrats, they followed the last of a stream of neighbors already on their way to Faneuil Hall.

"Perhaps you would have been happier if you had attended the meeting with Lord Wattington," Michael said, by way of another apology for having been detained with a patient.

"It was not only *not* a displeasure to wait quietly at home for you, Michael," Jeremy reassured him, "but something of a relief."

At this oblique remark, Michael turned to Jeremy with a puzzled expression. Jeremy intended to speak with Michael, but their walk en route to the town meeting was not an appropriate time. "I simply mean, that as cordial as the Wattingtons are, as charming and gay as Belinda may be, it was pleasant to have a quiet dinner and accomplish some of my work as well," Jeremy said, altering the implication of his previous remark.

Upon their arrival at Faneuil Hall, they saw many small groups of men, interspersed with some women, milling about the steps of the building whose first floor held a day market and second the meeting hall. There was a handsign posted, but before they could pass through the crowd to read its message, Mr. Howard, a neighboring merchant who owned one of the largest whale-oil manufacturing companies in Boston, greeted them with a firm handshake and a happy laugh. The hearty, affable older man seemed to be enjoying the commotion. "It appears that most of Boston's almost sixteen thousand inhabitants have turned out to hear the inevitable orations of James Otis and Sam Adams," he said with a sly grin in obvious hyperbole. "Therefore the meeting has been moved to the more spacious accommodations of Old South Meeting House."

"I expected that might happen," Michael said with an equally pleasurable smile. "Shall we walk together, Mr. Howard?" he offered.

"Most certainly, although you young men will have to slow your pace to accompany an old gizzard like myself. You may not be able to reach your seats among our kind, what with the masses of the 'middling' sort and a surprising number of those of the . . . 'inferior kind,'" he whispered, "who have been excited to attendance by all the talk and rabble-rousing by those who should know better."

"I have had my fill of reading the riotous propaganda against the Stamp Act in all of the Boston press," Jeremy added to his father's old friend. He noticed that Michael had grown quiet again.

"Yes, I gather," Mr. Howard said with a wry laugh. "I have no doubt that you have your work cut out for you, Jeremy. Your father must be bursting with pride, what with you stepping in to manage his affairs while he is in Halifax. And working in such a high position for the governor and his council. It was not too long ago that he lamented to me, I don't mind telling you now, that he feared you would remain in London forever. He felt as if he had lost both his sons. He had always assumed that it was your fine brother, Damon, who had the inclination to follow in his footsteps while you seemed more the, ah . . . the one with more artistic, scholarly leanings might he have said?"

"I have little doubt that he would have suggested such," Jeremy answered pleasantly; the tightening of his jaw that belied his equanimity was not noticed by Mr. Howard. However, a side glance proved to Jeremy that the same could not be said about Michael.

Just as Mr. Howard predicted, by the time they reached the Old South Meeting House, the pews were filled and many stood in the aisles and back of the hall.

"I shall help Mr. Howard to a seat up front," Michael spoke softly to Jeremy. "You and I can stand in the back if you do not mind." Michael seemed strangely animated by the crowd.

Jeremy was puzzled. It appeared to him that Michael was relieved that there was no apparent room in the front of the Third Congregational Church, where those of their class were always seated. "I do not mind at all," he answered. He for one was pleased to avoid the company of pompous and stuffy Lord Wattington for one evening; Belinda, of course, had not attended.

As Michael helped Mr. Howard down the long center aisle, Jeremy glanced about him. Most of the common faces of mechanicks, artisans, tradesmen and women, seamen and day workers were at best vaguely familiar to him. Surprisingly, he found himself moved by their animated, expectant faces and spirited conversations. They were so different from the "inferior sort" and the downtrodden who appeared as a blur in the dirty streets of the disease-ridden sections of London and Bristol.

Not that Jeremy believed that those of lesser classes had the background or the ability to dictate the weighty matters of government. In fact, last week, when Governor Bernard had spoken at length with him about his private plans for the reorganization of the colonial government, Jeremy had been duly impressed, for Bernard envisioned a reorganization closely modeled after that at Westminster.

In the Massachusetts Bay Colony, as well as the twelve others, it was only the governor's council, or its equivalent, of which his father was a member, that paralleled the House of Lords. The Assembly was close in form, if far in spirit, to the House of Commons. Bernard planned a bicameral government that would include a newly instituted upper house, comprised of titled and landed aristocracy as well as a new category peculiar to the colonies, which would include its wealthiest and most influential merchant class.

Although suffrage, or the right to vote, was contingent upon a property requirement, financial holdings, or position in the church, the rise of the artisans, many of whom had become quite affluent as a result of the French and Indian War, had allowed too many of that sort too much influence. It was their radical ideas that were at the heart of the uproar against the Stamp Act in particular, and of this growing "American" sentiment that was by its very nature treasonous, Jeremy thought. Worse yet, in his readings of the Boston press Jeremy already saw thinly veiled promises for universal suffrage being dangled at the most common of men, like a carrot on a stick, in order to sway them to the cause of these "middling sort" of clever radicals who knew how to manipulate the masses for their own means—

Jeremy felt a thick hand clap him on his back. "I had begun to wonder what had become of you two," said Mr. James Harrington, Michael's father and a wealthy barrister who headed the governor's financial office. His slate-blue eyes, as brilliant as Michael's and at the moment much more lively, sparkled. Mr. Harrington was generally in good spirits. For, like Jeremy's own father, Mr. Harrington's high position and loyalty to the Crown had paid off handsomely in gifts of enormous land grants in the frontiers and north of the Bay Colony. "I take it that it was my son who detained you while he was out treating some thug who had his arms broken in a brawl or something to that effect."

"I told you it was a woman in the South End who had been laboring in childbirth for two days. The midwife waited too long before she sent word for me. I couldn't save the baby—" Michael spoke to his father in a respectful tone but his face was deceptively unexpressive.

"The Lord's work. One less urchin to feed," Mr. Harrington interrupted, his smile diminishing only slightly.

Michael's eyes barely veiled their anger. "Nor the mother, sir. They both died."

To his credit, Mr. Harrington flinched slightly. "Which is why you should have left the whole affair to the midwife, who knows better than you doctors about such things," he pronounced. "Well, I daresay that at least you did arrive."

Jeremy knew that Michael's father had wanted his only son among four daughters to enter his law firm, and that he disdained not only Michael's defiance but his choice of professions, although a physician ranked high in social status. Mr. Harrington considered physicians to be charlatans and worse, yet even Jeremy was taken aback by the man's callousness.

Mr. Harrington smiled at Jeremy, who was forced to smile back. "Well at least this one had the sense to enter a real gentleman's profession," he said to Michael as his sharp eyes held Jeremy's. "Come now," he continued to both, then turned his head, covered with a high, powdered wig, to the front of the hall. "Lord Wattington and I went to much trouble to retain seating for you lads. In fact, Goodman Simpson had the audacity to ask for the seats for himself and his son!" he told them, his face growing red with indignation. Mr. Harrington wiped his heavy brow. "There is little room to breathe," he declared impatiently, looking about the crowd in the back of the room with obvious distaste. "The meeting is to begin in minutes," he added, then turned forward and hurled his corpulent body through a cluster of men in homespun shirts and leather trousers. "No manners!" he sniffed.

Jeremy stifled his laugh until he saw that Michael was attempting to do the same. Then he broke into a shared grin and chuckle as they followed bullish Mr. Harrington down the center aisle. As Jeremy followed Michael, in the wake of his father's turbulent path, he spotted Mr. Harrington already standing in the second aisle before the only open seats in the entire room. Jeremy gazed about the pews of seated citizens to his right and left. Midway down the aisle, he saw the double-headed brightness of red. One an ugly carrot color, the other plaited, silken crimson.

Why did his heart leap, he taunted himself. For surely he knew that Abigail would be amongst the small number of women who attended. And certainly she would be sitting beside her brother. He was both disappointed and relieved that Abigail's head was turned away in conversation with Adam Taylor. Jeremy had composed a half-dozen letters of apology to Abigail during the course of the week past. But each letter inevitably ended in a pledge of love that he dared not make.

He had not returned to her shop, even on the pretext of business. Rather, he had procured copies of the *Boston Word,* which he had read from cover to cover. Abigail was a fine publisher. While libelous and seditious statements appeared in her paper, they were mild compared to those in the larger and more influential press. Should he have followed his original instincts for revenge by closing down her paper or bringing suit, he would have looked ridiculous in the eyes of the governor and his council, for there were many more worthy opponents to challenge, like Mr. Edes of the *Gazette.* Moreover, he knew in his heart that he could do nothing to truly harm Abigail, and if that meant letting Levi be, then so be it. But he could not allow Abigail this knowledge, at least about the safety of her paper. For what other pretext would he have when he finally acquired the courage to face her again?

Unconsciously, Jeremy had halted. Levi turned,

saw him in his fine frock coat, and tightened his fists as he glared at Jeremy. When Jeremy met Levi's eyes, he took in the bitter stare.

So Levi knew of his abominable behavior, Jeremy thought. His guilt forced him to look away and walk on. He did not turn, because he could not have stood the challenge of Levi's inevitable smirk.

When Jeremy followed Michael to their seats, he paid his respects to Lord Wattington and the other gentlemen. Before he sat, he glanced back a dozen or so rows behind him. Abigail was looking straight ahead, but appeared not to see him. She was dressed in a blue and white frock and matching bonnet that became her. Her eyes shone like precious emeralds in her pink, heart-shaped face. Her full red lips were closed as she sat in repose. It was all he could do to refrain from shouting her name and leaping over the pews until he pulled her into his arms. Yet, when she began to move her head his way, Jeremy abruptly turned and folded his long frame into the space between Michael and Lord Wattington.

Abigail had seen Jeremy enter the church. She had watched as he greeted the aristocratic gentlemen and then turned in her direction. Her heart pounded so strongly that she was afraid that Levi could hear it. How beautiful Jeremy looked in his green frock coat and golden silk breeches. In the crowded room, his broad shoulders and height were even more attractive in contrast to the men about him. His bright brown eyes glowed in his sculptured face that appeared flush from the heat of the room. A lump formed in her throat, so large that it became difficult to swallow. How could her heart pound so for a man who had humiliated her? A man who obviously wanted nothing more to do with her? A man who stood for all the callousness and calumny of the Tories she so disdained? Levi had been right. Yet, as she tried to compose herself she realized that she was even more foolish than Levi had imagined. For at the moment she fantasized that if she were to gather the courage—to say nothing of the audacity—and march to the front of the church and call to him, he would come to her and sweep her into his arms, out of the church, and away from all reality. . . .

What was wrong with her? For even Katie, in their private talk late one night, had gently but firmly agreed with Levi. And even to Katie she had not been able to recount the humiliating scene that had occurred last Monday morn.

Jeremy had forced himself to pay attention to the various speakers at the beginning of the meeting. But soon, despite himself, he was caught up in the stirring arguments, especially those being recounted by James Otis. Although Otis said nothing Jeremy had not already heard or read, his way with words, his passion that no one could doubt was utterly heartfelt, caused Jeremy to listen with a new ear. Perhaps there was some legitimacy to Otis's arguments that Parliament had no right to tax the colonies directly, that this was the function of the local assemblies, and that the Stamp Act would be a further deterrent to trade because of the many taxes to be levied on shipping papers.

There was silence in the large hall as Otis spoke of payment in specie, gold and silver, that would mean an additional drain of that already scarce money source. There were cheers when Otis asserted that the troops to be supported by stamp proceeds would be used to help enforce this and other measures, *not* to defend the colonies as Parliament asserted. The loudest cheers came from many merchants, not a few among them known smugglers and proud of their flourishing rum trade, when Otis claimed that the trials for infringement of the law and other measures in vice-admiralty courts—like the one over which Jeremy's father presided in Halifax—which operated without juries, was just another blow to their rights as Englishmen.

As the radicals cheered and the Tories around him sat in stony, angry silence, Jeremy found himself confused. He'd entered the room so certain of his ideas. Now he had to think. Moreover, he was quite puzzled about Michael's reactions. For although Michael did not applaud Otis, Adams or the others, Jeremy, who glanced at him often during the two hours, was certain that his friend's sentiments were merely being expertly repressed.

During the time that Jeremy pondered, the floor had been opened to questions and comments from citizens, even those who did not have the privilege of voting. Within moments, the voices of logic and reason had given way to the ill-spoken, ill-mannered common folk. They attacked not only Governor Bernard, who was an easy target, but Lieutenant Governor Hutchinson, who Jeremy knew to be a fine, intelligent, and compassionate man who was ironically overly sympathetic to the colonial claims of injustice.

A thin, gray-haired, wizened man rose. He was dressed in severe black clothes that were reminiscent of the earliest Puritan settlers a hundred years before. "And what about the Anglican plot to bring us their bloody, idol-worshipping bishops!" he cried in a high-pitched, ardent voice. Thus began more clamor and tumult. Jeremy, an Anglican by heritage and occasional visitor to the colonial Episcopal Church, thought the comment too ridiculous to merit an answer. But soon a shouting match ensued. Eventually Sam Adams took control again, but not before Jeremy grew disgusted with the spectacle. This was what happened if the "lesser sort" were given a voice in a public forum. He thought of Abigail and wanted to explain to her his fresh insight as to why a regulated government, run by those who ruled best, was an absolute necessity for a civilized society. The common man, given free rein, would inevitably degenerate into a blind, unthinking, ugly mob!

Jeremy was relieved when Michael and the others rose. He wanted a strong glass of whiskey. As they walked into the aisle, a young man who Jeremy recognized as a "devil," or apprentice, at Ben Edes' print shop, approached Michael. Michael stepped aside and the boy whispered something in Michael's ear that brought a glint to his eye. Michael nodded and the boy was off. When Michael turned again to him, Jeremy could read nothing in his face that suggested what the boy had said. Silently they started for the door.

Jeremy caught a glimpse of Abigail, who was engaged in intense conversation with James Otis. She jotted words into a leather-bound book as they spoke.

As he progressed down the aisle Abigail came within touching distance, but Jeremy forced his eyes straight ahead and moved as rapidly toward the door as was possible in this crowded room.

"That was most interesting, I shall admit," Jeremy said to Michael as they stood in the warm night air on the cobblestoned street before South Meeting House. "Quite a show," he added with more joviality than he intended, for he was feeling perplexed about what he had heard and witnessed, and distraught about Abigail. "Shall we adjourn to our favorite tavern for a drink or two, old friend?" Jeremy asked as he slung his arm around Michael's shoulder.

Michael hesitated. He seemed agitated. Then he looked away. When he returned his eyes to Jeremy's face, his countenance was opaque. "I am sorry. But I cannot. . . . I must go to see a patient. . . . I am sorry. Perhaps tomorrow evening? And dinner then as well?"

"Oh," Jeremy said, openly disappointed. "So that is what Mr. Edes' devil spoke to you about."

"How did you know that he was—I mean, I didn't know you knew the boy, Dudley. Yes. His father is ill . . ."

Jeremy knew that Michael was flustered because he was an unpracticed liar. He was hurt that his best friend would see fit to tell him such an obvious untruth, but could not allow himself to speak so. "Well, it is a doctor's duty, my friend, is it not, to help the sick and needy," Jeremy said with more irony than he'd intended. Enough irony to cause Michael to flinch. "Be off with you then," Jeremy said heartily, "and we shall have dinner tomorrow and talk."

Michael clasped his shoulder and his eyes reflected his struggle. He too forced a hearty smile. "Aye. Tomorrow. I give you my word. . . . And we will *talk,*" Michael added, seemingly with intentional portent.

Jeremy headed for the Bunch of Grapes tavern, but turned away when he reached its door. He was thirsty for a drink—for many drinks—of strong whiskey, but in no mood to be in a crowded and boisterous room. He turned at random and headed toward the Long Wharf. Perhaps the salty air of the harbor would help him think.

As he stood before a magnificently masted sailing ship, Jeremy breathed in the cool sea air. He had returned to Boston little more than two weeks before, believing he knew his mind. But tonight he felt sure of nothing. He remembered the letter from his father that he'd placed in the pocket of his coat. There was no light by which to read it in this outermost corner of the wharf, but he would read it when he returned home.

He already guessed what the letter said. Surely his father would tell him of his plight with the colonial smugglers and common thieves who made their pockets full at the expense of the Crown. He would lament the accommodations and lack of accoutrements in Halifax. There would be words of greetings for the Wattingtons. Then, after some household and financial instructions, his father would say how proud he was of him. Behind those words was the message that he was *almost* living up to the expectations his father had held for Damon, for when he was alive Damon could do no wrong in his father's eyes. Now that he was dead he was the enshrined son who could do no wrong anywhere, to anyone, again.

Jeremy was shocked at his unkind thoughts about his brother, his own blood and image. He was not himself this eve.

A half-hour later found Jeremy standing off Dassett Alley in front of Abigail's house. Quietly, he crept into the backyard and stared up at the lighted windows. He did not know how long he stood beneath the apple tree, but finally he caught a glimpse worthy of his vigilance, for Abigail appeared at the window of the lighted dormer room. She raised the window and leaned out a bit, looking into the dark night. He heard her sigh so sadly that he had to bite his lip to keep from calling to her. Then, in too brief a moment, she lowered the window and walked off. Moments later the candle that flickered in her room was extinguished. Jeremy waited a moment longer and then turned and left.

As he stood at the front door of Belinda's fine house on Hanover Street, not far from his own, he reached for the knocker. Quickly his hand dropped and he turned and walked down the street undetected.

By the time he'd reached the tavern called The Salutation at the North End of the city, he was weary and equally thirsty. He had not been in this tavern in years. In fact, it had never been one that he cared to frequent, what with its seamen clientele. But here he was and here he would probably be unknown. For he wished no idle conversation tonight.

Jeremy was considerably cheered and even more

considerably drunk, when he observed a group of gentlemen leave the back, private room about an hour after he had arrived. They left swiftly and quietly. But as drunk as he was, Jeremy was certain that the man who exited at Ben Edes' side was no other than Michael Harrington.

"Another tankard, mate?" Henry, the sailor with whom he'd been sharing idle bar talk and bawdy jokes, offered.

"A double whiskey, I think, and chaser. But this round's on me, Horace," Jeremy declared loudly.

"You are an honorable gentleman and a mate who can hold his own with any man!" the sailor declared and clapped him hard upon his back. "And the name is Henry, but I take no offense, sir! None at all!"

When Jeremy woke up before dawn in his own bed, he hadn't the slightest idea of how or when he'd arrived there. He lifted his head but quickly laid it back on the pillow as the dizziness and nausea overtook him. Finally the room stopped spinning. He had the vilest taste in his mouth, but before he could reach for the pitcher of water that stood on the table by his bedside, he fell back into a restless sleep.

"Abigail," he cried out more than once during the night, but there was no one by his side to hear him as he dreamed.

# Chapter Eight

ABIGAIL WAS DEFTLY SETTING THE LETTERS IN TYPE when Katie appeared in the workroom of the shop. Katie, so slight and fragile, appeared all apron, as her belly seemed to enter a room a moment before she did. Abigail did not know much about these things, but she believed that Katie would bring the new babe into the world before the end of August, as the midwife said. Sarah wriggled in Katie's arms. For Abigail, Sarah's smile and delft-blue eyes lit the room. It was at moments like this that Abigail ached for a babe of her own. She forced herself to remember that it was seemingly not God's plan for her to bring children into the world, and to question God's intentions was arrogant at best.

"I am taking Sarah with us. When Jane is at market, Sarah and I will first go to the candlemaker's shop, then to the dry goods store. I will meet Jane at the butcher shop." Katie smiled. "Is there something you need that I might bring you?"

"No, there is nothing that I think of at the moment . . . soap? I do need another ball of soap . . ."

"Aye. Jane is stopping for that on her way to market."

"That is all of which I can think, then, thank you." Abigail thought that Katie appeared a bit wan, while Sarah, a bundle of energy, bounced in her arms. "Why not leave Sarah with me?" Abigail earnestly offered. "You can lay her in her cradle right beside me. It will make your morning easier."

"Thank you, Abigail, but she has been cutting a tooth, as you know, and I am not certain that she would sleep. If she cried you would not complete your work, and all the type must be set by the time Levi returns from deliveries, so that he can work the press. Is that not so?"

"You have certainly learned all there is to know about printing a newspaper," Abigail said, in admiration of Katie. She and Katie had already spoken of the role she could play in producing the weekly paper after the baby was born. Katie had long before learned to set type and did it almost as well as herself. "Aye, all that is so. But I could rock Sarah to sleep with one hand and continue to set the type with the other if necessary."

Katie walked to her and kissed her on her cheek as she put Sarah in Abigail's arms. Abigail inhaled the perfume of the baby's sweetness. But she held Sarah awkwardly, for she did not wish to dirty the baby's bunting with her grimy fingers. Katie laughed and lifted the baby. "Thank you for your offer," Katie said. "We shall leave you to your work and see you by noon. I do hope that it does not rain, for the skies look very threatening," Katie added with a sigh.

"Is that so? I have been so busy that I had not noticed." Abigail watched Katie walk to the door. "Good-bye until later, sweet sister and niece," Abigail called. She listened for the chiming of the bells as Katie closed the door behind her. Then Abigail sat in quiet solitude once more.

How very peculiar life could turn out to be, she reflected. Little would she ever have imagined, as a girl, that she would have grown to become an artisan and spinster. She had always assumed that she would marry and have as many children as was God's will.

When she began to be courted by Jeremy, in her fifteenth year, she had arrogantly assumed not only that it was her right to love and have him, but that she was meant to have such a fine, handsome, talented husband. For she knew herself then to be a pretty girl, and despite Jane's admonishments of the sins of vanity, she was very taken with herself those many years before. How she had loved to flaunt her thick, silky, long red hair at every opportunity. And as her body grew into womanhood, she would secretly study it in the looking glass. How secretly prideful she had been of her sprouting small but shapely young breasts, the curve of her slender waist that flaired into slender but womanly hips and thighs. But for almost the last five years, she had scrubbed her body which had matured even more fully, but she no longer thought of it as an object of admiration and eventual pleasure. Not since Damon's hands . . .

A year after Jeremy left, she had been courted. But

she had no interest. Fortunately, as she learned the printing trade and had a proclivity for writing, she had been valuable to her father and therefore he never insisted that she be wed. After his death it was no longer an issue. Now, in the little more than two weeks since she'd first seen Jeremy, she was transformed in a way that mortified her. For once again, since his kiss, did she steal admiring glances at her form before the looking glass in her bedroom.

Worse still, her senses seemed to have grown more acute. The soft skin and sweet smell of baby Sarah could bring her to tears if she allowed her true feelings to emerge. She began to hate the texture of her coarse work dresses against her skin. She was aware of the feel of her breasts against her sheets when she lay in bed, and had begun to imagine Jeremy's strong hands caressing them. She remembered the touch of his full lips upon her own, the breath of his shoulders as he held her in his arms, the heat of his body and pressure of his strong thighs against her belly. She had not been sleeping well, for her conscience nagged at her for these sensual and sinful thoughts and daydreams— Enough! She was doing it again!

Abigail forced herself to concentrate upon her work. She read aloud the lines of type she had just set for tomorrow's paper. Already Boston had been buzzing about the resolution made by the Assembly two days before. "On the 8th of June, the Massachusetts House of Representatives sent a Circular Letter to the Assemblies of North America, inviting Them to meet in a Congress at New York this coming October. The Purpose of the Congress is to consider of a general and united, dutiful loyal and humble Representation of their Condition to His Majesty, and the Parliament; and to implore Relief.''

The bells at the outer shop door chimed just as Abigail finished proofing the first paragraph. Distractedly, she walked from the antechamber to the front of the shop, the foolscap paper from which she set the type in her hand. "Good morning," she said, as she looked up. She said no more as her mouth dropped open, for there before her stood Jeremy.

"Good morning, Mistress Peabody," he said and gave her a small bow with his three-cornered hat in hand. His smile was tight. "Please forgive me for calling upon you without prior notice. But I was at the office of Mr. Edes' down the street and—if I have picked an inopportune time—" he stated apologetically.

Abigail was suddenly aware of her clean, pressed but stained yellow chemise and white petticoat. She felt tendrils of her hair at her face. She looked plain and shabby, she thought as her face warmed with embarrassment. "Eh . . . No, Mr. Blackburn. I have been at work, as you can see," she continued and glanced at her ink-stained hands which furthered her sense of appearing unfit for a visit. Wait, she thought. This is not a visit, but a business call. For she was a *working* woman and proud of it. If she did not appear in silks and laces, with soft creamed hands, like Belinda Wattington, it was because she was *not* a lady of Belinda's position. Nor did she wish to be! Her composure returned. "I have been setting type for tomorrow's paper. It is not a particularly good day for further business. But I realize that you have your job to perform. So please sit down and tell me how I can help you, even if it cannot be accomplished today."

Abigail sat on one chair and then Jeremy settled onto another. As he removed his pipe from its velvet pouch she studied him. Jeremy did not look well. Lines she had not seen before had appeared at the corner of his eyes, and his eyes themselves lacked the sunny brown brightness she knew so well. Beneath them she noticed that the sockets were darkened. He has not been sleeping well either, she suspected.

"Do you mind if I smoke?"

"No, go right ahead. I do so like the aroma of tobacco. I miss it, for Levi doesn't smoke as Father did . . ." How was it that thoughts of her father abounded in Jeremy's presence? Jeremy seemed to be having difficulty starting his pipe and he glanced up at her, but quickly lowered his eyes to his task again. She restrained herself from reaching out, taking the match from his tapered fingers and holding the flame for him as she'd done so often for her father. She must move him to the purpose of his visit and have it finished with as quickly as possible, Abigail knew. For the quivering in her stomach that belied her composure was a warning sign she would heed. "So, how may I help you, Mr. Blackburn?" she inquired.

He looked up at her. "Well, Mistress Peabody. I have obtained past issues of the *Boston Word*, upon the request of the governor. I have read each and every one. I do wish to compliment you on the overall highly professional tenor of your publication. It matches many I have seen in London, and although smaller than some papers in Boston, it matches the quality of the finest press in this city." He finished his little speech, which was sincere although planned. As Jeremy smiled at Abigail's pleasure, despite her attempt to conceal it, he thought of what he really wanted to say. He had noted her self-conscious appraisal of her person when he'd unexpectedly entered the shop. As he watched her, pretending that his pipe was giving him undue difficulty, he wanted to say that even as she sat before him in a simple work dress that had obviously seen many a day of labor, she was more beautiful than any woman he had ever seen. He wanted to push away the strands of crimson hair that fell about her face, caress her soft, high cheeks and her slender neck, and kiss those red full lips that she unconsciously, nervously licked. He wanted to take her in his arms and feel her softness against his body and smell the sweet fragrance that was her natural perfume, sweeter than the most costly blends from Paris. He wanted to kiss her eyes, those eyes that shone at him with the beauty of the sun lighting the sea.

". . . Mr. Blackburn? Are you well?" Abigail asked. For he had not seemed to hear her speak. He appeared pale and flushed. She feared he had a fever. Since the small pox epidemic of last summer, one couldn't help but fear a fever, even a small one, as an ominous sign. Abigail was truly alarmed.

Jeremy felt the color rise in his face as he realized that he'd been so lost in thought and passion. "I am fine . . . just a bit weary. Please do not worry about me," he said, too late realizing the implication of his words.

"I have no reason to *worry* about you," she said defensively. She had been too obvious in her sentiments, she realized. Soon he would mock her. He already had, although it was said in an even tone. "I believe you have Mistress Wattington to do that. Perhaps she does not allow you enough sleep—" The words popped from her mouth before she could stop them. She could not believe that she had voiced such an improper remark, as blatantly rude as it was nasty. She reached for the keys that hung on the rope around her waist. "Please, forgive me! That was rude and uncalled for—" Why was he grinning at her? His face had taken on a life it had lacked until this moment. She was confused, for surely he should be angry at her impropriety.

So she's jealous! Jeremy's heart leaped with joy, for that meant that he might still have a chance. "No, please, Abigail. Do not apologize for a polite concern for my health. I have gazed at myself in the looking glass and I do agree that I do look less than fit these days. I appreciate your concern." He puffed on his pipe to help keep his mouth from expressing the delight he felt. Now was the moment. "I am the one who owes you an apology. I behaved brutishly the morning of my previous visit. I would have come earlier to apologize but I was afraid that you could never forgive me for . . . I am terribly sorry, Abigail. Can you find it in your heart to forgive me?"

Abigail studied his face. She saw his sincerity in the gentle, caring eyes of the Jeremy she had once loved. She found it difficult to speak. She had to remember that what he offered was an apology for his behavior. Nothing more. Nothing else had changed. "Certainly. I do accept your apology. I think it would be helpful for you to know that I have not spoken of the, er, incident, to anyone. Nathan has quite forgotten, for you did much to allay his fears."

Jeremy allowed himself to smile freely. "He is a fine young boy, is he not?"

"Aye, he is most dear to me. To all of us . . ." It was happening again. She had to return their conversation to a more proper subject and make it clear to him that they must conduct their business and be done with it. "I am very busy, Jeremy. I do not wish to be rude, but it would be most helpful if you would tell me what you wish me to do, or whatever, so that I can return to my pressing work. I do appreciate your apology and am sure that from here on we can conduct ourselves properly—"

Before the clanging of the bells at the door stopped, Mistress Pomegrant entered the shop in a flutter. Jeremy rose.

"My dear Abigail, my dear Abigail," she hurriedly spoke in her peculiar combination of French and Boston accents. "I am so very grateful I found you in! For I am in a tizzy!" The long feather of her hat swung in emphasis.

"Please, madame, have a seat," Jeremy graciously offered.

Abigail made the introductions. Obviously Mistress Pomegrant was much taken with Jeremy, for she began to bat her eyelashes and fling her hands in the air as she told him about her dance school and how very sophisticated the city of Boston had become in the four years since her arrival from Paris. Jeremy flattered her and the plump, round woman, dressed in a low-cut silk gown that did not flatter her heavily rouged face nor overly rounded body, became as coquettish as a young girl. She seemed to forget Abigail's presence.

Abigail worked hard at checking her laughter. She saw Jeremy try to meet her eyes once or twice, but she dared not meet his for fear of breaking into impolite giggles. Instead she listened to Jeremy as he charmed the woman without making fun of her. Soon, it was to Jeremy rather than herself that Mistress Pomegrant explained her frantic excitement. For it seemed that the date on the handbills Levi had delivered to her home this morning was incorrect.

Abigail went into the office and returned with the order forms. She flipped backward until she found the last of the many changed orders from Mistress Pomegrant. She placed the book on the desk beside the woman and pointed to the form. As politely as she could, she said, "I am sorry, Mistress Pomegrant, but it says on the form that the opening of your school was to be on the afternoon of the twenty-fourth of June. And here is your signature that approved the order."

"Signature or no signature, it is impossible! For I had always intended for the school to open on the fourteenth of June! I can't imagine how your brother made such an error!"

"Excuse me for one moment. I shall check the book that contains your original order," Abigail answered, forcing a smile. As she returned to the antechamber she doubted that there had been a mistake made on their part. But since Mistress Pomegrant had changed her order almost a half-dozen times since her first visit to their shop, it was possible. Abigail walked to the shelf that held the books for which she looked. Something caught at her foot and she began to stumble. Fortunately, blessed with good balance, she regained her footing. Annoyed, she looked down at the stack of bound and twined paper that had caught her foot.

"Oh, no!" she whispered. For what stood a foot high was an order for the barrister George Carey, in Cambridge. An order that specified delivery as of *this morning!* How could Nathan have been so careless! Mr. Carey was a haughty and demanding man who looked down upon all artisans, whom he derisively called mechanicks. He had been known to refuse payment on any order that did not meet his pleasure. Abigail remembered a story recounted by Adam Taylor to Levi, as to how Carey had ordered a hutch and finely-wrought china cabinet for his parlor, and then refused to accept it because delivery had been one day late. As much as Abigail disliked the lawyer, they most certainly needed payment and his future business. She had to make delivery this morning! But how could she? Even if she retrieved Nathan from school, he was too small to carry the heavy bundle, and Levi was out with the cart drawn by his old nag until mid-afternoon. If Levi were forced to reembark for another trip to Cambridge they would never have the press running for tomorrow's paper in time.

As Abigail stood with brow knit, attempting to discern a solution to this unneeded crisis, she realized that she'd almost forgotten what had brought her to the shelf in the first place. Quickly, she pulled out the order book and turned until she found Mistress Pomegrant's original order. Just as she had suspected! The foolish old woman! For even on the original order, the date had been specified as the twenty-fourth of June.

Abigail had neither the time nor patience for this silly woman. She steeled herself and returned to the front room of the shop, ready to hold her position firmly now that she was armed with the evidence.

To her astonishment, Mistress Pomegrant was smiling and chattering away so that one would have thought she was at a social. Jeremy was smiling most affably as well. "Excuse me, Mistress—"

"Oh, Abigail dear! Mr. Blackburn is one of the most *delightful* gentlemen it has been my pleasure to have met since I left Paris! He has told me of the dance schools in London and has so graciously offered to recommend my school to the ladies and their daughters of our set!"

"That's very nice," Abigail said, glad that Jeremy had humored the woman to the degree that she might be less argumentative when confronted by her original order form. "But I would—"

"Oh, do put that book away, Abigail! I do not care to have an apology, for Mr. Blackburn has explained how your mistake is actually an advantageous one. For I did not know—I mean I'd forgotten, what with all my preparations—that of course I'd meant to open the school on the twenty-fourth although I asked for the fourteenth. For, *of course,* the summer social season does not begin until the last week of June." Mistress Pomegrant stopped for a moment and began to fan herself. "My, it is such a humid day, that I almost wish for the relief of rain. . . . In any case, Mr. Blackburn will be free to attend my opening the evening of the twenty-fourth, while he would not have been able to do so on the fourteenth. And he has so graciously offered to bring along many of his fine friends, including Miss Wattington whom he told me will *insist* that many of *her* fine lady friends be included!"

Abigail glanced at Jeremy with astonishment. Other than his continued charming smile at the round, perspiring lady who fanned herself as rapidly as she spoke, Jeremy appeared unreadable.

Mistress Pomegrant rose slowly. "So, Abigail, I will forgive you and Levi *this* time. Mr. Blackburn was so impressed with your printing that I suppose I shall return for further work, as long as I have your promise to be less careless about the particulars in the future! I must be off," she said and turned to Jeremy who had risen. *"Quelle plaisir, monsieur,"* she said fawningly, and gave Jeremy an awkward curtsy. "I shall see you the twenty-fourth, if not before," she twittered.

Jeremy gave her a deep bow. "The pleasure was mine, mademoiselle," he said. *"Adieu."*

"Good day, Abigail," Mistress Pomegrant said with a note of reproach in her voice. She turned and smiled again at Jeremy. He smiled so handsomely in return that Abigail saw the flush of color that rose across the woman's large bosom. *"Adieu, monsieur."* Her giggle was higher than the clinging of the bells as she opened and closed the shop door behind her.

Abigail and Jeremy watched as she turned down the street. Then Jeremy turned to Abigail. "May I see the order form?" he asked as he walked to Abigail's side and looked into the book. "Just as I thought," he declared. "Silly old fool . . ." With that he broke into a hearty laugh. *"Adieu, monsieur,"* he mimicked, down to Mistress Pomegrant's clumsy curtsy.

Abigail tried to think of the woman with charity and restrain herself. She couldn't and began to laugh as well. She laughed longer and harder than she could remember as Jeremy recounted their pretentious conversation.

"Fine for you to be so amused," he said in an obviously teasing voice. "For it is not *you* who will have to attend her ridiculous gala opening. It is at times such as these that I wish I was a physician like Michael Harrington!"

Abigail had to sit down, as she broke into another wave of laughter. "I am in your debt, Jeremy," she said when she was able to speak. "We really needed her payment. And even though the mistake was hers, we could not afford to have reprinted the handbills free of charge."

Jeremy's laughter diminished. "Times are that difficult?" he asked with genuine concern.

"Yes. And what with the tax on paper that will begin on the first of November if the Stamp Act is not repealed . . . I am not sure whether we will be able to continue to print the newspaper at this rate. Daily, craftsmen declare bankruptcy. There is little money and now that bills of tender are no longer legal . . . times are quite difficult for the average Boston citizen, Jeremy," Abigail said gently, for she had the feeling that he honestly had not been aware of such. People of his standing tended to believe that others lived as easily as themselves. Often this was not even a malevolent heartlessness, as Levi and others insisted. At least not to her mind. Rather, it was an ignorance as simple and unintentional as ignorances of common manners among the very poor.

Jeremy's countenance grew reflective. "I did not realize the extent of difficulties. I wish that you would perhaps teach me more . . ." He watched Abigail's expression harden and her brow furrow. She did not believe him. She did not trust him. But then, why should she not believe he was being as artificial as he'd been with that foolish woman moments before! "I meant that—"

"What?" Abigail asked. "I am sorry. My mind fell to other matters. I discovered an order that had to have been delivered to Cambridge this morning, but Levi is already gone until mid-afternoon—" Why was she speaking to Jeremy of such matters? "I am sorry, for this does not concern you. You have been of more help already than I could ever have—"

"Please, Abigail, do continue. It was my pleasure. Truly, for it has been ages since I have so thoroughly enjoyed myself, even if, I am ashamed to admit, the joke was on that ridiculous woman!"

His eyes were so lighted with pleasure that Abigail couldn't help but drop her guard. "This problem is not nearly as humorous as Mistress Pomegrant, I'm afraid."

After she had told him of the situation with Mr. Carey, Jeremy appeared more delighted than before. His eyes twinkled as he smiled at her. "This is simple. It is not that I am so masterful a problem solver, but this too is an easy one. For you see, Mr. Carey was a fellow student at the Inn of Court in London, where I studied law. He was a supercilious prig, even then. But immodestly, I must tell you that it was only due to my help that he passed more than one course of study. I shall go home and get my carriage, drive you out to his fine office in Cambridge, and deliver the order with you. I know that you would not mention it, but if I remember correctly, he is not one to part with silver, even if due, easily. So I shall help you procure payment immediately."

"I couldn't. Really, I couldn't impose so upon you." Why was he being so very kind, as if he really cared—

"I am tired of reading and am not due to see the governor until late afternoon. I have been feeling peaked, as you yourself commented upon. A ride in the fresh air to the village of Cambridge would do me a world of good. Can you deny that?"

Abigail didn't know what to say. His argument was so persuasive. "Aye. I mean, I cannot deny that you look peaked. But what of our business?"

"We can conduct that in the fresh air and comfort of my carriage." Jeremy's jaw was set, his eyes determined. She did not have the energy to argue. It was essential to deliver the order to the barrister, and Jeremy did offer a better solution than she could derive. And it would be so nice to ride into the country, for so seldom did she have the opportunity to enjoy the daylight. "Are you certain it is not too great an imposition?" she asked shyly.

He rose and smiled warmly. "It will truly be my pleasure. Think of it as repayment for my help with Madame What's-her-name!"

Abigail gave in happily. "I must leave a note for Jane—" She looked down at her hands, then at her chemise. "I must change my clothes as well, if I am to present myself in Mr. Carey's fine office."

"Yes. I believe so. Though you look more—I mean,

I do agree. I shall use the time to get my carriage and shall return to pick you up in no more than half an hour. Will you be ready by then?" He realized that if he spoke too openly, as he almost had, about how lovely she looked in *anything* she wore, that Abigail would more likely than not change her mind.

The smile that lit her face was one he had not seen since his return. He remembered how Abigail had always loved the idea of an adventure.

"Oh, certainly. I shall not keep you waiting, I promise!"

"Good," he said. Then as he walked to the door, he turned and bowed deeply. *"Adieu, mademoiselle,"* he said with the same affected tone that had so flattered the simpering Mistress Pomegrant. Jeremy's deep, melodic laugh and her own giggles sang out harmoniously with the chiming of the bells as he closed the shop door.

Jeremy raced home with more energy and spirit than he'd felt since his return, as his mind planned the afternoon with great care and greater delight.

Abigail quickly ascended the steps to her bedroom. She would wear her green calico, for certainly she did not want to embarrass a gentleman of Jeremy's position by looking less than proper. She felt happier than she had in some time. In the back of her mind a voice told her that she was making a mistake, that she should not spend any time in Jeremy's company—but she had to deliver the order, she protested to that voice. She began humming a tune to herself and soon that inner voice was drowned out by happy thoughts of the beauty of the countryside.

# Chapter Nine

FOR THE SECOND TIME WITHIN HOURS, ABIGAIL WAS forced to hold her laughter in check as Mr. Carey escorted her and Jeremy down the drive from his office, a large one-room structure attached to his fine stone house, to Jeremy's waiting carriage. Jeremy took her hand and helped her step up onto the plush, red velvet seat.

"Delightful seeing you, Jeremy," George Carey said in his booming bass voice, that sounded especially incongruent emanating from a man of such slight stature. "I had not heard word of your return," he continued. "We will definitely meet for dinner at my club week from next Thursday, then, shan't we?"

"Yes, most definitely. We shall talk of old times," Jeremy said with a joviality that pleased the lawyer but did not fool Abigail.

"As well of the dreadful scourge of those who would have Boston up in arms against our honorable Crown if they could. There is much scurrilous activity, about which you have probably not yet been properly informed. We need you, old chap, to help bring sense back to the colony! God knows we're almost overrun by the inferior sort these days. Not to mention the recent audacity of those groups of mechanicks!" He turned to Abigail and gave her a polite smile. "No insult intended, my dear. But you know as well as I that not all artisans seem to know their appropriate place in society. . . . Don't you agree?" He looked back to Jeremy. "Of course she does. I must take a look at Mistress Peabody's newspaper one of these days. You must bring me a copy, Jeremy, when we meet! Well, safe trip back and I must be off. Abigail, I can be assured that I will have the new order and my calling cards by our agreed date? I understand how this order was delayed, as a personal favor to Jeremy to pay me a surprise visit. How very clever of you, Jeremy. I must admit that when I saw Mistress Peabody standing at the door I did not expect to find you hidden behind the bush! Jolly good, I say! Good day to both of you." Carey gazed up at the sky. "I don't think it shall rain after all," he said and turned up the path to his house.

Jeremy expertly drove the carriage pulled by his magnificent black horse. When they reached the outer marked boundary of Carey's estate, Jeremy slowed down. He and Abigail looked at one another and burst into unrestrained laughter.

"So that is why you made me go back into the shop for my order book!" she exclaimed between laughs. "Is it true that calling cards and the other sets of paper you recommended to him are the current rage in London?"

"Let us say," Jeremy hesitated and grinned, "that I have seen their use before I left by some of the equally pompous gentlemen I met there. Perhaps Carey will be the first to begin a craze here!"

Abigail clapped her hands in glee. "Oh, Jeremy, how can I thank you? I am sorry that I argued how foolish a plan it was for you to claim that you asked me not to deliver his order until today, in order to surprise him with a visit. It worked just as you said—"

"Though not before he hurled an ungentlemanly expletive or two, I am afraid."

"I have heard worse," Abigail said and grinned.

Jeremy remembered the terrible words he'd spat at her five years ago. The laughter left him.

"Jeremy, what's wrong?" Abigail asked. He had visibly paled before her eyes. "Are you feeling ill again?" she asked.

Jeremy looked at her lovely face set in genuine concern. He hadn't intended to begin his plan at this very moment, but his remembered sorrow had unintentionally given him a perfect opening—that is, if he could maintain his countenance, especially when he had to face the alarm in her brilliant, large green eyes. But it was for both of them that he was doing this. "I don't know," he said quietly. "Despite the warmth of the day and the sun that has again broken out from behind the clouds, I felt a sudden chill."

Abigail forgot propriety and quickly moved across the velvet seat to him, her hand touching his forehead. "You don't feel as if you have a fever."

"Oh, I'm sure it is nothing at all," he declared bravely, knowing that this would make her all the more convinced that he protested too strongly. "I think it is that I am hungry. I had quite forgotten to eat breakfast today . . ." He pulled out his pocket watch. "And it is almost one. Perhaps we could stop at an inn that I know nearby—" He looked at Abigail with what he hoped was an apologetic expression. "Oh, I am sorry. You have much work to do and I dare not impose upon you to have luncheon with me. I'm sure I can wait to eat until I arrive home. It will only be another hour or so." He watched her face from the corner of his eye as he pretended to be noting the stately grounds along the road. "Look at that garden to the right," he pointed. "Isn't it lovely?" he asked, pretending to be changing the subject.

"Yes, it is. I have often heard tell of this road of fine mansions. Now I know why it is called—are those primroses?" she asked, not wishing to tell him what the road was called.

"Tell me what you intended to say before you so cleverly commented about the flowers?" he asked with a soft, bemused smile. They were both being so careful, he realized.

At that moment Abigail decided. "I was going to say that I do wish that you would stop to eat some food. Perhaps it is your hunger that is making you so peaked." She meant this most sincerely.

"Are you certain?"

"Aye."

He grinned, careful not to appear as well as he felt at this moment. "Under one condition, I will."

"And that condition might be?"

"That you will join me. You have not had your

midday meal either and you are a hearty eater, or used to be. Am I not correct?"

Abigail felt her cheeks warm as he so casually referred to their past association. "I was . . . and sometimes still am . . . though it does not befit a lady, does it?"

"It most certainly does! I am glad some things don't change." Again he had treaded into dangerous waters; he could tell by the growing pinkness of her cheeks. It was so difficult but he hoped that by the time the afternoon had ended their mutual skittishness would be over. "Tell me now what you stopped yourself from saying before you mentioned the flowers," he asked. "But first let me tell you that the inn at which I wish us to dine is a few miles in the other direction, toward Watertown. Does that meet with your approval?"

"Oh, yes. It is lovely to be riding in the country and to have the opportunity to see the lovely estates, and glimpses of the formal gardens. The air feels so fresh. Even the clouds seem to have lifted."

His heart warmed. He guessed that Abigail had neither the time for, nor did her station afford her the luxury of, leisurely rides in the country, or boating rides or picnics or so many of the activities he so took for granted. Activities like the balls and receptions that he found so tedious. To see them through her shining, almost childlike eyes—just the hope of having his beautiful Abigail at his side, in lovely gowns of silk and lace that would become none better than she, thrilled him. He could share so much with her, enjoy so much through her eyes. He had been lonely for so long. Despite all the women, all the events of high society, all the wine and carousing, he'd been so alone. He fought back the tears behind his eyes.

"Jeremy! Are you certain you are well enough to drive? I could take the reins if you are not feeling up to it. For I have driven the cart often, when I have made deliveries with Nathan when Levi was unable to—"

"I am fine!" he reassured her, for her brow was knit. He was moved by her concern. He could hardly imagine Belinda making a similar offer. "It was a particle of dust from the road. Now tell me what the road is called?" he demanded in mock impatience which made her brow unfurl and her lips flower into a pretty smile.

"Only that it is called Tory Row," she answered hesitantly.

"I suppose that is fitting. It is true that the wealthiest of Bostonians have their country estates set along this road from Cambridge to Watertown. But I am much too hungry to discuss politics with you at this moment, if that meets with your approval. I believe we would both enjoy observing the country sights more fully— Look! To your left. A doe and baby deer."

As Abigail smiled softly at the tender sight, Jeremy looked from the road to her face. She was so lovely and seemed not to know it. His eyes briefly traced the graceful form of her body. How he wished to hold her in his arms!

Abigail watched the doe and its baby in genuine wonderment. Then she kept her eyes on the countryside, for she dared not turn to Jeremy. She was afraid that her face would give away the joy she felt riding beside him in the elegant carriage as they traversed the beautiful countryside. Had she ever expected to experience such contentment again? . . . She had to regain her reasoning. She was getting lost in fancy, she feared. Jeremy had been wonderful today. Perhaps they could even slowly become friends again, but certainly nothing more. For he was to marry Belinda Wattington. More than that, nothing had changed between them. It never could.

She was feeling like a lovesick girl and she was too old to allow herself these idle vanities. She believed she'd seen herself through his eyes a moment before. For the first time in years, she had felt almost beautiful. And she had wished more than anything, may the Lord help her, that Jeremy would take her into his arms and kiss her. She had felt that strange sensation in the pit of her stomach when he smiled, for surely no more handsome man had ever been created. She had to stop feeling such dangerous impulses.

"What are you thinking of, Abigail?" Jeremy asked.

"I have just been observing . . . It is so very lovely . . ."

"Yes, it is," Jeremy answered. But not more so than you, he thought.

They continued to ride in an easy silence, each lost in the serenity of the countryside. Besides the comforting sound of the carriage wheels upon the dirt road, the sweet chirping of spring birds, and an occasional gust of wind that blew coolly onto their faces, there was nothing to disturb them from the pleasure of the moment and sweet thoughts of one another.

"You are not going to finish your cherry tart?" Jeremy asked as he sat across from Abigail in the lovely inn.

Abigail finished chewing and laid down her fork. She sighed, then grinned. "I am so very full! I cannot believe how much I have eaten," she exclaimed so sincerely that Jeremy began to laugh.

"Yes, you did seem to enjoy the pheasant and carrots and sweet potatoes and—"

"Please, I beg you, do not go on!" She patted her middle. "I am not sure that I shall be able to step up into your carriage."

"And I am not certain that I will be able to help you since you surely weigh another stone after this feast!" he said. His dimples deepened in a happy smile. "I do suggest, from experience may I add, that you wash some of it down with another glass of punch."

"I am afraid that I shall not only be much heavier, but tipsy as well, if I drink much more. It is a most delicious beverage. I have never tasted it before. Or have I told you so already?"

"I believe you mentioned it," Jeremy said. He had to keep from laughing because Abigail was a bit tipsy already. Although it was quite acceptable for ladies as well as gentlemen to drink, Jeremy realized that Abigail still obviously abided by the old, sterner ways of the Congregationalists. He did not wish to get her drunk. "Perhaps just a sip more, then we shall go."

"Aye, just a sip," she agreed. "I am thirsty from so

sweet a tart," she said. She drank almost a half glass of the punch from the pewter cup.

As they approached the carriage, Abigail, allowing Jeremy to lead her with his hand on her forearm, noticed that the white clouds that had covered the sky in Boston had followed them to the country.

"I do not think it will rain," Abigail pronounced.

"Nor do I. And since we are in agreement, I have an idea. There is a stream across the lane that is quite beautiful. Would you care to take a short walk before we begin our journey back?"

"I would love to. Perhaps I will feel less discomfort if I walk a bit of my gluttony off," she said. "That is, if you will continue to tell me about your adventures in London."

"You are not bored yet?"

"Bored?" she asked in amazement. "I love to hear you speak. You describe the city and its people so well that I can almost see it!"

"If you're certain . . ." he said. It was such a pleasure to share some of his happier moments in London with someone who listened and cared. Or seemed to. "The third Christmas I was there, I was invited by a school chum to his father's castle in—"

Abigail interrupted him with wide eyes. "A castle? You were invited for Christmas to a genuine castle!"

"It was rather a small one, actually." Jeremy realized how silly his answer sounded and they fell into laughter once again.

They crossed the stream and had sat under a large oak tree talking for longer than either of them realized. So engrossed were they in one another that neither noticed the threatening black cloud until Abigail was startled by the first clap of thunder.

"We must hurry back to the carriage," Abigail said, jumping up from Jeremy's skirted brown coat.

"I think that we will not make it back. It is too dangerous to be out in the lightning." Already the rain began, in slow but large drops. Jeremy looked around, and then spotted a barn in the field behind them, about a hundred yards away. "I think we best run for shelter there," he said pointing. "It is a spring storm and therefore shall probably pass quickly. Do you agree?"

"Perhaps you are right," Abigail agreed. For a moment she worried that her delay would cause disquietude at home. But she could do nothing to rectify that at the moment. A flash in the sky and then a quick, loud clap of thunder frightened her, causing her to grab Jeremy's hand. Since she had been a child, the only fear she had suffered was of thunder and lightning. Although she had tried her best, she had never quite outgrown it. She did not wish to allow Jeremy to see her mounting fear. "Yes, let us hurry," she said as calmly as she could.

As quick as the roar of thunder came the rain, pouring down upon them as the wind rose.

"Can you run?" Jeremy asked.

"Oh, yes! I haven't run in years but I used to almost beat Levi in races when we were children," she called out as she held onto his hand and lifted her petticoat with her other hand. "Oh, I wish I hadn't eaten as much," she complained as she felt her body heavy against the rain and wind. Jeremy laughed heartily in response.

The rain grew heavier as they approached the barn. Already they were soaked to the skin. Jeremy saw that his jacket had hardly protected Abigail from being drenched. He should have insisted she button it, he thought, as he raced ahead of her and threw open the barn door. Abigail followed him in, her breath heavy from exertion, and collapsed upon a pile of hay. He closed the barn door behind them, but it was so dark that he reopened it just enough for them to have some light.

Then he stripped off his waistcoat and collapsed beside her. "I do not believe this day," Abigail said as she tried to catch her breath. Then she burst into laughter.

Jeremy was relieved and delighted, for he had feared that she would be angry at him for having suggested they walk rather than return immediately to Boston.

The barn's dankness was accentuated by their soaking wet clothes. Jeremy turned onto his stomach. In the light that filtered through the door, he saw that Abigail's chemise had become almost transparent. It clung to her breasts like a wet, second skin. As she lay laughing, her hands behind her head, her nipples had become taut with chill, and her sweet rounded breasts rose and fell so seductively that he felt himself grow hard. It was fortunate that he lay on his stomach, he realized. Tentatively he reached out and touched her hair, which was heavy with rain. "I think perhaps you should unplait it so that it will dry more quickly," he said softly.

Abigail's laughter subsided and she lay still for a moment longer. She could feel the chill that began to run through her. She was cold but it felt oddly different from a normal chill. Oh, how she wished he would wrap his body around her and warm her. "Yes, you are right," she answered in little more than a whisper. She sat upright and pulled off her soaked bonnet. Then she undid her hair and felt it fall heavily to her waist. She pulled it off her shoulders, behind her back. Her teeth started to chatter.

"You are chilled, and it is my fault," he said, looking straight ahead rather than at her.

"It is not your fault. But I am chilled." Her body began to shudder visibly.

Jeremy looked at her and lost his resolve. Besides he had to warm her or she might catch her death of cold, and his skirted coat and waistcoat were of no use. He opened his arms as he moved onto his side. "Let me hold you until you've lost your chill," he whispered.

Abigail hesitated for a moment. Then she slipped into his waiting arms. With unpracticed but native instinct, she fitted herself easily against his body. She was surprised at how his body felt like the heat from a hearth as he wrapped himself around her. Abigail sighed as she curled herself further beneath his warmth. They lay still and wordless as her chills slowly diminished. The rain continued to beat heavily against the side of the barn.

Jeremy tentatively stroked her hair. When she made no protest, he stroked it with a stronger hand, that ran down the soft curve of her neck to her shoulder. Abigail purred and responded by fitting her body more tightly against his; her movement seemed as natural as that of a child. He raised his torso by resting his weight on his elbow and his head on his hand. He stared down at her as she lay with eyes closed and a sleepy, childlike expression of calm upon her face. Her full red lips were slightly parted and the white of her teeth glimmered through. He traced the tip of her nose with his finger and she grinned and opened her eyes. Jeremy lowered his face until his lips were upon hers. He kissed her gently at first. So gently that he ached with the beauty of her response as she softly returned his tender kisses with her own. He was afraid to go further for he wanted her so much. He knew she had to feel the heated hardness of his maleness against her soft thighs. One more kiss, and then he would rise, he thought.

As his mouth met hers again, Abigail could restrain herself no longer. She flung her arms around his neck and pulled him to her with all her strength. His body tightened for a moment but then relaxed as his hips pressed hard against her own and his mouth took hers in a way she had never known but instinctively responded to in kind. Her mouth opened as his tongue began to explore her own, bringing a pleasure sweet and aching at the same time. His hand slid from her shoulder to her breast, and a wave of chill coursed through her, but these were not chills of cold, for her body felt feverishly hot as his fingers gently played with her nipple until she cried out with a desire only he could quench.

Jeremy moaned, and wrapped his legs around her hips. He forced his lips from hers, kissed her chin and then her neck, and followed kiss upon kiss until he came to her chest. He untied the strings that held her chemise and pulled its neckline away until her sweet rounded breasts and pink nipples, hardened in desire, filled his eyes. He smiled with pleasure and brought his lips to one soft breast while his hand went to the other.

Abigail felt his lips upon her nipple and cried out again in pleasure as wave after wave of sweet sensation rode through her. As his lips finally came to her other breast the waves heightened, chilling her and making her feverish simultaneously. She ran her hands through his thick, fine hair as she drank in the redolent scent of his manliness. Her mind was so filled with sensation that no thoughts could work their way through, except the words she so desperately wanted to say. Jeremy, oh how much I love you, she thought, but couldn't release. She pulled his head to hers and he kissed her again, teasing her lips until she wanted to cry out. And when she did, his mouth had covered hers, their tongues intermingled so that her cry echoed back at her.

Abruptly, Jeremy sprang up, and she wanted to cry at the pain that the cold air and absence of his body brought her. He helped her rise, for she was unsteady, as he seemed to know.

He held her hand between his own and caressed it. He looked deep into her eyes. His eyes shone so bright. She wondered if her own did as well, because her vision was blurred in a strange way. "Jeremy—"

"Please, let me speak first," he said in a strangely husky voice that she immediately loved. "Abigail. I want you more than I have ever desired any woman. I love you. I always have. I know that it was ugly in the past between us, but all of that is now long ago. I want you . . . I want more than anything for you to be my wife."

It had to be a dream, she thought as she listened. How long had she dreamed that the nightmare Damon had created would go away and Jeremy would be hers as he was meant to be. Aye, aye, she wanted to call out to him. She didn't need more words. She wanted to tell him that he was— What was that he had said? She must have misunderstood as she listened and thought simultaneously. "What did you say?" she asked and found her own voice strange to her ears.

"I said that I forgive you for your . . . er . . . your moments . . . your affair with Damon. It had to have been *my* fault, for I was much too proper and shy and did not give you what you needed. I assumed because you were still a young girl—oh what does it matter! Why talk about it! I love you more than life itself! I forgive you! Never will the subject enter my mind again, I swear!" Jeremy was stunned when she pulled her hand from his and jumped up. What had he said that offended her? He was so certain that she loved him. "What have I said—I mean what have I done— have I presumed incorrectly—what?" He found himself speechless suddenly.

Abigail thought her heart would break. She'd been so certain that he'd somehow come to his senses and realized that Damon had been an evil liar who had nearly raped her. He forgave her, he said? *He forgave her!* That meant that he believed that she had willfully lain with his brother! She wanted to cry but her heart turned to stone.

"Please, Abigail! Speak to me. Do not stare at me with such hateful eyes," he pleaded.

"You have never loved me, Jeremy," she said with nothing but coldness in her voice. "You are engaged to be married. I do not blame you for this . . . incident. It is more my fault than yours. I only ask that you excuse my wanton behavior and take me home. I hope that you will find it in your heart to forget this . . . this indiscretion on my part, and never speak of it. May I ask that of you?"

"What? I don't understand." He felt the tears of disappointment and confusion fill his eyes but didn't try to force them away. "I love you. You love me. I don't understand. Please, don't leave me like this!"

His tears tore at her heart, which she believed was beyond pain. "There is nothing to explain. You don't love me. You never have or you couldn't— It doesn't matter. You are to be married to a lady of your class. I wish you well. Please! Take me home now." She looked out the barn door. The rain had stopped.

Jeremy glanced across the barn as well. The rain had stopped. Abigail stood with her hands wrapped around her, then began to fix her chemise. She straightened her petticoat, pinned up her wet hair, and covered her head with her bonnet. She looked as presentable as possible under the circumstances. She did not meet his eyes, but the stubborn expression on her otherwise impassive face told him that it was useless to plead further. She did not love him. Perhaps it was Damon she loved all the while. She had been making love to Damon! He was Damon's identical twin and therefore Damon risen from the dead! That had to be so!

She had not meant to hurt him *this* time, that he knew. It was his own fault. He was not the immature man he had been five years ago. He would not punish her for what she could not control any more than he'd been able to contain his love for her. "It was all a mistake, I agree," he said softly and with as much dignity as he could command. "I beg your forgiveness. For you are correct. I am soon to be married. I cannot explain what overtook me. I shall never refer to this . . . moment . . . and will forget it quickly. Of that you may rest assured. Nor need you fear retribution. What I have not told you since I first saw you in early morning is that it is my judgment that the *Boston Word* is not as libelous or seditious as other publications with greater circulations and prestige. I think I would be remiss in my responsibility to the Crown and governor if I used the prosecution of you as publisher as a foolish personal vendetta. You have my word."

Abigail didn't know what to say. She had searched his face as he had spoken. She did not doubt his words, any of them. She wished he had never returned to Boston. She would maintain her dignity, she swore to herself. She would not shed a tear. She would be silent on their return trip if she could not force herself to speak pleasant, inconsequential words. "Thank you, Jeremy. I accept your word. I believe that we should leave now, don't you?" she asked as steadily as she could.

"Yes. I think we are in agreement on that as well."

Abigail turned to the door which Jeremy swung open. They walked across the wet field wordlessly, looking straight ahead.

# Chapter Ten

"I WISH TO SEE MISTRESS PEABODY," SPOKE THE YOUNG woman in the thin, light, glossy pink silk dress, tied with a rose silk sash. Her black hair, fixed in ringlets to her shoulders, was in the latest English fashion.

"She is occupied at the moment. May I help you, Miss . . ." Katie politely asked this finely dressed woman who looked vaguely familiar. Yet Katie could not place her, other than to know that she was obviously an aristocrat. Even in the midday heat and humidity of this late July day, the girl was the model of perfection. Her silk fan that she waved gracefully to and fro seemed more a fashion complement than a device for relief from the heat.

"Miss Wattington," the young woman stated with a haughty smile that didn't reach her black eyes. "No. I am afraid you may not."

Katie watched the woman stare at her large stomach with a distasteful expression. "I will see if I can fetch her, then, Miss Wattington," Katie said. After she repeated the name it came to her that *this* was the girl Jeremy was to marry. Why was she here to see Abigail, Katie wondered. And why would a girl only slightly older than herself stare at her belly with such disdain? For wasn't carrying a child one of the most glorious miracles of God? Katie felt sorry for Belinda Wattington, despite her fine clothes and superior airs. How could it be that a man who had so loved Abigail could plan to marry a girl of this sort?

"Why are you staring at me instead of finding Mistress Peabody?" Belinda snapped at the pale, faded girl with the obscenely large belly. Why would a woman in her condition present herself before the public? There was such immodesty among the lesser sort that it sometimes astonished her. To think that Jeremy had been familiar with this family, and it hadn't been when he was a mere boy, for that perhaps could be excused. But, as her father had told her, Jeremy would be a fine husband if kept in tight rein. Hadn't Sir Bentley Blackburn himself told her father such?

Katie walked to the door leading to the workroom. She turned back to Belinda. "I did not realize I was staring at you, miss. I do apologize if I have made you feel less than comfortable. I shall get Abigail at once. Please, have a seat."

"I prefer to stand, thank you," Belinda said without looking up as she searched through her brocade pull-string bag.

Abigail was so concentrated upon her typesetting that she didn't hear Katie approach. When she looked up, Katie stood beside her with an uncommon frown upon her face. "What's wrong, Katie? Are you feeling ill?" Abigail asked. Katie had been looking quite pale and peaked the past week.

Katie smiled and patted her belly. "Both of us are just fine," she answered, and her face glowed for a moment with pride. Abigail still found it hard to believe that Katie's babe wasn't expected for another month. It was the twenty-fifth of July and Abigail couldn't believe that Katie could possibly carry the child for another month. "Then why the disturbed expression?" Abigail asked.

"Miss Belinda Wattington is in the shop. She wishes to see you. She would not tell me why. She seems to be a most unpleasant young woman," Katie declared uncharacteristically.

Abigail rose from her stool. "I shall see her right away." Abigail wiped the perspiration from her brow. "It is terribly hot. May I ask you a favor? Could you ask Jane to fix us a pitcher of cold lemon drink?" Abigail waved her hand in Levi's direction, across the room. Levi was busy working the press with Nathan's help.

"Jane is at a church charity committee meeting. But I shall be happy to do it. I certainly would enjoy a cool drink as well." Katie followed Abigail across the room.

"That would be most appreciated. But then I insist that you take your rest. I fear that the afternoon heat is too much for you, Katie. Do you promise?" Abigail asked. Katie smiled and nodded.

Katie walked past Abigail and entered the house. Abigail turned her attention to Belinda. "Good afternoon, Miss Wattington," Abigail said as she entered the shop. She watched the elegantly dressed woman evaluate her. Abigail knew how she must appear, dressed in an old muslin chemise smudged, she guessed, with fresh ink. Abigail stood erectly before the girl and stared her directly in the eye. This past month and a half, a part of her had toughened in a way she'd never dreamed possible. She was a working woman, not a fine lady of Jeremy's class. She would not kowtow to Belinda nor anyone else. "What is it I can do for you?" she inquired politely but with no deference.

She looks little better than a chambermaid, Belinda thought. And yet she doesn't even display the good manners and smile one could expect from a mechanick. It seemed impossible that Jeremy could have ever fancied this woman. Besides her bright red hair and green eyes, there was nothing else striking about her. She was far thinner than was appealing and small bosomed. Men—who could understand them! "I have come to have something printed in your public announcement column, Mistress Peabody." She handed Abigail the foolscap she had pulled from her bag. She watched as Abigail read it, and smiled as she saw the woman pale. By the time Abigail looked up she had composed herself, but Belinda had her satisfaction, even if for but a moment.

When Abigail looked up, she saw the woman smiling spitefully at her. Abigail hoped that she had not given herself away, but feared from Belinda's expression that for one moment she had slipped. But what did it matter? Since that afternoon in June, Abigail had accepted that Jeremy could never be hers. This announcement was no surprise. In fact, she had expected to read of their marriage weeks ago. But why did Belinda bring it to her to print when her sort would be unlikely to even read the *Boston Word?*

Of course, Abigail realized! It was so obvious and silly that she couldn't help laughing aloud. Belinda had personally brought the announcement of their impending marriage on the fourteenth of August, to gain the satisfaction of seemingly rubbing salt into a wound. How foolish of the girl, to even think that she had been a threat to her in any—

"I beg your pardon, Mistress Peabody. May I ask what has struck your humor about my wedding announcement!" Belinda demanded in a shrill voice.

"Nothing. I beg *your* pardon, should I have given you that impression. I was merely remembering a joke that my brother had told me a moment before. It will be my pleasure to print the announcement of your wedding date," Abigail said evenly, her eyes giving nothing away.

"I am pleased. For you see, Mr. Blackburn has been most insistent that I set the date," Belinda pushed, trying her best to break Abigail's façade.

"Your announcement will appear in Friday's paper. But it will appear in the *Gazette* on Thursday as well, will it not?" Abigail knew she was behaving childishly to play at this girl's game, but she could not resist.

"Yes . . . uh . . , yes, I suppose it will at that," Belinda stated, color rising into her pale cheeks as she flustered.

"Well, good day then, Miss Wattington. I hope your marriage brings you all the happiness you deserve," Abigail said and smiled so sweetly that she could hardly keep herself from laughing. Belinda's small dark eyes narrowed as she tried to decipher whether Abigail's remark was intended to be facetious or polite.

"Yes . . . well . . . ah, thank you," Belinda replied. She attempted a polite smile but was too confused to carry it through. Why did Belinda have the distinct impression that it was *she* who was being dismissed? "Good day to you too." Belinda glanced beyond Abigail and saw the pregnant girl standing at the door that evidently led into the house, with a pitcher and cups in her hand. The girl had an amused expression on her face. Apparently she had been standing there for some time. Well, she for one would not let their kind cause her to forget her manners. "And good day to you, too, Goodwife," she called.

"To you as well, Miss Wattington," Katie sweetly replied.

Belinda abruptly turned on her heels and flew out the door.

Abigail turned to Katie. Katie did not know how Abigail would react and was thrilled to see her burst into a gale of laughter. But then Abigail's laughter increased until tears rolled down her cheeks. Then she broke into a loud sob and raced past Katie. Heartsick, Katie turned and watched Abigail race up the stairs. She heard the slam of Abigail's bedroom door. Even two flights down, she heard Abigail's muffled sobs. Katie turned to follow her up the stairs, but then decided that Abigail needed time alone. Katie decided to bring the cool drink to Levi and Nathan. Before she entered the workroom, she composed her face. It would do Abigail no good for Levi to learn what had happened and upset her further, however deep his concern. Katie entered the workroom with a smile.

Katie knocked and called to Abigail, "May I come in?" She could hear Abigail's continued sobs, softer now but still as painful to her ears.

Abigail didn't know if she wanted to speak to Katie. Evidently Katie had heard the entire exchange between herself and Belinda. Since that afternoon with Jeremy, Abigail had avoided any sisterly night talks with Katie under the pretext that Katie needed her sleep or that she herself had much writing to do. She knew she hadn't fooled Katie, who merely demurred with great sadness in her eyes. Nor had she fooled Jane, who after the first few days stopped harping at her for barely eating and thereafter watched with worried eyes. Abigail knew that Jane had become so concerned that she no longer engaged in her usual playful sharp banter with her. Even Nathan sensed that Abigail was not herself and responded in his quiet way with extra kisses and hugs.

Strangely, only Levi seemed oblivious. But then, Levi appeared preoccupied with something he wouldn't reveal. Most nights he left shortly past dinner and returned late in the night. The times Abigail had encountered him upon his return, he appeared highly excited, his cheeks flushed and his eyes gleaming. At first Abigail had assumed it was drink, but Levi had not been drunk, at least not so drunk that she could discern so. She suspected that Levi was frequenting Blue's Tavern where that disreputable McIntosh, the cobbler and leader of the South End Mob, held court and—

"Please, Abigail. Won't you let me in?" Katie called through the closed door.

Abigail took her handkerchief and blew her nose once again. She wiped her eyes as well, but it did little good, for the tears would not cease. She rose into a sitting position on her bed. "Yes. Do come in." Abigail studied the cotton lace of the canopy above her bed, trying to compose herself. She felt Katie sit down heavily on the edge of the bed beside her. Finally, she looked into Katie's pale, concerned face, her blue eyes filled with worry. "Oh, Katie!" Abigail sobbed, and fell against Katie's frail shoulder.

Abigail did not come down for dinner, claiming a disturbed stomach. Katie took the broth Jane had fixed up to her. Abigail thanked her but did not talk. But then, what more was left for her to say, thought Katie, after she had poured out the story about Jeremy and that rainy day in June. Katie had appealed to her to go to Jeremy and tell him the truth about his brother, but she would not hear of it. Now, Katie merely kissed Abigail on the cheek and returned downstairs.

Levi was dressed, his hat in hand, and came to kiss his wife good-bye. He told her he would try not to be home too late, and Katie knew better than to question his evasive behavior of the past few weeks. Besides, she was anxious to see him on his way, for she needed to speak with Nathan alone if she was to enact her plan. She kissed her husband good-bye and wished him to give her regards to Adam and Charles.

Jane was sitting at the hearth, knitting. "How is she?" Jane asked, her usual ebullience faded by worry.

"She is sleeping now," Katie answered. "I think it is no more than a bad stomach."

"Humph!" Jane retorted. "And I think I am the Queen of England! I am surprised at you, Katie, that you would keep—oh never mind," Jane said as she looked at the sweet, tired girl. "I suggest you follow Abigail's example and get yourself a fit night's sleep as well. You look far too pale to my eyes, child!"

Katie feigned a yawn. "I am quite sleepy. I think I will do just that. But first I will say good night to Nathan. He was most helpful to Levi on such a busy day as today."

"Aye, he is a fine boy. I am too weary to rise, so give him a peck from me as well, would you?"

Katie closed Nathan's door behind her. She knelt down beside his bed. The boy had already fallen asleep, a book perched on his stomach and the candle still burning. She shook him gently. "Nathan," she whispered.

He opened his eyes and smiled. "Yes, Katie," he said in a small, sleep-filled voice.

Katie leaned closer to his ear. "I have a favor to ask of you," she whispered. "But it is a secret and you must promise to keep it before I tell you."

Curiosity wiped the sleep from his voice. "I promise," he whispered back. "Cross my heart and swear on the Bible!"

Katie chuckled at his earnestness. "Your promise will be more than sufficient," she replied, stroking his dark hair. "Now listen very carefully. Much later tonight, you and I are going to pay a visit to a fine house on Hanover Street. We are doing so in order to help Abigail. You have noticed that she has been quite sad for a long time now, haven't you?"

The boy's gentle dark eyes filled with compassion. "Aye, I have. I feel so sorry. I have tried to cheer her, you know."

"Aye, I do. So have we all. I think I know what we can do that will make Abigail more happy than she has been for a very long time."

At ten-thirty, when Katie, wrapped in her cloak, crept down the darkened stairs and knocked softly at Nathan's door, the boy was dressed and ready. He held a small lantern in his hand. Katie took his free hand and together they slipped out the door into the darkened street.

# Chapter Eleven

JEREMY SAT BESIDE BELINDA ON THE FINELY UPHOL-stered sofa. He tried to pretend interest as she chattered on.

"I do so love the way this room looks since your father had it finished with this exquisite Chinese wallpaper," she said as she appraised the luxurious room. "I intend to do the same once your father returns from Halifax and we acquire our own town-house. Does that please you?" she asked in a syrupy voice.

"Whatever pleases you, pleases me, my dear," he answered. Especially if it will help to silence you, he thought. Again he was sorry that he had not had the fortitude to cancel this impending marriage—but it was not so much a lack of fortitude as a lack of interest.

That rainy night in June, after he had driven Abigail home in silence, he had numbed himself with the help of a bottle of whiskey. For the next two weeks that was how he had gotten through the nights.

Strangely, he awoke each morning sober enough to lose himself in his work each day. Despite his hearty constitution, he soon began to see the effects of the whiskey upon his face and body. Even Belinda, who was far too self-absorbed to notice much, commented upon his dissipated look. The fact that he did not seek to spend any nights in her bed during those weeks did not seem to bother her, for he had agreed to allow her to begin her wedding plans.

Usually, there was no gala event involved in a Boston wedding. Once the couple had applied for a marriage license, or in the case of those who could not afford the costly document, placed a bann in the public notice column of a newspaper, the ceremony was shortly held in a church and the matter was done with. Lately, it had become the practice among the "better sort" to follow the fashion of London, by making a costly and complicated event out of an otherwise simple process. Some, like Belinda, not only applied for a license but made a public announcement as well. Rather than a simple reception after the ceremony, she and her mother planned an elaborate party that was to be the social event of the summer season. He feigned interest, but all her petty talk and plans went in one ear and out the other.

Little more than two weeks after his nightly whiskey binge, Jeremy had woken in his usual numbed state. By late evening he'd noticed that the numbness had not worn off. It seemed to have become a permanent part of him. He was relieved. After that he was able to drink in moderation without fear of feeling coming back to torture him. He had then decided that it was as easy to marry Belinda as not to, for she would make no worse a wife than those of his acquaintances. Love was not an issue, nor would it be so ever again.

"Jeremy!" Belinda called. "You weren't listening to me," she said with a pretty pout.

Pretty she was, Jeremy thought. And since she was his and would soon be so by law and in the eyes of the church, it was a shame that he did not desire her. He desired no one. Not even the hot, flirtatious nymph, Prissy, could tempt him, much to his deepest regret—and Prissy's as well, since she barely spoke to him these days.

"Jeremy! What is wrong! You are doing it again! Just staring into space."

"I am sorry, my dear." He gave her a false smile she happily accepted. "In fact, I was thinking how very lovely you are."

Her smile brightened her face. "Were you really? How nice. Now, what I was telling you when you were off somewhere . . ." she began, pouting once more.

"I am fully attentive now. I promise."

Placated, she began again. "Remember how Father spoke of suspected collusion between this group that call themselves 'The Loyal Nine,' of which Mr. Edes is the leader, and Sam Adams, James Otis, and possibly Sam's cousin John?"

"Yes," he answered, his curiosity aroused. For seldom did Belinda speak of more than trivia. "What of it?"

"And remember how Sir Jeffery said that although he didn't have proof he was sure that they were organizing the most common sort and ruffians on the South Side for their purposes?"

"Yes, so what is your point?"

"Well, I didn't choose to speak of it at dinner because that is men's talk, but I believe he is correct. Today, when I was shopping and doing an assortment of errands, I noticed a definite note of arrogance among the shopkeepers and just in the air, shall we say, among the most inferior sort."

He should have known that she would have but dribble to speak of. "Isn't that a bit vague, shall we say," he replied, trying to hide his irritation.

"Allow me to go on," Belinda replied archly. "When I entered Peabody Printers to place an announcement of our wedding in the public notice column—"

"You did what?" Jeremy asked, amazed.

"I just *told* you. In any case, that woman with child out to here," she said as she gestured with disdain, "boldly stood in the shop. And when she *finally* brought Mistress Peabody to help me, that woman, dressed in clothes no self-respecting lady would be seen in, actually was surly and impudent to me—to say nothing of that expecting girl, who watched and stood smirking—"

"*Why* did you present an announcement when you'd already submitted one last week to the *Gazette?*" Jeremy said sharply enough to bring a flush to her pale cheeks.

"Why shouldn't I have!" she countered, her brow arched in the way it did when she was angry. "And why are you cross with me when that common woman—"

She was pushing at dangerous buttons. For the first

time in weeks he was feeling emotions. He had to check himself and push them away before it was too late. He swallowed hard and took a breath before he spoke. "Mistress Peabody is hardly a woman of the common sort, if by that you mean inferior. She is a skilled artisan, a publisher, and a rather good writer," he replied evenly.

"She is still of the middling class. I think of them as mechanicks, as my father and your own does. They are hardly our equals and should fast learn their places and some common respect if you ask me!"

Prissy rapped upon the door. Jeremy was grateful for her interruption. He gave her the first genuine smile in weeks. "Yes, Prissy, come in."

She did not return his smile. "Mother asked me to see if you or the *lady* wished another brandy?"

Jeremy took in her sarcasm and had to bite his lip to keep from laughing, especially under the circumstances. "Would you care for another brandy, my dear Belinda?" he asked gallantly.

"Are you going to join me if I do?" she asked as she glared at Prissy.

"No, I think not. For I have much work ahead of me tonight." Then he realized that if she did not have another, Prissy would too soon depart. The evening was so warm that Prissy was dressed in a very sheer chemise that barely covered her taut full breasts. Suddenly he was enjoying himself. "Perhaps I will join you, after all," he stated, and draped his arm around Belinda's shoulder. "We would both enjoy a brandy, then, Prissy," he said with a smile. He watched Prissy take in his arm around Belinda's shoulder. If looks could kill, he thought. He felt bad for toying so with Prissy, for he genuinely liked the girl. But she had played enough of her own games with him to receive a mild one in return.

"Yes, *sir,*" she said with false obsequiousness, and sashayed across the room, undulating her fully rounded hips for his temptation. She poured a brandy and brought it to them. Jeremy assumed she was going to hand it to Belinda. Instead she came around the edge of the sofa and leaned forward so that he had full view of her enticingly full breasts. "Here you are, *sir,*" she said and handed the glass to him.

"Well! If that doesn't prove—" Belinda began.

"Prissy," Jeremy said trying not to laugh. "One always serves the lady first. I believe you knew that."

"Oh, so sorry, sir," she feigned, her eyes belying her look of forgetfulness. She leaned in again, removed the goblet from his hand and handed it to Belinda. "Here!" she said.

Belinda was livid. "You must teach this girl etiquette if she is to serve!" she insisted, speaking as if Prissy were not in the room. "Missy," Belinda addressed her, "you are to say, 'Here is your drink, *Miss Wattington.*' Then I say 'Thank you,' you curtsy and with a smile you say, 'You are welcome.'" Belinda handed the glass back to Prissy. "Now let's do it properly."

Jeremy interceded. He took the glass from Prissy and handed it to Belinda. "I am sure that Prissy will remember, for she is a quick girl, is that not right, Prissy?" He secretly winked at her.

"Yes, sir, that is right. I shall remember in the

future, Miss Wattington," Prissy answered sweetly. She walked to the table, poured another brandy, properly offered it to Jeremy, and curtsied politely. "Will that be all, sir?" she asked.

"I believe so, thank you."

Prissy curtsied to Belinda at an angle that he knew intentionally offered him another display of her ripe breasts. Perhaps one of these nights, he thought, watching as her hips swayed lustfully from the room.

"Jeremy, you are much too easy on the servants—"

"Perhaps, my sweet. But I merely wanted to rid us of her." Jeremy rose and pulled closed the parlor door. He wanted to push Belinda on her way and knew just how. "I have been too distant from you tonight," he said, looking at her with pretended ardor that pleased her, as he knew it would—at first. He sat down beside her and pulled her into his arms. "Perhaps I have been too diligent about my work these past weeks. What do you think of my forgetting it for just this night and spending the time with you?"

"Oh, that would be so nice!" she said with a rush of excitement. "I have so many details of the wedding I wish to discuss with you."

He took the brandy from her hand and placed it on the side table. "Talk was not what I had in mind," he whispered and brushed his hand against her cheek. "I was thinking of a night of unadulterated lust," he whispered in an intentionally husky voice. "There are positions that I learned of in London that are most exciting . . ." He nibbled at her ear. "I can feel myself becoming aroused just thinking about you in my bed, against the soft sheets, as naked as a babe and—" He pretended to try to pull her hand to his groin.

"Jeremy, stop," she cried, just as he'd expected. Quickly she composed herself as he let go of her hand.

"I am so sorry," he said with false contrition. "It is your beauty that carried me away."

"That is all right. I do understand. You are a man and can't help but—" She caught herself, apparently. "What I mean to say is, that as much as I adore your . . . longing for me, I was thinking that it would be wrong for me to take you from your work, and I have so much planning to do tomorrow, and my—" She gazed at the grandfather clock. "It is already ten-thirty. I must take my leave, despite my desire to stay with you."

He rose and led her to the door. "I certainly understand," he agreed. "Soon we will be married and I will have you in my bed every night." He gave her a peck on the cheek. "Wait here. I will call your driver. Or perhaps I will walk you out myself, dearest, as much as I hate to see you take your leave."

Jeremy turned and saw Prissy hiding behind the door to the dining room. Impudently she winked at him and he winked back. "Shall we?" he said and led Belinda out the door.

Jeremy downed two glasses of whiskey in rapid succession. He sat with a pamphlet issued from the press of Mr. Edes, but he had little interest in reading it at the moment. Not that he hadn't found himself thinking about the issues expressed in this work and the constant deluge of argument in the Boston press. Since he had returned to Boston he had begun to understand that there was more than rhetoric involved in the arguments against the Crown and Parliament, for he had seen firsthand some of the duress that afflicted all but the wealthiest Bostonians or those in government positions.

Now that he had sent Belinda home, he was free to think, and he did not wish to think about her or Abigail. For even Belinda's unnecessary visit to Abigail—so transparent in intent that it was laughable —was a subject that crossed the stone wall that he'd constructed to protect him. And even as Belinda unknowingly crumbled a stone or two, the knife-like feeling plunged through to stab him. Only now, with the calming effect of the whiskey, did the comforting numbness reseal the gap.

He wished that he could speak to Michael—not about Abigail, for he had vowed to never mention his hurt to anyone, but about politics and life. However, Michael was rarely available to him these days, and when they did have a brief conversation, Michael would parrot whatever Jeremy said. More often than not, Michael offered almost transparent excuses to decline Jeremy's invitations.

In part, the unspoken breach between them was his own unintentional doing. For that night, that rainy night when the last vestiges of his hopes had died and he had sought consolation in the burning liquor, Michael had stopped by for a visit. That Jeremy was drunk had to have been obvious to his friend, but how drunk he was, Michael never comprehended. Vaguely, Jeremy remembered that Michael had appeared quite agitated and had wanted to talk. Jeremy had just the glimmer of recollection of that evening. It seemed to him that he had been less than supportive, although he'd be damned if he could remember what it was

Michael had spoken of. Almost two weeks later, when Jeremy had finally come out of his alcoholic trance, he'd stopped by to visit Michael.

Michael had been in a rush to some appointment about which he was reticent. Jeremy had assumed it might be to court a girl, perhaps even the barmaid he'd seemed so taken with that night at Giles's Tavern. What else would explain his secrecy and nervousness? Jeremy had offered Michael a ride in his carriage but Michael had declined, saying he needed the fresh night air. When Jeremy had asked if he was perhaps headed for a secret meeting in a tavern, it had seemed to him that Michael had blanched, but it had been too dark for him to be certain, and moments later they parted.

Why did that joke so upset his friend? Meeting in a tavern—why did the very phrase suggest something to Jeremy that seemed almost a dream-like memory?

"Can I get you anything before I retire, sir?" Prissy's voice startled him. He hadn't been aware that she'd entered the study.

"No, I don't think so," he answered distractedly. A meeting in a tavern . . . why couldn't he put his finger on it? He rose and poured another glass of whiskey as he continued to try to think, but already his brain was growing foggy.

"Sir? . . . Jeremy?"

Was Prissy still in the room? He turned and saw her curled on the large leather chair, her legs bare and tucked beneath her, causing the skirt of her chemise to rise and present him with a glimpse of her creamy full thigh. Why was she— He remembered, especially the last wink they had exchanged. She was a tempting sweet, but one which he did not intend to taste tonight. "Prissy, I think it best if you remove yourself from that chair and take yourself to bed."

She rose and started for the door, wordlessly. Then she turned, walked to him, and threw her arms over his shoulders. She stood upon her bare toes and pressed her body tightly against his own. He could feel the mounds of her breasts and the heat at the delta of her belly. She pulled his face down to hers and kissed him, her tongue plunging hotly into his mouth as her hands caressed his neck and her ardent nipples came to life against his chest. She was so very tempting. His hands dropped to her firm, round buttocks and she pushed herself tighter against his thighs.

"Prissy, no. I'm sorry," he said, as he gently extricated himself from her.

She stood and looked at him, brown eyes filled with genuine tears and sweet red mouth quivering. "Why?" she asked. "I was so sure—"

"I know. And it is my fault. I apologize for misleading you—"

The knock at the door startled them, although it was soft.

Prissy straightened her chemise. "I'll get it," she said, regaining her composure.

"No, that's all right. I will. Who could be calling at such a late hour?" he said. A glance at the clock told him it was almost eleven. "You best run up to bed." Perhaps it was Michael.

The soft knock at the door was more insistent as he strode toward it. Jeremy swung open the door. There

before him stood Levi's pregnant wife and the boy
Nathan. Katie looked frightened and pale; she was
hugely pregnant. The boy looked sleepy but did his
best to appear as an alert escort. "Please, Goodwife
Peabody, Nathan. Do come in." Why were they here
at this hour that found most women and children safe
within their beds? Had something happened to Abigail?

"I am most sorry to disturb you at such a late hour,
Mr. Blackburn," Katie said in a particularly soft and
appealing voice. "But I must talk to you. I brought
Nathan along because I felt it was unsafe for me to
traverse the streets alone at such an hour—"

"Yes, that was a wise idea, although I'm not certain
that a boy," he looked down at the proud Nathan,
"even one as strong and manly as Nathan, could
provide the protection—you know that the streets
have become dangerous in these past years." He
looked at her drawn, pale face. Of course she knew.
Obviously she had some serious reason to see him.
And here he stood lecturing the tired, pregnant
woman. "Please, come into the parlor and sit down."

As Jeremy turned, he saw Prissy, hiding at the
stairs. "Prissy, good. You came down to answer the
door I take it," he said as a way of obliquely explaining her presence. "Prissy, this is Goodwife Peabody
and Nathan."

"Katie," she said, with a smile at the girl. "Pleased
to make your acquaintance. We are sorry if we awoke
you."

Prissy smiled warmly at Katie. "Oh, no. I was
actually on my way down to the kitchen for a glass of

milk. Nathan? Would you care for a glass of milk as well? And I do believe I know where some ginger-bread can be found. What do you say?"

Nathan looked to Katie who nodded in approval. "That would be very nice, thank you," Nathan said eagerly.

"Thank you, Prissy," Jeremy said and vowed that he would make a point of giving the good-hearted girl a genuine apology for his behavior tonight.

"This way, then, Goodwife Peabody."

"Please, call me Katie, Mr. Blackburn," she said as she followed Jeremy into the parlor.

"Call me Jeremy, then, Katie," he said as he closed the doors behind them. "Please, sit down. May I offer you a beverage? Some milk perhaps?"

"Nothing. Thank you. You are already more than gracious," she said as she sank wearily upon the fine sofa to which he had led her.

"Tell me frankly—" He could withhold the words no longer. "Abigail. She is not ill or—"

Katie smiled softly. In fact she seemed to glow. "No! I am sorry if our appearance alarmed you. She is quite well, physically at least. But your alarm makes me all the more certain that my late visit to you was imperative."

"How so?" he asked, relieved but more confused.

"I will explain. But first I must ask for the liberty of speaking quite frankly and terribly intimately to you. Will you allow me to do so?" she asked with trepidation in her pale blue eyes. "Even though I am Levi's wife?"

"And obviously a brave and admirable lady. Abigail told me much about you that day—"

Katie watched his kind smile turn to anguish. "Thank you. She has done the same about you. In fact, I am breaking her confidence in hopes that I can help both of you. If you will indulge me, I will begin by telling you a story. A story of an event that happened almost five years ago . . ."

He wanted to stop her, but somehow he couldn't bring himself to upset this fragile, gentle lady. Something in her face told him that he could trust her. Trust her he would. At the very least he would hear her through.

Katie watched a drained, anguished Jeremy fight his own mind, his dead brother, and everything that he had believed for almost five years, as he stood at the table and drained a glass of whiskey. She accepted the glass of cool water he wordlessly placed in her hands. She drank it down quickly. Her hands were trembling and she felt dizzy and nauseated. She attributed it to tiredness and the fear of Jeremy's reaction when he heard the truth.

She watched his jaw pulsate in his tormented face. "Why did she not tell me herself, if what you say is true?" he demanded.

"Because of her foolish pride. As I said, she believed—still believes—that if you loved her you could never have thought—"

"But Damon presented such details that it never occurred to me . . . that he could have been so devious . . . so evil . . . my own twin!"

Jeremy sank into the chair across from her and the harsh, wracking sound of grief broke through him as he covered his face with his hands and began to cry.

"Why?" he pleaded between bitter sobs. "Why would he do that to Abigail? To me?"

"I have asked myself the same thing. I guess that he was troubled. And so envious of your happiness that he couldn't help himself. Then, when he was discovered by Levi, he must have been so frightened that he invented his story more to protect himself than to further harm you or even Abigail."

"If he did as you say, as Abigail says, then I hope he is burning in hell!" Jeremy proclaimed. He broke into fresh sobs again.

"No, you don't," Katie admonished softly. "He was your brother and you loved him. You must hope that God forgave him, that before he died he asked God's forgiveness."

"No! He has ruined my life. And Abigail's. All these years of loneliness and torment. I hope he is burning in hell!"

Katie knew that these were words of the deepest hurt. Time would temper them. She could not sit and watch Jeremy's shoulders shake with the wracking sobs of his pain. He needed someone to touch him and help him feel less alone. Slowly, Katie rose to walk to him. "Oh!" she cried out as the pain shot through her, and she sank down again.

Jeremy immediately raised his face, and seeing how deathly pale she'd grown, jumped up and raced to her side. "Katie, what's wrong?" he asked, frightened. Fear choked his sobs.

"I don't know . . . I think that perhaps my water broke . . . the baby is coming . . ." She looked down and turned paler still. "Oh, I am so sorry! Look what I have done to your fine sofa!"

"Damn the sofa!" Jeremy insisted. "It is you whom I'm worried about. We must get a doctor!" He put his arm around her trembling shoulders and felt the cold that seeped from her body. "Prissy! Nathan! Mrs. Latham!" he shouted. He felt her go faint in his arms. He yelled their names again.

"Jeremy," she whispered. "I will be fine. This is my second baby. But I must tell you something," she whispered so softly that he had to lower his head to hear her. "You said your life is ruined. That is why I came. It is not. You are still a young man and Abigail is not yet twenty-one. You have your whole lives before you. Do you hear me?" she demanded as strongly as she could.

"Yes, I hear you." He kissed her on her forehead as Nathan, with Prissy on his heels, ran in, followed by a confused Mrs. Latham in her nightclothes.

"What is the—oh, my Lord!" Mrs. Latham exclaimed.

"Don't chatter. Quickly, Prissy, go fetch Michael Harrington and tell him he needs to deliver a baby immediately."

"But what if he is not at home? What shall I do?"

Suddenly Jeremy knew the answer to the puzzle—a secret meeting in a tavern! The Salutation in the North End! "If he is not at home you must go to The Salutation tavern on Salutation Street off North Street. Do you know where it is?"

"Aye, I think so. He will be at the bar?"

"No, in the back room. They will say he is not, but tell the keeper that it is an emergency. Run into the back room on your own if you have to! Now get going."

"I will, sir," Prissy called, already running from the room.

"Nathan," Jeremy turned to the stricken boy. "My coachman is off for the evening. Do you know how to ride a horse, son?"

"Yes, I do," Nathan answered.

"Then run to the stable in the back of the house and saddle the black mare. Do you know how to mount a saddle?"

"No. But I can ride bareback. Truly, sir!"

Jeremy had no choice but to believe the boy. "Good. Then ride home and bring Abigail and Jane with you, immediately. Try not to alarm them more than necessary if that's possible. Tell them I have sent for the doctor."

"What about Levi, sir?"

"Bring him too, of course. He has a wagon, does he not?"

"Yes, sir."

"Then get going, son!"

Nathan raced out of the room.

"Boy," Mrs. Latham called after him. "I shall show you the fastest way through the kitchen." She followed him out. "I shall heat water and bring towels, Mr. Blackburn!"

"Good!" he called out. He returned his attention to Katie who lay limp in his arms and was growing colder. He looked down and saw that a red substance had spread across the seat and through her petticoat. Blood!

"Hurry, Mrs. Latham!" he shouted. "For she is bleeding! Hurry with the towels, please!" Should he lift her and carry her to his bed? He did not know what one was to do. She was almost unconscious. Swiftly he lifted her body, which was light despite the weight of the child, just as Mrs. Latham rushed back in with a stack of towels in her hand. She blanched.

"Oh, my Lord! There is blood all over you and her! Quick, take her to my room."

"No, I shall take her up to my own," he insisted. So she wasn't quite as terrible a woman as he'd assumed. So much of what he'd believed seemed to have been wrong—but he had no time to think of that now as he raced up the stairs with Katie in his arms. "I know nothing of childbirth," he called to Mrs. Latham at his heels. "Is there always this much blood?"

"No, Jeremy," she said, calling him by his given name for the first time in years. "May the Lord protect her and the child—there should be no blood at all, not at this point. There should be no blood at all."

# Chapter Twelve

"BUT WHY WAS SHE AT JEREMY'S!" ABIGAIL CALLED aloud to no one as she hurriedly dressed. "It is my fault. She must have gone there to speak to him after I told her— It is my fault!—"

Abigail flew down the stairs. Jane was dressed and waiting for her at the door. For the first time, Jane looked like an aging woman, her face deeply lined in worry. "Where is Nathan?" Abigail asked.

"He has gone to get the cart and horse. You must drive it since Levi is not at home yet. Nathan will ride Jeremy's mare back. Where *is* Levi! He's been up to no good for some time now! I've kept my peace about it and that was most certainly a mistake— I will give that boy a thrashing— I tell you, he's not too old or big for Jane to take over her knee—"

"It does no good to rave and rant now, Jane!" Abigail said so sharply that Jane quieted. "I must go and find him. For if Katie is about to have the babe— I will take Jeremy's horse and ride to Blue's Tavern. Nathan can drive you to Jeremy's in the wagon."

"Do you intend to ride through the town bareback at this hour? A young woman alone down at the wharf? I will not hear of it! Write Levi a note telling him what has happened and he will meet us there."

Abigail quickly scribbled a note. "I must find him," she insisted and ran through the back door before Jane could further protest. "We will meet you at Jeremy's," she called behind her.

Levi and Charles walked through the disreputable blocks of Anne Street. Even at this late hour of almost eleven, girls, some as young as Katie, dressed in bright-colored, short dresses weaved among them, offering themselves for a small sum. Levi spotted a fancy coach which had stopped in a deserted alley. As he and Charles approached, they noticed first the richly dressed young men, then the coat of arms on the side of the polished carriage. They soon picked up the drift of conversation. For a whore, still young enough to be pretty, was attempting to pull her arm from one gentleman's grip.

"I have changed my mind, sir," she whined. "I do not wish to go with the two of you. I do not do that sort of thing," she pleaded.

The man who held the reins laughed. "Come now, wench. You do that and *more,* I am certain. We told you we will pay you well." He shook a bunch of clinking coins in his money bag. "Get in and do not tarry," he insisted, as the man closest to the girl grabbed her other arm and began to pull her into the carriage.

"Get in or we will just as easily slit your throat and leave you to die in the alley," the man puffed as he pulled at the resisting girl.

"Please, sir, let me go!" she pleaded and cried.

Both men laughed in response and the man with the reins jumped out of the carriage, still holding the girl firmly in his grasp, and clamped his strong hand over her mouth. "Cry all you like, girl!" He laughed heartlessly as he hoisted her into the carriage.

"Those Tory bastards!" Levi exclaimed bitterly, as he and Charles watched from about ten feet away. "They think they can take anything they fancy!" He began to rush forward. "Gentlemen!" he shouted.

The men turned to see from whence the voice issued in the dark alley.

"Don't, Levi," Charles pleaded, restraining him momentarily. "It is not your business!" he whispered. "Nothing will happen to the girl that she has not experienced many a time. They will pay her handsomely perhaps."

"Who goes there?" the gentleman with the reins called out anxiously.

Levi broke free from Charles and ran to the carriage. "Let that girl go!" he demanded.

"What are you yelling about?" said the same man, his pockmarked face clearer under the light emanating from a nearby window. "This lady is our guest. I do not know what you overheard but it is all a game."

"If it is a game, then why does your young friend have his hand clamped to her mouth?"

As Levi spoke, the man holding the girl had slipped his knife from his pocket and pressed it against the terrified girl's side. The girl, feeling its sharp edge, looked down and the glint of metal at her side confirmed her worst fear. She quickly understood what she was to do, as the man unclamped her mouth.

"See," the man then said to Levi, his knife pressed harder at her ribs. "Ask the girl yourself if it is not a game," he said with a sickly smile.

"I am fine, sir," the girl said in a trembling voice to Levi, as her eyes pleaded otherwise. "Thank you for your concern, but these fine gentlemen are friends of mine. Truly . . ."

"Oh, I understand," Levi said. He smiled disarmingly. "I apologize for my misinterpretation of what I thought was transpiring." He tipped his hat. "Good night to you all then," he said and turned away, taking two steps toward Charles, who stood yards away against a darkened warehouse door.

"And good night to you," the man at the reins said jovially.

Before he had finished the sentence, Levi had leaped into the carriage from behind, taking them by surprise.

"Damn fool!" Charles muttered, watching but unsure yet whether to run to Levi's aid.

Levi pounced upon the man who held the girl and grabbed him by the throat. "Release her," he demanded, and with that the girl leaped from the carriage and ran down the street past Charles.

Levi saw the glint of the knife a moment before the man attempted to plunge it into his chest, and struggled until he pulled the knife from the weaker man's hand. The driver's whip stung so sharply at his shoulder that Levi cried out in pain as Charles rushed to his aid.

Levi jumped from the carriage as Charles arrived at

his side, the man's knife in Levi's hand, pointed at the two gentlemen. "Tory bastards!" he shouted. "Come down from your fine carriage and fight one-to-one—man-to-man—if you are more than girls dressed in men's breeches!"

"It is the hour of eleven," they heard the night watchman cry as he turned into the alley and marched toward them, his boots heavy on the cobblestones.

"Help, help!" the man at the reins cried, shocking Levi and Charles. His friend who had held the girl quickly joined in. Levi heard something drop beside his feet, but it was dark and—

"Help! Thieves! Help!" the gentleman yelled, as the watchman ran their way. Soon another approached from the direction in which the girl had fled.

"Let's get out of here!" Charles insisted, tugging at Levi.

"Flee? Why, when we can have these men arrested for attempting to kidnap a girl—"

"You fool! Don't you know what they're doing?" Charles tried to warn him, but it was too late. Charles felt his arms pulled behind him by one of the burly watchmen, while the other did the same to Levi, who made it worse by struggling.

"Why are you upon me, when it was I who saved the girl from—"

"Be quiet and stand still," the watchman who held him demanded gruffly, poking Levi with his stick for emphasis. Levi stopped struggling. "Now tell me, gentlemen, what seems to be the problem?"

"These Tory bastards—" Levi began, only to be poked with the stick again.

"Not you," the watchman said. "I am speaking to the *gentlemen*."

Levi was dumbfounded.

"Thank you," spoke the man behind the reins. "We are so grateful for your arrival in time, for these hooligans tried to rob us—"

"That is a lie!" Levi yelled. "They are lying Tory scum—"

"If we are lying then look by that ruffian's feet and you will find the blue velvet moneybag he stole from me at knifepoint and then dropped as you approached."

"Stand still, I warn you," the watchman said as he kneeled searching the ground with his hand as he kept his eye on Levi. In a moment he stood and raised a blue velvet moneybag, dangling it before their eyes. "Is this the bag, sir?" he politely asked the gentleman.

"That is it. Had you not come he would have slit our throats I fear!"

"You are under arrest," the watchman said as he cuffed Levi's hands behind his back and regarded him with the air of disdain one has for a common thief.

"And this one?" asked the watchman who held Charles.

"That one held the knife at us while the other searched our pockets," the man who had held the girl claimed.

"You are under arrest," the burly officer said to Charles, and cuffed his hands.

"They are lying! Listen to me. He threw the moneybag on the ground as you arrived on the scene—"

"Quiet, young man. You may tell your story to the judge in the morning."

"Officer," the man behind the reins called. "There is more that you should know. The red-haired one spoke to us of a group of friends who intend to commit treasonous acts against the Crown. He made us tell him where we lived and said he and his group would be arriving in Cambridge deep in the night, soon, to burn down our houses!"

"Oh, did he now?" the watchman said with excitement. Perhaps this was more than a routine arrest. Lieutenant Governor Hutchinson would learn about this, at the very least. Perhaps that meant a promotion to daywatch. "Will you gentlemen swear a complaint to such?" he officiously asked, already knowing the answer.

"Of course, sir!" one answered and the second repeated.


"Now there's one I could happily take to my bed," a tall, rangy sailor said to the mastmaker at his side, as he admired the red, wild-haired beauty that flew into the tavern.

"Watch your mouth," the mastmaker, a graying, sturdy fellow, snapped, as he turned and saw Mistress Peabody approaching. "That is no strumpet. That is Levi Peabody's sister."

Abigail rushed to the bar in the taproom. "Excuse me," she called to the man who tended the bar. "I am looking for my brother, Levi Peabody. Have you seen him—"

"Good evening, Mistress Peabody," the mastmaker

said, gently touching her shoulder. Abigail looked at him with surprise added to her already troubled face. "I am Tom Burns. We were introduced by your brother once at your printing shop." He offered his hand and was shocked to discover hers was as cold as a winter night at sea, despite the warmth of the summer eve. "Pay that no mind, can I help you, miss?"

"Aye, thank you," she said, attempting to smile. "Has my brother been here this evening? It is crucial that I find him."

"He has indeed. He left awhile ago with Charles Osborn. We had a few tankards of flip—but he was not drunk if that is your concern. I expect that he should be home by now. Is there something I can do to help?"

"I don't think so. You already have. . . . If by some chance you should see him again this night, please tell him that his wife is already bringing their child into the world. Tell him she is at Jeremy Blackburn's home on Hanover Street. That we are all there. Would you please?"

"Certainly, miss. I guess you left him a note at home saying that?" She nodded and he realized that it was more than a simple childbirth. His wife had brought nine into the world with little alarm. His sisters, both of them, had not been so fortunate. One had died in birth last year. He realized that apparently Abigail was out alone, so late. The streets were dangerous these days. "Miss? Have you walked here alone? It is unsafe. Let me see you to this Mr. Blackburn's house."

"Thank you, but it is not necessary. I am on horse and shall ride back quickly. Thank you so much, Goodman Burns."

With that she flew out the door, her crimson hair trailing behind her, just as quickly as she had flown in.

"How is she?" Abigail asked Jeremy at once as she ran into the hallway. Jeremy's haggard face fueled her fear.

"Michael Harrington is upstairs with her, as is Jane." Abigail was already halfway up the stairs. "I have tied your horse to the post outside," she called. Even with her hair tangled and her face smudged with grime from her ride, Abigail looked more beautiful than any woman he had ever seen. The fear that filled her emerald eyes and strained her face had made it even more difficult for him to restrain himself from taking her into his arms and giving them both a moment's comfort. What could he do to help anyone? He was frustrated by having to wait. He ran out to take the mare into the barn. At least that would be something. Then he remembered that Nathan sat forlornly in the kitchen. Jeremy retraced his steps and found the boy. "Nathan, would you like to help me quarter and water the mare, and your nag as well?"

With an attempted smile, the boy followed him out. "Did Abigail find Levi?" he asked.

Jeremy realized that he had forgotten to ask, so grateful was he to see her at the door safe and sound. "I don't know . . . I expect not or else surely he would have arrived with her." He saw the boy's face grow more troubled. "But I am certain that he will arrive before long," he said as he tousled the boy's hair.

Abigail knocked quietly but entered before anyone could respond. Jane and another older woman dressed in nightclothes flanked the bed, while Michael Harrington hovered over Katie. A pretty, young girl sat on the floor in the corner of the room, her fist in her mouth and tears in her eyes. Jane looked up and tried to smile at Abigail but failed miserably. Abigail was suddenly struck by the ominous silence, for surely Katie should be wailing as the baby pushed within her body to be born. Unless—

Fighting her dizziness, Abigail hurried to the foot of the bed. Katie stirred! Thank the Lord, she was alive, Abigail thought as tears of relief poured down her cheeks. She brushed them away. This was not a time for self-indulgence.

Abigail walked to Jane, who took her hand. From this view she was horrified to see the bloody towels stacked in a pail in the corner. "The baby?" Abigail whispered to Jane.

She watched as Michael's bloody hands suddenly pulled a red-haired, fat baby from between Katie's legs. The baby was covered with afterbirth, as Abigail had seen before. But something was wrong. It's body, beneath the afterbirth, shone almost blue. It wasn't crying. Why didn't Michael slap its bottom to make it—

Michael looked up at them. His strained face and haunted eyes gave him away. "Please, Jane, another towel. And the cradle."

"But the baby isn't crying, why isn't it crying?" Abigail asked in quivering voice.

Michael looked from one woman to the other. "I'm sorry. The baby boy is stillborn. . . . I did my best to save it."

"Take care of Katie, good doctor," Jane stated stoutly, fighting back her tears. "She will bring many more healthy ones into the world. And we thank you for your best efforts, but God's will is His own," Jane declared as she cleaned the stillborn baby boy, kissed him once and then placed him in the cradle. She took a clean towel and covered the babe so that the truth could no longer be denied.

Abigail stood numb, until the silence was broken by the loud cries from the young girl in the corner.

"Hush, Prissy," the older woman spoke. "It is God's will. Leave this room at once, daughter!" the woman scolded harshly, but Abigail realized it was for the girl's own good as well.

"Thank you, Mrs. Latham," Michael said. "I would appreciate it if all of you would leave the room now, except for Jane, whose help I may need."

Silently, Abigail started for the door behind Mrs. Latham. "Abigail!" Katie called out to her, as if from the dead. "Abigail . . ."

"Go on with you," Michael said more harshly than he meant. "She is delirious and does not know that she called out."

"I am staying," Abigail stated quietly. She did not wish to give the doctor trouble, but she couldn't leave when Katie needed her.

"Aye, doctor," Jane said. "Let her stay and I shall take the child away. Abigail can be of great help to you, for it was she who saw Katie through Sarah's birth, not I." Jane lifted the cradle and stopped before Abigail. She raised the towel so that Abigail could see the sweet face of the baby that looked as if it slept contentedly. Abigail kissed its already cold forehead, fighting back her tears. She kissed Jane's cheek as well, then walked to the chair beside Katie and sat down. Never before had she felt so weary, as she reached and took Katie's hand into her own.

The clock had just struck two when a bleary-eyed, haggard Michael entered Jeremy's study and carefully closed the door behind him.

Jeremy rose from the chair, poured a stiff whiskey and handed it to Michael, who wordlessly accepted it and sank into a chair. Jeremy poured himself a glass as well. "How is she?" he asked.

"She has lost much blood. She comes in and out of consciousness and has a raging fever. If she makes it through this night—" Michael watched Jeremy's face whiten further.

"You mean she may die?" he whispered, even with the heavy door closed.

"She may. It is up to God now, I am afraid. Abigail seems to somehow give the girl the will to struggle. She is still at Katie's side, although Katie has been asleep or unconscious for the better part of the last hour. Still, when she wakes she searches Abigail's eyes and almost smiles back, though she is too weary. Abigail sits and talks to her. Almost girlish chatter. She is quite a lady, that Abigail. As strong as they come," he said with a tired smile. "Where are the others?"

173

"Nathan has been put to bed in Mrs. Latham's room with baby Sarah. Prissy apparently cried herself to sleep in her own bed. Jane Stewart and Mrs. Latham sit by the hearth, talking and comforting one another the way women can. And I have paced the house feeling utterly useless! I have thought about many things as well. Tonight for the first time I fully appreciate why you chose to become a physician. It is more than admirable—"

"So admirable that I have lost the child, and the mother may die before the sun rises," Michael said bitterly.

"That is weary talk, Michael. For think how many you do save . . ."

"Perhaps. But we have so far to go in the study of medicine. Perhaps someday a doctor will save and heal more than he loses. But that will not be in my lifetime, I'm afraid." He drank a strong swallow from his glass.

"At least you try. What good have I done for *anyone?* I work for the Crown and a governor who instructs me to sue for libel and sedition editors whose very arguments I find myself agreeing with more each day. I look around me and see the privileged among us grow more greedy as those with less grow more desperate." Jeremy watched Michael's mouth drop open in shock and his eyes flicker with renewed life. Then Michael tried to erase his own sympathies from his face.

"What do you mean?" he asked evenly.

"Oh, don't give me that tripe," Jeremy said and laughed softly. "I figured you out tonight—by accident—when crisis forced me to think hard. I know you are one of 'The Loyal Nine' or at least one of their followers. How else do you think Prissy found you in the back room of The Salutation where apparently your group meets? The night of the town meeting I wandered in there and was at the bar when I saw you exit in the company of Ben Edes. Only, I was too drunk then to remember, until tonight."

Michael burst into laughter. "But when I tried to talk to you over a month ago . . ."

"Again I was so drunk that you, as a doctor, should have seen me to bed rather than tried to conduct a rational discussion, my dear friend." Jeremy gave him a sardonic grin. "It was the night after Abigail and I spent the afternoon in the country . . ."

Michael watched as Jeremy's eyes darkened and he seemed to be fighting back tears. "I did not know you had visited with—"

"Have you not wondered what brought Katie to my house tonight?" he abruptly asked.

"Yes, I had," Michael yawned. "But so much has happened that I haven't had time to think."

"I know," Jeremy replied somberly. He downed his drink. "She came to tell me that for the past five years I had believed an insidious lie that almost—"

Michael's eyes flooded with relief but then he looked down at the carpet. "She told you the truth about Damon? How he tried to rape Abigail, and when Levi discovered them in time to stop him, how he lied to you to save his own skin."

Jeremy was speechless for the second time that night. Suddenly fury flooded his brain. "God damn you!" he shouted. "You knew!"

Michael quickly rose and grabbed him by his shoulders. He shook Jeremy hard. "I will tell you everything. But if you wish to scream and curse at me, please wait for another night, for there is a dead baby and a dying woman in this house," he whispered anxiously.

"I'm sorry . . . You're right . . ." Jeremy whispered contritely. "Please! I will be quiet. Just tell me why!"

"Do you recall that I had just become a doctor and was at Damon's side as he died in that alley?"

Jeremy rose. He walked to the mantel and stared at the unlit wood in the hearth. "Yes."

"Damon swore me to silence. It was a deathbed promise he extricated from me. You don't know how it has haunted me all these years, especially since your return from London. After you had gone off to London and wrote eventually how you intended to remain there, it had become less of a burden. I have wanted to tell you the truth since your return. But it was a promise at his deathbed. His last request."

"But if you knew, then he had to have told you *before* he was stabbed. Why did you not tell me then? For he died two nights after—"

"Because I believed I could convince him to tell you himself. I had no knowledge of the story he fabricated that turned Abigail and Levi into the villains. I did not know that you had gone to her house and accused her of vile deception. I didn't learn any of that until the night of Damon's death, when he got stinking drunk and spilled it all out in a drunken slur. That was why he was wandering about the South End Wharf alone, for the truth had so disgusted me that I stormed home. But even then, I was so enraged that I returned

176

to find him and threaten him myself. I intended to tell him that if he did not tell you the truth by the next evening, I would. I found him beaten and stabbed, lying in the alley. I passed Levi and his friends, heard them brag—"

"So Levi did murder him! That much is true—not that I can say I would have acted much differently if Abigail had been my sister."

"No, I think not. They did not see me as they passed, but Levi drunkenly bragged to Adam Taylor that when Damon woke in the gutter it would be a long time before he would be able to attack another woman again, even if he wanted to! Then one of the boys whom I did not recognize made a lewd remark about Damon's future sexual ability. If they had killed him, or left him to die, they would not have been joking as they were. They beat him, fairly severely I would say, but nothing was broken that would not mend or heal."

"Why did you not testify so at the trial?" Jeremy walked to pour another whiskey. He held the bottle in offering but Michael shook his head. Jeremy realized that Michael could be needed upstairs at any moment.

"Because I was certain, as I said, that Levi had neither stabbed nor robbed Damon. I was afraid my testimony would further incriminate him. And I believed, that as you yourself said, that if Abigail had been my sister I might have done much the same thing, physician or not. Although I doubt I would have required a gang behind me."

Jeremy rubbed his aching temples. Everything Michael said made sense . . .

"And in effect I did perjure myself, for I was asked

if I had seen anyone at the site of the murder. In essence I had, but I couldn't admit what I'd heard. As much as Damon was despised—there is *so much* about your brother you always refused to see—I was afraid that the jury would feel obliged to find Levi guilty if I spoke what I knew. Especially since the true story of Damon's attack upon Abigail was never introduced, although there were many rumors flying about the city."

"I was so stupid and blind!" Jeremy spoke as he sank back into his chair.

"No, you weren't. He was your brother. More than just a brother, your twin. You had a blind spot predicated on love. It is that simple. And that sad."

"If only I could believe that Abigail could ever forgive me. But why should she? God, how vilely I treated her. Even when I told her I loved her that day, I pompously offered to *forgive* her her sins! No wonder she was so furious and hurt. I see it all now, so clearly . . ."

"There is time for you to beg her forgiveness. To explain. I must go see how Katie is. I am sorry that I cannot be more comfort to you now. We will talk again, very soon, my dear friend." With a sad smile, Michael rose and departed from the room.

Jeremy sat and stared at the hearth. It was too much for him to think of now. He rose sluggishly. He would see how Mrs. Stewart and Mrs. Latham were holding up, and have a cup of tea. Perhaps he could urge the women to take some rest; perhaps he could be of use to someone, somehow.

# Chapter Thirteen

THE LIGHT POURING THROUGH THE LACE-CURTAINED parlor windows awoke Jeremy the next morning. He raised his head from the sofa pillow. Waves of pain pounded his skull but he grit his teeth and rose. He had no time to waste. Through blurred eyes, he looked at the grandfather clock. It was even later than he guessed, for it was nearly eleven.

He found Nathan in the kitchen. "Would you run to the coach house and ask Tom, the coachman, to ready my carriage? Tell him I will not need him to drive me. Thank you, Nathan."

"Aye, sir, right away," the boy answered, apparently pleased to have a job to perform. Jeremy knew just how the boy felt . . . such a fine boy. Already he had grown quite fond of him.

"Some breakfast, Mr. Blackburn?" Mrs. Latham asked, as she stood by the table watching Jane feed pretty little Sarah. Abigail was noticeably absent. He assumed that she was still upstairs with Katie, which he took as a fortuitous sign. Prissy was nowhere in sight either.

"Just a cup of tea will do, Mrs. Latham, thank you." Despite the weariness that lined her face, Mrs. Latham gave him a pleasant smile. Jeremy returned one in kind. Had it been he, or she, who had been transformed since Katie appeared at his door, he wondered. Another subject on a long list to be mulled when he had the time. "How is Katie?" he asked anxiously.

"I was upstairs just before, Jeremy," Jane answered. "She seems to be sleeping comfortably. Abigail is beside her still," Jane smiled with a hope that her eyes belied.

"Yes, and Prissy went with Dr. Harrington to pick up some medicine at the hospital. He had thought of bringing Katie there, but decided she was too weak and would receive better care here at home," Mrs. Latham informed him.

"Would it be possible for me to slip into my bedroom and retrieve some fresh clothing?" Jeremy asked her.

"I have already done just that for you, sir," Mrs. Latham answered. "They are laid out upon my bed."

"Thank you. . . . Thank you again, both of you," Jeremy said. "I have some urgent matters to attend to, but I will be back within an hour or two," he explained. "Do you think I might slip upstairs in any case and just look in? It would give me some peace of mind until I return."

The ladies smiled at one another in that mysterious womanly way. "I cannot see why not," Jane said.

Jeremy opened his bedroom door soundlessly.

Katie seemed to be sleeping peacefully, although she appeared unhumanly pale. Abigail sat in the straight-backed chair at Katie's side, but her body leaned against the bed and her hand was entwined with Katie's, as her head lay against Katie's pillow. He watched her face, relaxed in exhausted sleep despite her awkwardly contorted position. "I will make it up to you, dearest," he swore silently, and closed the door as carefully behind him as when he had entered.

As Jeremy jumped into his carriage and pulled away from the Wattington house, he began to laugh. He had intended to break off his engagement as politely as possible. He was ready to admit to any culpability Belinda or her parents chose to place upon him. Of course he had had no intention of telling them the truth. He had known it was too much to expect a polite reception, but Belinda's shrieks, crocodile tears, and proclamations of love and undying passion were too much. He couldn't help but laugh. This infuriated Lord Wattington so, that the corpulent man grew livid. Words led to other words and before Jeremy knew what he was saying, he'd told the pompous old man exactly what he thought of him, his shrew of a wife, and sniveling daughter. Jeremy knew that because Lord Wattington was such a powerful man and a confidant of the governor, his job might be taken from him. But he didn't really give a damn. It had been years since he'd felt so free.

Jeremy sobered as he drove through the crooked streets. He knew someone was missing this morning, but he had been so anxious to break his engagement that he'd not remembered. Where was Levi? Why had he not appeared sometime in the night? Jeremy had a hunch. He turned the corner and headed for the state building in the heart of town.

Jeremy used his influence to get the bailiff to release Levi and Charles. Levi almost didn't leave with him, so suspicious was he of Jeremy's motives.

Once they were outside, Jeremy was not sure how to break the news to him. Quickly, he decided that the harsh truth at once was the best. Levi's face tightened and he seemed to lean on the weight of Charles's arm, but he said nothing at first.

"How is Katie?" he asked after a moment. "And what the hell was she doing at your bloody house!" he said with blazing eyes.

"She is not as well as she should be. So please, hold your temper, for explanations will come later. Please get into the carriage so that I can drive you there at once."

"Would you like me to come with you?" a bedraggled, heavy-bearded Charles asked him.

Levi pounded Charles on the back. "No, I don't think so. I shall see you later, after I've taken Katie and the family home. Meanwhile, I suggest you see your lawyer friend, the one who tries to help *decent citizens*. We cannot allow those Tory bastards to get away with it!" he said and then glared at Jeremy.

They spoke not a word on the ride back to the north side of town. When they reached Jeremy's house, Levi jumped out of the still-moving carriage and strode toward the house, with nary a thank you. As Jeremy drove the carriage away, he wondered to himself if he could ever grow to like this impetuous and arrogantly feisty carrot-headed man, even if he were Abigail's brother.

Knowing there was little he could do inside, Jeremy lingered at the coach house with Tom and Nathan. Then he and Nathan went to the stable and brushed the horses. The boy's chatter was comforting, as he talked about his father who had been a "famous" sailor.

Supper was a dismal affair, although Mrs. Latham, with Jane Stewart's help, had prepared a fine meal. Michael had stopped by to check on Katie, who was still only semiconscious, and he had been persuaded to stay. Only Levi took more than a few bites, although Jane implored all of them, especially Nathan, to eat. Prissy brought a plate of food up to Abigail, but later returned with it untouched.

If it weren't for the glazed look in Levi's green eyes, and the paleness that accentuated his freckles, Jeremy might have thought that the man was more upset about what he called his false arrest than by the fact that his son had been stillborn and his wife was barely clinging to her own life. For Levi railed about the whole incident in language that was not befitting ladies at the table. Jeremy finally could stand it no longer. He opened his mouth, intent upon bluntly ending Levi's obnoxious and unfitting behavior. As he was about to speak, he caught Michael's glance. He studied his friend's face which said to him, hold your peace. Jeremy heeded, but shortly after excused himself and retreated to his father's study.

Minutes later, Michael followed him in. "I know

what you are thinking," he said, cutting Jeremy short. "But you must understand that what you are seeing is the evidence of shock. The young man is so terrified that all he can do is bluster and blame his unfortunate arrest for his not being with his wife when his son was stillborn." Michael sat in the leather chair. "Worse yet, while he sat beside Katie's bed all afternoon with Abigail, Katie did not once return to consciousness. It is only the strong man who can allow himself to cry without fearing that he will thereby be permanently broken. It is something that women do with ease but which comes to us as a feat greater than the strongest display of physical prowess."

Jeremy thought about Michael's words. "You are right. . . . I know that too well myself. I will try to be more patient. But I don't think I will ever like that man."

"Perhaps not. I do not much like him myself, for he is a braggart and impulsive . . . yet my heart goes out to him at this moment. . . . How about a glass of brandy, my friend?"

"Certainly." Jeremy poured them both a drink. "Though I must say," he added as an afterthought, "that if the story he told us about trying to save the whore is true, he is also a caring and brave man. Would I have interfered in such a situation? _You_ would have, that I know. But I'm not certain about myself," he mused.

"I don't share your doubts. How about that drink?"

Abigail stirred as she felt Katie's hand move within her own. It had to be night, for the room was dark except for the dim lantern light. Abigail raised her head and looked at Katie's face. Katie's eyes were open! Abigail wanted to cry out in joy, but Katie called so softly to her that she had to place her ear close to Katie's lips to hear.

"Katie, you will be fine! You've come back to us!" She felt Katie try to raise her head. "Don't. You're too weak. I'll be quiet and listen."

"Abigail . . . listen . . . my . . . my baby died?"

Abigail's eyes filled with tears. "Yes, sweet sister. But you'll get better and have many other fine fat ones! Do you want me to go fetch Levi? He's downstairs—I don't have to leave you. I could just shout for him. We're all here—Jane, Sarah, and Nathan . . ." She watched Katie's lips trying to form words.

"Abigail . . . two things . . . important . . . please . . . take care of Sarah . . . and Levi . . . I worry about Levi . . . especially after I'm gone . . ."

"Don't speak such nonsense—"

Katie slowly raised her hand to Abigail's lips to silence her. Abigail choked back her tears.

"The other thing . . . Jeremy . . . he does love you . . . I know, for I . . . I . . ." Katie's eyes closed and her hand fell to her side.

"Katie?" Abigail whispered. "Katie, wake up . . . oh, Katie, you've got to wake up!" Abigail placed her head against Katie's chest and held tightly to her icy hands. "You can't die, Katie! You can't die and leave me! I love you, Katie!" Abigail sobbed. The tears poured from her eyes until Katie's gown was soaked.

185

Hands tried to pull her away but she wouldn't let go until somehow Jane's voice reached her. "She's gone to heaven, Abigail. Let go of her, because she is beyond all disappointment and suffering now."

Abigail fell into Jane's arms, and slowly Jane led her from the room. Michael closed Katie's eyes and covered her with a sheet. Levi stared uncomprehendingly at what had happened, until he fell to his knees at his wife's side. Abigail saw none of this as she sobbed so hard in Jane's arms that she didn't even hear her brother's tortured wail.

Jeremy caught Abigail as she collapsed and carried her into his father's bedroom, laying her on his father's enormous, elaborately carved bed. She looked so small and broken, he thought. When Abigail stirred, Michael made her drink a medicine that would make her sleep. "She is suffering as much from exhaustion as from grief," he explained to Jeremy and Jane, who watched distraughtly.

Levi wished to take Jane, Nathan, and Sarah home. Michael insisted on driving them safely there in Jeremy's carriage. Reluctantly, Levi acquiesced, as he had earlier agreed to leave Abigail sleeping where she was for the night.

Sometime around one in the morning, Mrs. Latham suggested that she prepare Jeremy's bed in the parlor for the night. But he insisted that since she had changed the sheets and aired the room hours before, there was no reason he could not sleep in his own bed. He didn't say so, but he felt that if the spirit of Katie remained in the room, it would be as gentle and soothing as she was in life.

Jeremy stirred. He felt a presence in his room. He did not believe in ghosts, but he'd felt a current of air— He wondered if he were dreaming.

"Jeremy," the voice whispered in the dark, causing him to jump despite himself. He must be dreaming, for it was Abigail's voice.

"Jeremy, are you awake?" she whispered.

"Abigail, is that you?" he whispered back. The touch of her hand upon his confirmed that he was either awake or this was the most vivid dream he'd ever had. And then, suddenly, she was in his arms, and he drew her to him. It was no dream. "Let me light the candle," he whispered.

"No, don't. Not yet. For I must say what I need to say in the comfort of the dark. . . . I love you, Jeremy. I always have. I don't care if you are to be married. I don't care if you feel I have wronged you. Please . . ." Her voice quaked so, that it almost broke his heart to let her continue. "I need you to hold me. To make love to me. For I believe at least a part of you still loves me . . ." She lowered her heated face to his. Her lips shyly begged his mouth for kisses.

God, how he needed her! But first he had to tell her the truth. To think that she loved him enough to find the courage—her love, her need as strong as his own. How it awed him, knowing she still assumed that he believed all of the ugliest accusations he had flung at her. "Abigail—" She covered his mouth with her trembling fingertips and then her warm, gentle lips, until he grew silent and urgently responded to her delicate, exploring mouth. He felt her draw back the bedcovers. Then she nestled against him, and he could feel the heat of her body through the soft folds of her nightclothes.

His eyes grew accustomed to the dark and he was able to see the outline of her slender form above him on this bright, starry night. He watched as she rose and in one fluid motion slipped her nightdress over her head. She tossed it upon the chair on which she'd sat in vigil beside Katie. He reached for her and she slid into his outstretched arms and molded her body onto his. "Abigail—" he started again, but she covered his mouth with her own and he could no longer speak as his tongue hungrily explored the soft recesses of her irresistible mouth. He stroked her shoulders and slowly traced his hand down the curve of her satiny back until his hand rested at the graceful flair of her hip. He caressed the softness of the back of her neck as he kissed her eyes, nose, and cheeks until she emitted a sigh of pleasure and he felt himself growing hard. Gently, he nudged her legs apart with his strongly muscled thigh and she sighed more deeply. Her breath quickened as the tip of his hardness touched the moist heat of her womanhood.

He rolled her onto her back and straddled her, as he raised his torso, his elbows carrying his weight. He drank in the sight of the rise of her small, jutting breasts and brought his lips to each of her pink nipples that grew hard as he played at them, teasing them into further tautness as he listened to her breath catch in her throat and her body jerk in pleasure. His fingers traced the roundness of her breast and then followed

188

down the flat of her belly to the red tangle of curls and to the growing heat of her trembling thighs that parted at his touch. She opened to his fingers that rested at the junction of her vulnerability. As his fingers began to explore her delicate, steamy moistness, he felt her open further to his probing, and she instinctively arched and flowered until his finger touched her very core. He caught her tortured, muffled cry of desire with his mouth.

As her body undulated in waves of pleasure from the gentle, insistent touch that drove her wild, she felt the thrill of his swollen manhood hot against her thigh and wanted to know the rest of the miracle now, with the man she had always loved. She shifted her body, and his hand gently spread her legs further apart and then slipped beneath her, raising and caressing her buttocks as he slowly entered her.

His mouth retraced its path of kisses from her lips, to the nape of her neck, to her collarbone, sending her into deeper waves of pleasure until his lips played at her nipples, then suckled one breast and then the other, making her shiver as the ecstasy she had never known coursed through her, all the way to her toes. She heard sounds of pleasure and realized they came from her own throat. She felt him grow larger inside her, until he filled her. He thrust slowly at first and then he was deeper inside her than she'd ever imagined possible. She met his every stroke with unbridled desire, and he moaned and thrust harder and faster, each thrust bringing her greater waves of this new, feverish sweetness until she could no longer think. She had to let her body answer his own until she was carried to a crest.

His tongue filled her mouth as passionately as his powerful manhood filled her insides, until she was no longer just herself, and they were meshed as one. The sweetness and thrusting engulfed her until she saw colors of extraordinary magnitude explode behind her eyes and she shuddered with pleasure at the precipice until she tumbled and then floated off to somewhere she couldn't name. Eventually she returned to earth, to Jeremy, as she clung to his muscular shoulders. A scent of muskiness permeated her senses with its sweetness. She sighed deeply, trying to mutter words, but was unable. She thought that if she were to die at this moment she would die contented.

Then he was filling her again, and his thrusts grew stronger and deeper, bringing a fresh wave of desire to her. Her body met his strokes even as he moaned from the depth of his chest and then cried out. His body shook as violently as a storm until, with another moan and a sharp shudder, he collapsed into her arms.

They lay together, their bodies glistening with a veil of perspiration, as they tried to catch their breath. Jeremy kissed her again, so gently. Then he rolled upon his back and brought her against him, her head resting beneath his chin. She heard the pounding of his heart beneath her ear as she nestled closer against him, her thigh tucked between his sinewy thighs.

"Abigail . . ." he whispered. "I love you more than you could ever imagine." He kissed the top of her head and stroked her silken hair. "Abigail?" Why did she not answer his whisper? Was it a still-maidenly shyness that she reverted to after her first moments of womanly passion? She curled closer against him nevertheless. Then he felt her body relax as her breathing grew soft and regular. "Abigail?" She cuddled closer and sighed softly. He almost laughed aloud when he realized that she'd fallen asleep in his arms.

Never had he felt more fulfilled, as he listened to her sweet breath rise and fall. For while she had made love with the innate instincts of a passionate woman, she still slept like a little girl. He stroked her hair again and gazed upward with a smile. "Thank you, Katie," he whispered, for somehow he felt as if she knew from her place in heaven. Others might have found them blasphemous for consummating their love in the very bed in which Katie had died just hours earlier. But in the brief time he had been blessed to know Katie, he couldn't help but believe that it would have made her very happy.

# Chapter Fourteen

JEREMY STIRRED AND REACHED ACROSS HIS BED TO DRAW Abigail to him. She was not there. His frown gave way to a smile as he realized that she'd probably slipped back into her room for propriety's sake. He wanted to touch her, but for the moment had to content himself with the memories of their lovemaking, that found them falling asleep in one another's arms as dawn broke the darkness. Jeremy listened to the chirping songs of the morning birds. He heard stirring downstairs, but knew that Mrs. Latham would not disturb his or Abigail's sleep. He rose and stretched his body tautly until he began to feel his blood flow. He slipped on his blue satin gown and quietly crept from his room to hers. As he slid open the door, he saw that Abigail lay fast asleep, her hair loose and spread across the pillow, reminding him of a lovely maiden in his favorite Botticelli painting. He tiptoed to the bed, and leaning over her placed a light kiss on her parted lips. Abigail stirred and opened her eyes with an expression of alarm that immediately changed to pleasure as she recognized him and then to embarrassment as she apparently remembered. She pulled the bedcovers to her chin and cast her eyes at the window. Understanding her reaction, and touched by her modesty, Jeremy sat beside her for a moment. Then he gently turned her face to him. As he tilted her chin, he lowered his lips to hers. His lips caressed her own, and he drank in the sweetness of her natural perfume as he stroked her crimson hair, golden-flecked in the morning light. "Abigail—"

"No, Jeremy, please! Let me speak," she said, and forced herself from his touch as she scrambled upright against the large pillows. She knew she had to say the words now, before it was too late, or she might never be able to utter them again. "I must apologize for my bold behavior last night. I was half out of my mind with grief . . ." She felt her eyes fill as she remembered how Katie had died in her arms. The lump in her throat made it difficult for her to continue. Jeremy sat quietly beside her, his eyes so gentle and glistening that she thought her heart would break. "But that is not an excuse and I would never allow myself to pretend that it was Katie's . . . that it was because of . . . I came to you with a love I have long felt."

Jeremy watched as her color heightened and she again averted her eyes to the window. He wanted to end her agonizing embarrassment, but he sensed that she needed to say her piece first.

She turned back to him, her jaw jutted and her green eyes bright with determination. "What I am trying to say is that I do not regret what transpired between us. It was my doing and I am glad for it." Her cheeks reddened again. "If I had it all to do again I would do it the same . . ." She took a deep breath, then stared at him with a bold determination that was belied by her trembling lips. "I would say that our lovemaking was even more wonderful than I'd . . . experienced," she said, challenging him to deny her worldliness.

It was all he could do to keep from laughing. "I am pleased you feel that way," he interjected with a practiced neutral expression. "What you are trying to tell me is that you know that I am about to be married. *And* that you do not expect me to alter my plans because of our, er, night of mutual pleasure and comfort. Is that not correct?" he said with an air of understanding her intentions and accepting them as a matter of fact. He watched the delicate jaw of her heart-shaped face tighten as she fought back her tears and smiled brightly.

"Aye, that is what I meant to say."

"Well, that is wonderful and terribly sensible of you," he pronounced cordially. He slapped his hand upon the mattress for emphasis. "Then I take it you would have no objection to remaining my mistress after I am married!"

Her mouth dropped open and her eyes widened as the color fled from her cheeks.

"And you were so wonderful, so *skilled* a lover that I do believe we could reach further into the plea-sures—" The pillow flew at him so hard and fast that he almost fell from the bed. Then she was upon him, beating her hands against the pillow that covered him.

He fell backward. Laughing hard, he reached around and caught her wrists, restraining them. He began to rise, but a wave of fresh laughter left him immobile.

Was he laughing at her, mocking her? Abigail wondered. But if so, why such gales of laughter that not even the heavy pillow could muffle. She pulled it from his face as he lay beside her, shaking with mirth until he began to cough, then choke. Automatically, she reached for the pitcher of water that sat on the table beside the bed. She began to pour him a glass, as he still laughed and choked. So he thought it was a subject of such lightness and hilarity! She grabbed the pitcher and dumped its cool water over his head. "That should dampen your spirits, you!" She tried to jump from the wet bed.

Spunky, he thought, as he pulled her back down and laid her in the center of the puddle. "You silly goose!" he said, his laughter subsiding as he pinned her still and smiled. "I love you! I broke my engagement yesterday morning! I've always loved only you!" She struggled against him and he was afraid she wasn't hearing his words. "I'm going to marry you! Marry you as soon as you like! Tomorrow, today, whenever you'll have me!" She lay still and looked at him with a dumbfounded expression. So she had finally heard him. "Katie told me all about the terrible, evil lies my brother told and I ignorantly believed . . ."

She watched his laughter die as his eyes filled with bitter remorse. He swallowed hard as he tried to blink back the tears that nevertheless rolled down his cheeks. So much had just transpired that she struggled valiantly to catch up as her mind replayed his words. So *that's* why Katie had come. That's what Katie was trying to tell her, Katie's very last words—suddenly it was all so clear. He had removed his arms from her wrists and now his hands covered his face as he wiped away the rolling tears. The nightmare was over. Abigail rose and gently pulled his hands to her shoulders and began to kiss his tears away. "My love," she whispered, as her own tears of joy flowed freely.

Momentarily he withdrew from her kisses and stood. So she had heard him and understood. She forgave him! He pulled her from the soggy four-poster bed and lifted her to her feet. He peeled the dripping nightdress from her body, tossed it to the floor, and swept her into his arms. As she clung to him and they kissed ardently, he carried her around to the dry side of the large canopied bed. He lay her against the pillows, pulled off his own soaked gown, and sat beside her. With a smile he returned his mouth to hers but resisted the pull of her arms to him.

"Jeremy," she said softly, a smile of pleasure mixed with lingering confusion. "So you knew even last night when I appeared in your room—"

He laughed happily. "That you were a virgin? Of course." He stroked her cheek as his eyes filled with the beauty of her body, more lovely than the finest works of art. He met her eyes. "I did not hurt you, did I?" he asked with lingering concern.

"Oh, no!" she exclaimed, so artlessly that he laughed in response. "I adored it! It was even more wonderful than I had ever—"

"Imagined," he interjected. "As you started to say earlier but disguised in your attempted charade as a fallen woman," he said with an ironic smile.

"And am I not a fallen woman now?" she asked with uncharacteristic coyness.

"Let me think on that." He brought his mouth to one sweet pink nipple as his hand cupped and fondled her other breast. He felt the tremors in her body that spoke of her arousal. "If you are not, you will be in the next hour," he said as he slid his hand down to caress the pretty tangle of red curls. Gently he slid his fingers between her legs and she opened her alabaster thighs to him and moaned in pleasure. He traced his kisses down her belly to the red thatch of hair, and as she began to writhe he planted his kisses on each of her tender inner thighs until his lips moved to the most delicate spot of all. She tensed for a moment, but as his tongue caressed her, her legs widened and she opened herself to his lips and tongue like the most tender flower opens to the sunlight. With gasps of pleasure and undulating hips, she gave herself to him as her hands caressed, then grasped at the back of his head, until she arched her pelvis and cried out in the ecstasy of this newfound pleasure.

Her breath became more languid as she lay in his arms. Then she rose on her elbow and smiled at him with a smile he could only describe as both heavenly and lustful.

As the sunlight flooded the room, Abigail looked at her Jeremy's chiseled face with deeper love and knowing than she'd thought possible. In the dark of the night she had felt his strong body, broad shoulders which tapered to narrow hips, muscular thighs and manhood. Now she wanted to see and touch him in the daylight. Lightly, she kissed his lips and then traced her fingers across his wide brow, down his straight, fine nose, and then across his lips that began to nibble at her fingers, making her giggle. She played at his lips, then moved her fingers to his strong chin, kissing his deep cleft and then dimples as he smiled in pleasure. All the while her other hand caressed the silky skin covering the strong muscles of his shoulders and neck.

For a moment she stopped and her eyes traveled from his matted chest and taut ribcage to his hips and then to his manhood, which appeared soft and delicate as it lay beneath his golden-brown bush of hair. Her heart quickened at his beauty and she wondered if she were too bold. She met his golden-brown eyes which seemed to shine with love and pleasure. As if he had read her thoughts, he brought her hand to his furry chest and nodded almost imperceptibly. She pecked his lips, then lowered her head to his softly matted chest, and began to kiss his brown, flat nipples as he had done to her. His sigh encouraged her and she forged a trail of kisses from his chest to the mat of hair beneath his waist, as he fondled her breasts. She lifted her head and shyly studied his delicate manhood resting against his thigh. Wondering how it grew as it had last night, she looked up at his face, but couldn't find the words to ask. Jeremy grinned at her. "I'll show you," he said, as he gently guided her hand to its soft, silky head. "One of the wonders of nature," he whispered. "Watch." Slowly, he guided her hand in soft strokes, until she understood and continued on her own, watching with awe as it began to grow and turn a handsome shade of deepening color.

It continued to grow until her small hand could no longer contain its hard girth. Jeremy groaned with pleasure, and his pleasure so filled her that she wanted to bring him more. Instinctively, she leaned above the tip of his hardness and gently kissed it, tasting its salty flavor. She opened her mouth and gently began to caress his tautness, fearing at first that she might hurt him. Gently, his tapered fingers upon the crown of her head encouraged her, as she took more of him into her mouth and he moaned more deeply and raised his hips to her mouth. "Oh how I love you, my lovely green-eyed temptress," he whispered in a deep gravelly voice that excited her.

He pulled her up to him and his mouth devoured her own as he rolled her onto her back. He nibbled at her nipples that hardened as he moved from breast to breast, taunting, sending paroxysms of pleasure coursing through her while his hand slipped between her legs and she felt herself already wet and wanting him.

This time he entered her quickly and thrust hard and deep, each thrust causing her to cry out and arch to meet his next. He almost withdrew from her and she wanted to pull him back, but before she knew it he plunged into her more deeply than before. She writhed and gasped. He held her tongue with his mouth and raised his hips only to plunge into her again as she followed him into unbridled bliss.

"Is it always this wonderful?" Abigail asked as she lay snuggled against Jeremy in satiated exhaustion.

Jeremy tousled her hair and gave her a bear hug. "Always?" he mused playfully. "Let us say it has its ups and downs," he answered with an ironic grin.

Abigail didn't understand in what way he was teasing her and amusing himself. "Ups and downs? I don't know— Oh!" she laughed as his double entendre finally hit her. She felt herself begin to blush, which caused him to chuckle.

"Not quite the courtesan, are you? Despite your blatant, wanton passion of the past hour," he said, watching her color heighten further.

"Oh, Jeremy, tell me! Please! In all honesty! Did I behave too—I mean—"

He pulled her to him and kissed her softly on the tip of her nose. "You responded to me as a healthy, loving woman responds to the man she loves."

"Truly?" she asked, wondering if he was trying to protect her dignity, until she looked into his golden-brown eyes that held her in such tender regard that she no longer needed to question herself or him. "I was thinking before, about the fact that I came to you in the dark of night, in the bed in which Katie had . . . Katie had died. And I wondered if the Lord would punish me for my sin . . ."

He wanted to tell her that he too had thought of their consummation in Katie's deathbed, but sensed that she needed to express her feelings independent of his own. So he allowed her to continue without interruption.

"But then, this morning, after you told me that Katie had come to your house to tell you . . . that she had told you . . . then I remembered Katie's last words. Literally her last. They were about you. Us.

Katie said to me, 'Jeremy, he does love you. I know for I—'" Abigail swallowed hard and her eyes blurred as she looked deep into Jeremy's eyes. "She didn't have the chance to finish her thought . . . but I believe I know what she was going to say. She was going to tell me that she'd told you the whole story although I had sworn her to secrecy. It was probably the only time Katie broke a promise in her entire life . . ." Abigail wiped away her tears.

"I agree, for it was very difficult for her to tell me the story. For that *very* reason, I believed her."

"Aye. We have Katie to thank, for had it not been for her belief in the power of love—" Abigail had to stop. They remained gazing at one another silently but so lovingly. "It is for these reasons that I decided," her voice grew stronger, "that perhaps in others' eyes I have sinned, and maybe in God's eyes as well, for He knows all. But I do believe that if Katie knows, and somehow I believe she does, she feels nothing but joy and love for us." Jeremy hugged her so tightly that for a moment she thought she would not be able to breathe. Then he loosened his hold and leaned back against the pillow, a sad smile on his face.

"That was exactly what I thought this morning when I awoke in my bed; it felt as much hers as mine at that moment. I thought that if her spirit knew, how happy she would be for us. What an affirmation of life and its possibilities, that Katie seemed to understand so much more fully than either you or I. It is a lesson we must try to remember all our lives."

"Do you believe that we will have long lives?" she asked, reminding him of the speculative conversations he'd missed for so many years.

"I believe that I shall live to a ripe old age and that you shall long outlive me." She began to laugh with a delighted expression on her face.

"Oh, I do believe so," he answered quite seriously. "Until last night, I dreaded the idea of a long life and years of continual loneliness."

Abigail stroked his cheek, as her eyes grew sadly pensive. "Were you truly that lonely? Even though you were to be married?"

"For almost five years I don't believe I have known a day that did not end in loneliness. And you?"

"No. I cannot say the same in good conscience. For I have had my family, especially before Father died. . . . And even after, I still had Levi . . . and Katie . . . and Nathan, and dear Jane. God always . . . What I felt was a longing for you, and a deep sadness for what seemed to be a nightmare from which I could never awake." She smiled at him through her tears. "But not the terrible loneliness you suffered, my dearest."

"Mine goes back to even before I met you. You know that, don't you?" He saw the knowledge of his deepest self, and caring he'd thought he'd lost forever, in her lovely face. "Your father was the first person I believed really cared, besides my brother—"

She was frightened by the dark hatred that glowed in his eyes.

"My dear, *loving* brother," he snapped. "I only pray that he burns in eternal hell! I—"

"No! I will not hear you say that! I will not see that look, even more malevolent than that which you cast upon me—"

"Abigail, I didn't mean to—" He took her hands into his own.

"I do not mean it that way, Jeremy. For the look of love that is on your face has banished that hurt forever. Believe me. But I will not see you continue to tear yourself apart. Damon did not *win* after all! Can't you see that? His evil was no match for Katie's love, nor did it extinguish the embers of our own these past years, did it? I harbor no animosity toward him. I hope Damon has received forgiveness and rests in peace. And if you are to love me fully you must hope the same, can't you see?" She watched his face as he struggled with her words. Then, as if a heavy weight had been lifted from his heart, he looked up at her and smiled.

"Again, my dearest Abigail, you are right. It should please you to know that Katie said much the same words to me. But it is with your forgiveness that I can begin to forgive as well. . . . But, speaking of forgiveness, what about Levi? He hates me as much as he hated Damon, you know."

Her calm gave way to a troubled countenance as she thought. "I know. Levi is a kind, considerate man, although I know you have seen little indication of such. But it is not possible for me to talk of feelings and matters of the heart with him. Levi is always so afraid of being stricken, or having someone he loves hurt, that he strikes first. He can be too impulsive, but he would not hurt a fly." She searched his eyes. "You know that he did not kill Damon? He was not even in the area. He swore so to me. Other than that afternoon when he found Damon—when he beat him and

**203**

might have harmed Damon if I had not pulled him away . . . After that he never saw your brother again. You do believe that now, don't you?"

"Yes, I believe that," he answered, hoping his eyes did not belie his words. For had he not learned from Michael that it was not Levi and his friends who had robbed and murdered his brother? What use was there forcing the truth that Levi and his friends had indeed beaten Damon bloody? Could he now blame them? Still, he knew that while Levi was a loving and loyal brother, he was a hothead and not entirely honest. For how else could he have sworn so to Abigail and later to sweet Katie?

Jeremy would have to protect Abigail and himself from Levi and yet protect her from the truth about her brother. Such irony, for it was true that he had never been able to see his own twin clearly. Since Katie forced his own epiphany, his sudden flash of recognition, he had been remembering so many small moments when he could have seen his brother for what he was, but had chosen not to. Although Levi was not Damon, Abigail's love and blind spot regarding her brother was strikingly familiar. Jeremy would have to be on guard for both of them, leaving Abigail to her adoration of her brother.

"Are you certain you believe that, in your heart, or are you just saying so for my sake?" she asked, frowning, having picked up some of his thoughts but fortunately not guessing the heart of the matter. He hated to be less than totally honest with Abigail, but this was for her sake. "Jeremy. I will ask you once again. You must tell me what you truly believe. Do you believe that my brother murdered yours?"

"No, I do not," he answered truthfully, grateful for the wording of her question. "For Michael Harrington told me that he had seen Levi and his friends elsewhere just before the attack on my brother. He told me so the night he came to try to save Katie and her baby. Does that allay your doubts?"

"Aye, it does." She smiled sadly, for how could one be happy in a joyous way concerning such a horrible event.

"Which brings me to another matter. Do you think we should tell Levi of our impending marriage today—" What was he thinking of, the man so deep in loss. "How insensitive of me. Of course not today, but when? Why are you frowning?"

"I'm frowning because I think it will not be a matter of days. I think we must handle Levi gently. In a few weeks perhaps—"

Jeremy jolted upright. "A few weeks! We have waited five years! I cannot wait a few weeks to marry you. I will not!"

"That's not fair! You're being rash! It wouldn't be fair to Belinda, as well. I know she is a silly girl, but she is entitled to her public face, without undue ridicule, as much as the next—"

"Did *she* show the same charity toward you when she spitefully came to your shop, as she *later* informed me, to rub our impending marriage in your face?"

Abigail grinned. "You mean you did not know she intended to do so?"

Jeremy arched his brow indignantly. "*Of course* I did not know. Do you take me for such a cad that—" He saw Abigail try to stifle her giggles, which angered him further. Then he realized. He broke out into sardonic laughter at the absurdity of what he'd just said. "Of course you thought so, for that would have been just another of the boorish actions I've been guilty of—and not as bad as many—" He threw up his hands in a *mea culpa* gesture and she leaped into his arms. They hugged and laughed simultaneously.

"You are right as usual," he said, as he nuzzled her neck. "So you tell me how we shall conduct ourselves and I will follow."

"I love you so," she said and kissed him gently on his cheek. Then she leaned back so that she could tell him of the plan she was already formulating. "I must go home at once. Levi needs me and we must make the . . . funeral arrangements."

"Will Katie be buried in Copp's Hill Cemetery in the North End?"

"I think not. For we would all like to be buried near Father in the Granary."

"Would it be permissible for me to attend the services? I would like to, unless you think that Levi would take offense—"

"I cannot see how he could do so, under the circumstances."

Jeremy hesitated, but then decided that the question had to be broached, that in fact Abigail had let such an obvious point slip by only because her mind was so full. "What will you tell Levi, and Jane for that matter, when they ask what brought Katie to my house at such a late hour the other night?"

Abigail leaned forward, her hands around her knees, and slowly shook her head. "I did not think of that. . . . I don't know. To Jane I could perhaps tell the truth without implying other developments at this moment. . . . Levi is a different story. I will have to deal with that when the question arises. I can't plan a lie—"

"I could drive you home and tell Levi the truth."

"No!" she declared with alarm. "Please, I know my brother best. Right now what I must do is prepare to go home."

He hugged her and kissed her lightly, careful to refrain from any touch that might inflame their passion again. "I will have Tom ready the carriage so that I can drive you home."

"No. I think it best if you allow Tom to drive me."

He was about to argue, but she was right. "Then when will I see you? I know tonight that you will want to be with your family and friends . . ." Already he felt as if he was losing her.

"And you," she said with sweet sadness. "I will send you a message regarding the funeral services. You may be shocked to find that we in the Third Congregation will not be dressed in black, as part of our protest against Parliament. We will wear sober, but homespun garments made in Boston."

"I have heard such. I suppose it makes no difference, but I am used to black mourning suits and dresses as a sign of respect for the dead. It seems a foolish—" He stopped himself. This was not the time to engage in a political debate.

"Foolish what?" she asked defensively. "A foolish gesture? A seditious act, perhaps!"

"Abigail. I said nothing of the sort. I think it is an inappropriate subject at the moment, in any case."

She was instantly contrite. "I'm sorry." Why was she always so quick to jump?

"Forgiven, *this* time," he said with a conciliatory smile, but she could see his annoyance. "I will see you at the services for Katie. But when will I see you alone?" he asked, looking as if he already missed her.

"I will have to think on it. For besides the funeral, I am quite worried about the charges against Levi and Charles. I am frightened to think what might happen to them—"

"At least that is something I can help with," he said, pulling her into his arms as they rose from the bed. "I believe his story. I remember hearing a strikingly similar one told by some 'fine gentlemen' in a club in London. They found it hilarious that the men they falsely accused, were . . . punished severely." He could not tell her how the men were punished, that their hands were cut off. "I will be Levi's *secret* benefactor, by necessity. And of course, Charles's as well. I will inquire this morning as to the names of the Cambridge 'gentlemen.' I will visit them and you may rest assured that they will voluntarily drop the charges. Levi will never know my role. Trust me."

"You have been so very good to us. I have not thanked you yet, but I do know that if anyone could have saved Katie or the poor babe it would have been a fine, skilled doctor such as Michael Harrington, whose services we could not have afforded. In fact, please tell him that we will arrange to pay him on an agreed-to basis—"

"And insult my best friend and an admirer of yours that way? He would not hear of it. It would indeed make him feel worse; he feels so helpless that despite all his training he could not save either of them. Your friendship would be his greatest repayment, I assure you. As for me . . ." Jeremy shook his head with disgust. "Not another false accolade! After all I have done to you, and indirectly to your dear father—"

"I will not listen to you flagellate yourself for something in which you were *just as much* a victim!" she declared angrily, with a shake of her head. "If there is blame to be meted, some of it is mine as well. For it was nothing but false pride that prevented me from speaking the truth to you—"

"You were little more than a girl. A frightened girl who had been abused, and then I came to you like a raving maniac—"

"Aye, that was so then. But almost five years have passed. You have been back for over two months. You even had the courage to declare your love to me, but *I* didn't trust you sufficiently. Katie tried to reason with me, but I was my headstrong, unbending self. I said that if you had loved me you never could have doubted me."

"But were you not right? Shouldn't I have *known* that my brother's story was a lie? That the girl he conjured was not the Abigail I loved?" he asked with distraught frustration at all the years he had lost.

"Aye. If you were a god rather than a man, perhaps. For it was your brother, your twin, who so cleverly, so convincingly fabricated such a vile story—"

"Still, that is no excuse. Damon was— I shan't say it again. But I was as bad in my own ignorant way."

"If that is so, why did you believe Katie? Did you expel her from your house?" she asked, hands on hips.

"Of course not!"

"Did you call her a liar or misguided?"

"I told you that from the moment she began to talk I knew she spoke the truth."

"And if *I* had told you the truth, that afternoon in the barn. Would you have closed your ears and mind to me?"

"I don't know . . ." he rubbed his brow unconsciously, trying to answer from the heart and follow her rapid logic. "I think I would have listened . . . I can't swear to it, but I believe I might have . . . yes, I think I would have . . ."

Abigail sat down on the edge of the bed. "Then I rest my case, sir," she said softly. "Is that not what you barristers say?"

He walked to her and cupped her face with his hands. "You are wonderful, my dearest Abigail." She watched as some of the anguish dissipated from his eyes. His smile, so gentle and deep, warmed her as much as their newfound lovemaking had. Then he grinned. "But I must say that I am pleased that women may not become barristers."

"Why is that?" she asked archly. "We women are capable of so much more—"

"Before your eyes begin to flame again, let me tell you why." She was so bright, and as quick to ignite in indignation as kindling in a hearth. She would be a handful, but never would he be bored, of that he could depend. "I was going to say because if you were a barrister and I had to face you in court, I would find you an adversary far more challenging than I prefer!"

She intended to demur, for who had ever heard of such a thing? But she thought upon it for a moment, and despite her quickness to vanity, decided he was correct in his assessment. She broke into a broad grin. "Why are there not women barristers? Perhaps I should inquire about the study of law . . ." She jumped up and clapped her hands as she laughed with excitement. "I could be the first woman lawyer in the colony! You could leave that ridiculous job you have and we could open a practice together!"

He looked at her with a mixture of amusement and alarm, for once Abigail got something into her head there was no stopping her. "Please, my love. You are a fine publisher. Stick to that for the time being?" She hugged him in response. What did she mean by his "ridiculous job," he thought, growing annoyed.

Abigail felt him tense ever so slightly. "What is wrong?"

"You called my job ridiculous. I have a high position working for the governor and you call that ridiculous?" he said feeling himself grow truly angry, in part because of his own thinking these past weeks, which he would not admit to her.

"As you said before, this is not the time for political debate, is it?"

He smiled wryly. "Trapped by my own words again. Perhaps I would have been happier with a foolish, simpering woman after all," he teased, then ducked at the pillow that flew at him.

The clock rang and they both looked at it. It was already nine. "Goodness," Abigail declared. "I should have been home already."

"I will slip back into my room. In a few minutes, pretend that you have just awakened and ring for Mrs. Latham. I shall have Tom ready to drive you home." He slipped on his gown and she wrapped her arms around him.

"One more kiss, please," she asked shyly. He kissed her deeply, finding it difficult to force himself from her.

"You shall make me an old man before my time," he whispered in a teasing tone. She looked at him with puzzlement. Then she laughed as her cheeks heated at the second double entendre she'd ever heard.

Mrs. Latham, who stood with her ear to Sir Bentley's door, couldn't hear the words, but the intimacy of the laughter was beyond mistake. With a smile upon her plain face, she slipped down the stairs. It would not be long before there was a new mistress in this austere, lonely house. God worked in strange ways, for with the untimely deaths of Katie and her son, He had brought new life into this house, and into all their lives.

She had been lonely and friendless for so long that she had forgotten that life could be different. But now she had Jane Stewart as her friend, Nathan to dote on, and the sweet Jeremy she'd remembered as a young boy. Even Prissy's sullen ways had changed, and during these days of crisis Mrs. Latham had realized that she had underestimated her daughter as well. Aye, it wouldn't be long before Abigail Peabody was the wife of Jeremy Blackburn and a joy to all of them. Sir Bentley was far enough away, ensconced in Halifax, to offer no problem.

Mrs. Latham's smile changed to worry as she reached the bottom step, for there was one cloud on the bright horizon. Her instincts told her that Abigail's brother would be trouble. She never knew how, but she knew that Damon had almost destroyed Jeremy and Abigail. She prayed that Levi would not try to do the same.

# Chapter Fifteen

## August 13, 1765

ABIGAIL CAREFULLY PLACED THE CANDLE BETWEEN HER diary and the book of poems she'd borrowed from Jeremy's library two evenings before. The days had been so busy, and during the early hours of the evenings she had worked diligently on an essay that was bluntly critical of Governor Bernard's plea to the Massachusetts Assembly to politely acquiesce to the Stamp Act. The completed essay appeared in today's *Boston Word*.

She had not seen Jeremy since Tuesday evening, when she had borrowed the volume, *Several Poems Compiled . . . By a Gentlewoman in New England.* That night, while she waited for him to bring the carriage around, she had skimmed through the slim volume and had discovered a lyrical poem written by Anne Bradstreet almost a hundred years before. Instantly she knew that this would make the perfect wedding gift for her beloved Jeremy. When Jeremy entered the study, she quickly shut the book and pretended casual interest in this volume that was published, posthumously, in Boston in 1678. Jeremy had been only too happy to lend the book to her and had seemed not the least surprised nor suspicious. For often, in the three weeks of secret nights, they sat and read to one another as they rested from their extraordinary lovemaking.

Abigail was going to copy the poem into her diary. Then she could decide how best to present this very personal gift to him. Jeremy had been pressing her to set a wedding date. Despite his attempts to be patient, he was finding it difficult to understand why she continued to keep their love a secret from her family. She tried to explain to him that Levi had been especially troubled since Katie's death, but loyalty to her brother prevented her from speaking negatively about him, even to Jeremy. Yet, the truth be it, in the past three weeks, she'd found it extremely difficult to speak with Levi on any subject that was not directly related to their printing business or newspaper. But she had no time to think about that now, if she were to copy the poem before Jeremy's coachman, Tom, met her in the alley behind the house. Living such a deception was increasingly taxing, and Abigail had been feeling more tired than usual as of late.

She inked her quill, but then paused to read the poem in totality, once again, before she began to copy it in her delicate script.

## TO MY DEAR AND LOVING HUSBAND

If ever two were one, then surely we,
If ever man were loved by wife, then thee.

**215**

## DAUGHTER OF LIBERTY

If ever wife was happy in a man,
Compare with me, ye women, if you can.
I prize thy love more than whole mines of gold,
Or all the riches that the East doth hold.
My love is such that rivers cannot quench,
Nor ought but love from thee give recompense.
Thy love is such I can no way repay;
The heavens reward thee manifold, I pray.
Then while we will, in love let's so persevere,
That when we live no more we may live ever.

Abigail smiled to herself, but then felt the tears that often and without warning filled her eyes when her thoughts turned to Katie. How Katie would have loved this poem! For had she been a poet, Katie herself could have written such a verse. It was so hard to remember that Katie was gone, while at the same time her absence left a constant gap in their lives. For herself, Abigail tried to remember how very precious life was, and how very blessed she was to have her remaining family and Jeremy.

Levi, however, seemed to have turned himself from all feelings, even to baby Sarah. His passion for politics and loyalty to the colonial cause had gone from fervent to fervid, from reasoned to so zealous that he'd begun to frighten Abigail. These days there was a hard, driven gleam in his eyes that she felt was dangerous. But perhaps she was being oversensitive. Better that he channeled his anguish into a fine cause than into drink or gambling as too often happened.

She had copied all but the last line of the poem when there was a knock at her door. Quickly, she slid the volume beneath her Bible. "Come in," she said.

"Abigail," Levi said, as he stood at her door, hesitant to enter. He had his three-cornered hat in hand and his "Sons of Liberty" medallion around his neck. He was apparently ready to go to whichever tavern the group was meeting in tonight.

"Excuse me for disturbing your writing," he said in the formal tone in which he tended to address her lately, "but I neglected to tell you that I have business to attend to tomorrow that will take much of the day. I do not think we have any pressing orders that cannot wait until the next. And I have already instructed Nathan as to what orders I would like him to deliver when he returns from school."

"And you shall be out late again this evening, I take it?" she asked casually, already knowing the answer.

"Most likely."

"May I ask what this business is that will take you from our work tomorrow?"

Levi studied the floor. "I cannot say at the moment." He looked up to her and she was again troubled by the glint in his green eyes. "But I can assure you that you will know by midday tomorrow, at least some of it. Good night, sister," he said and turned abruptly. Then he turned back and stared at her. "Are you feeling well, Abigail?" he asked with a caring, concerned expression that reminded her of the brother she had known before Katie's death. "You appear pale and tired."

"It has been a busy few days, as you well know," she answered. "But I am fine, just tired. I have not been sleeping well." She smiled gently. "Thank you for inquiring."

"Then perhaps you should put your writing away and go to sleep early tonight," he said with continued concern.

She was so weary of lying to him. She had to speak to him about Jeremy, explain everything *finally*. The day of Katie's funeral, when he had asked why Katie had gone to Jeremy's, Abigail had lied and suggested that Katie so feared that Jeremy would take action against the *Boston Word* that she had gone to plead their case. Abigail had spoken without forethought, and had thereby foolishly further flamed his hatred of Jeremy. For, of course, Levi blamed Jeremy in some indirect way for Katie's and the baby's deaths, just as he blamed his inability to save them on his false arrest. When Jeremy had had the charges dropped, as he said he would, Levi's fury at the Tories and the aristocrats in general was further fanned. He had left the courthouse with a sense of deepened bitterness and false power, truly believing that it was his righteous indignation that had brought about the withdrawal of charges against himself and Charles.

She must speak with Levi! Perhaps now, when he'd shown the first signs of the old Levi, was the moment to seize. "Levi? There are matters of importance of which we have to speak. Could we do so now—"

His expression hardened again. "I have important

business. Your lecture will have to wait, I am afraid!" he turned on his heels and slammed her door.

"Levi, wait!" she called, but it was too late, for she heard his boots stomping down the stairs. At this rate he would wake baby Sarah, who had been cranky for the past few days. Abigail felt her anger rise. She'd had just about enough from her brother! He was not the only one who was profoundly hurt by Katie's death. He had to stop acting like a recalcitrant child. She would talk to him by the first of the week. Then, whether he approved or not, she would set the date for her marriage!

As the front door slammed, Abigail heard Sarah's wails, two stories below. She should go downstairs and help Jane with the baby. Jane remained the family's anchor, and continued to be as plucky and commanding as usual, but Abigail saw the indelible sorrow behind her twinkling eyes. Abigail wanted to tell Jane about Jeremy, but a sense of shame before the old-fashioned, virtuous woman had prevented her each time she had started to broach the subject.

Oddly, Jane had never questioned her about Katie's visit to Jeremy. Abigail knew that Jane and Mrs. Latham had become fast friends. Jeremy told her that Mrs. Latham confessed that she had known of Abigail's frequent visits for some time. She told him that she blessed their impending marriage. She also told him that since Jane had spoken to her in a most general way about Levi's hatred of Jeremy, she had kept their secret from Jane so as not to cause her divided loyalties unnecessarily. Mrs. Latham added that she knew, from an occasional fond comment Jane made about him, that Jane would be most happy about their union. Abigail was not surprised by this bit of news. What puzzled her was that Jane, who had never missed an opportunity to mention that she had passed Jeremy on her way here or there, had made no such mention since the night of Katie's death. Jeremy mentioned, just Tuesday evening, that he'd passed Jane on his way to the State House that day. Was it possible that Jane *knew*—

Another knock upon her door ended Abigail's musing for the moment. Abigail knew it was Jane, for she heard Sarah's chattering. "Come in, please, Jane," Abigail called.

Jane stood in her nightclothes and cap, baby Sarah likewise dressed and gurgling happily in Jane's arms. "I just wished to say good night to you," Jane said with a yawn.

"You have been going to sleep quite early these past weeks," Abigail said. "Are you feeling ill?"

"Ill? Me! Heavens no! But we must face the fact that I am not getting any younger. Don't say it! I am *well aware* that I do not look a *day* past forty, but nevertheless, the fact is that I shall be fifty-two on the first of September," Jane declared as she patted sleepy Sarah's back.

"And might that be a tactful reminder, *again,* of your upcoming birthday?" Abigail asked and grinned. How she loved Jane! Jeremy was the only other person who could make her feel so lighthearted.

"Have I mentioned my upcoming birthday?" Jane replied innocently as her eyes sparkled. "See that. It is the first sign of old age, for my memory is fading, as I have *no* recollection of the subject at all."

"Is that so? Then I am truly alarmed!" Abigail pretended so finely that she caught Jane off-guard.

"How so?" Jane asked, frowning.

"Because I fear you are fast sinking into deep senility."

"You do?" Jane asked, drawing Sarah to her protectively.

"Aye. For you have mentioned your fifty-second birthday *at least* six times in the past week!" Abigail said and burst into laughter.

"Humph," Jane replied, stone-faced. "Perhaps I do need a good night's sleep. Imagine *you,* besting *me.* I bid you good night!" With that, Jane closed Abigail's door behind her. Abigail chuckled as she put her diary into her small, brightly lacquered chest that had been her father's last birthday present to her. She glanced at the clock. It was ten past the hour of nine. She hoped that Jane would be fast asleep by nine-thirty, the time she was to meet Tom's carriage.

Abigail crept from her room to Jane's door. She didn't have to place her ear against the door to hear Jane's loud snores. Abigail quietly headed downstairs.

Jane heard the back door close. She looked from her second-story window and saw Abigail race into Tom's waiting carriage. Happily she smiled to herself as she cradled Sarah in her arms. "Never you underestimate us old ladies, young lady," she cooed to Sarah. "Frances Latham and I still have a trick or two up our old sleeves. Soon you will be at your first wedding, Sarah. What do you think of that?" Sarah gurgled back happily. "I agree," Jane answered. "Jeremy Blackburn, your uncle-to-be, is a fine man. And *so* handsome! It won't be long before you have a cousin

221

to play with. Humph! At the rate those two are going, and what with your pig-headed father, I only hope the ceremony takes place before the birth! It wasn't like that in *my* day, pretty Sarah, I do tell you. But if that's what it will take to *finally* get those two wed, then I give them my blessings, may the Lord forgive me!"

Mrs. Latham greeted Abigail at the door with a friendly smile. "Sir Jeremy awaits you in his study. Let me take your wrap," Mrs. Latham said as Abigail slid from her shoulders the white cotton shawl that Katie had knitted for her last summer. "How is baby Sarah feeling? Has her tooth poked through yet?"

Abigail smiled. "Aye, it has. Tonight before I left she was happily chattering in Jane's arms."

"And Nathan? Will he come tomorrow to visit with Tom? You know that Tom's taken quite a shining to that boy, as have we all," Mrs. Latham said as they walked toward the study.

"I know. And he to all of you. He's grown very close to Tom Smith and I think he fancies Prissy, although he'd die before he admitted such!" She did not say that although she was pleased about the mutual fondness that had developed, it saddened her that it was due, in part, to the fact that Levi barely gave Nathan a moment of his attention these days.

"And Mrs. Stewart? We have not seen one another in a few days. She is well too, I take it?"

"Aye, but I am afraid she tires easily of late. She has so much more to do since Katie . . . died." Abigail's sunny smile faded into an expression of rumination. "And I have been so busy that I've been of little aid, I'm afraid. Jane was already asleep before I left, as she has been each night since my first visit, days after the funeral. . . . Mrs. Latham? Have you spoken—I mean, I would like to speak with you about Jane. Is she ailing and not telling me—"

"I'm sure it's your imagination, Abigail, for she has appeared most hearty to me. We have become fine friends. If she were ill, I presume that she would have told me so," Mrs. Latham said evenly. "It is probably no more than the hot days, and as you yourself said, the added responsibilities since Katie's passing, may she rest in peace." Even as she spoke, Mrs. Latham thought that this deception had to stop. For rather than Abigail *discovering* that Jane was pretending to go to bed early and feigning ignorance of her romance and impending marriage to Jeremy, as Jane had *feared,* Abigail's questions and countenance convinced Mrs. Latham that their scheme had worked *too* well.

They stopped before the heavy, wooden sliding door of the study. Abigail leaned against the wall. "Mrs. Latham," she said with a sigh, no longer trying to hide her concern. "I must speak frankly with you. I have not been sleeping well. I believe it is conscience that keeps me awake, for I have not been raised to such deception as I have been engaging in these past three weeks . . . nor to be less than honest with Jane, who has been more like a mother to me than—"

"But you have not lied to her, child, have you?" Mrs. Latham asked, trying to ease some of Abigail's guilt.

"Not a direct lie, but I believe that there is little difference between sins of omission and sins of commission. Am I not correct?" she asked, for she knew that Mrs. Latham was a Congregationalist as was she, rather than an Anglican like Jeremy.

Mrs. Latham did not know how to answer. She was sorry that she was not as quick-witted as Jane Stewart, who, she had no doubt, would say exactly the right thing without giving herself away. "I'm afraid that I am not as schooled upon the finer points of doctrine, my dear. But I do think that intent plays some role. For you are not deceiving in malice. You are doing so in order to give your brother time to begin to mend from his tragedy. And you are attempting to protect Jane from having to act against *her* conscience. I would think that was an act of Christian charity. But I do think—" Mrs. Latham hesitated. Soon this girl would be her mistress . . . but Abigail was not that kind. Already they were friends. Mrs. Latham found herself thinking of Abigail as if she were a second daughter. "Are you certain you want my advice?" she asked.

"Oh, most certainly," Abigail declared, sensing the woman's reluctance. "I have grown quite fond of you, Mrs. Latham," she said shyly. "And I hope I do not presume, but I believe you feel the same. I will appreciate your frankness and sound advice."

"Then I will speak freely." Mrs. Latham placed her hand on Abigail's shoulder in a motherly fashion. "I think that you must speak with your brother as soon as you can. Then I believe that you must set your wedding date." Her voice grew to a whisper. "I believe that Mr. Blackburn would sleep more restfully as well, once he can present you to the world as his wife."

Abigail kissed her on the cheek and pressed her

hand. "Thank you, Mrs. Latham. I had decided the same thing tonight—"

The door slid back loudly, startling them. "There you are!" Jeremy boomed. "I had begun to worry as to what was keeping you." Jeremy looked from Abigail to Mrs. Latham. Both had slightly furtive expressions on their faces. "Ah . . . I see. You two ladies have been gossiping. And on *my* time!" He tried to look at them askance, but his grin gave him away.

"Oh, no!" they both protested unsuccessfully.

Jeremy stepped backward and started to slide the door closed. "Don't let me disturb you two ladies. Perhaps you'd be more comfortable at the kitchen hearth than standing in the hall? Do stop in before you leave, Abigail," he said with a teasing air and smiling face.

"Jeremy!" Abigail exclaimed, and pushed hard at the door as she laughed.

With a deft move, Jeremy swung Abigail into the study, causing her to break into giggles. "Excuse us, please, Mrs. Latham," he said and slid the door closed behind them.

By the time a smiling Mrs. Latham reached the kitchen, Jeremy had carried Abigail to the loveseat and kissed her so passionately that her laughter had turned to a throaty sigh.

"Jeremy, your eyes are quite red. And you look so tired," Abigail said as they cuddled on the loveseat. "You've been working too hard, again," she complained.

"You're a fine one to talk," he countered, "for while you're a rapturous sight at your worst, you do look a bit peaked." He squeezed her slender waist. "And you've become a little too thin," he added. "We must fatten you up!" he teased.

"Thank you, but I am happy just the way I am. And don't change the subject."

"Which was?" he asked straightfaced.

"Which was how tired *you* are." Abigail pointed to the stack of newspapers, pamphlets, broadsides, and handbills piled high on Jeremy's desk. "Have you found any coded plots to overthrow the King or poison Governor Bernard today?" she asked sardonically.

"Abigail, please! I am in no mood for sarcasm. An entire afternoon of listening to the raving and ranting of the Honorable Governor Bernard on just such subjects was more than enough!" He didn't mean to take his frustration out upon her, but he was in no mood for her continuous baiting.

Abigail was taken aback by his sudden flare of anger. He was tired. And the more she and Michael Harrington talked to Jeremy, the more he read, the more he listened, the greater his understanding had become of their just colonial cause. Abigail knew so, although Jeremy was yet unable to openly commit himself. She shouldn't push him. She knew better but couldn't help it. In a private moment last week, Michael had discreetly but firmly told her so. But she was so impatient. For the colonial cause needed all the reasoned minds and dedicated citizens it could gather to its fold and the more from Jeremy's and Michael's social station the better, for the aristocrats had the power to be heard more loudly than a hundred poor men. That was a fact of life. "I'm sorry," she said cautiously, "it's just that I can't help but think—"

"I know exactly what you think, for you've told me directly a hundred times. And Michael as well, although he is far more circumspect. He still will not admit to me that he is one of the followers of the group that started as 'The Loyal Nine' but now calls itself 'The Sons of Liberty.' But you can be sure that it is 'The Loyal Nine' who are directing all these *patriotic* displays, like the raising of 'liberty poles' and distributing childish handbills such as this." Jeremy rose and walked to his desk. He returned with ·a handbill that was a cruel cartoon of Governor Bernard and Lieutenant Governor Hutchinson licking the boots of the prime minister and leader of the Parliament, George Grenville, and King George III.

Abigail studied the cartoon and chuckled. Jeremy pulled it from her hand in disgust. "I don't understand how you, who takes such pains to compose reasonable, well-developed, cogent arguments in favor of nullification of the Stamp Act, can chuckle at such common, vulgar humor. This is the kind of demeaning humor meant to appeal to the inferior sort—I mean—"

Abigail squared her shoulders and rose with an anger that flared in her eyes when she turned back to him. "I understood exactly what you *meant!* What you meant was that the aristocratic leaders of 'The Loyal Nine' and their upper echelon of artisans and merchants are no longer the only proponents of the colonial cause in Boston—or in the rest of the colonies for that matter. Others have taken up the cause and begun to have a voice as well. *Even* those of the lowest level of the social order, as well as the small tradesmen, *mechanicks* like myself—"

"Wait a moment," Jeremy said, halting her. He rose and placed the cartoon back on the desk. "You are an artisan. And a writer—a fine one at that. I *never* used the term mechanick—" He began to pace the room.

"No, you haven't. Not directly to me. But you know as well as I that 'mechanick' is the word members of *your* class—the 'better sort' I believe you call yourselves?—use when they speak derisively of us who—"

"Are you holding me personally responsible for those gentlemen who admittedly hold such an attitude? Shall I then believe that those who refer to me as 'gentry' in opprobrium, or those who call me 'Tory bastard' in blunter contempt, are reflective of your attitude?"

"Of course not," Abigail answered with irritation. "I don't even know how we got on this foolish course of discussion! Why are we fighting?" She walked to his desk and angrily fanned through a stack of papers.

"We're not fighting!" Jeremy yelled, his eyes narrowed and his jaw tightened. "We were having your damned political discussion!"

They stared at one another from across the room. If she were a man, Jeremy thought, they'd be about to draw their swords. If we were children, Abigail thought, we'd be rolling on the floor in a tussle. They burst out laughing simultaneously.

"I'm sorry," Abigail offered as they walked across the room to meet one another in front of the sofa.

"It is I who owe you an apology. My nerves are on edge tonight. Please forgive me, Abigail." He took her in his arms.

"I will forgive you if we may sit down and begin over as two rational adults." She kissed his lips gently.

"As long as we leave some time for additional kisses and things of that sort. Shall we shake upon it?"

She offered her hand which he took and gently pulled her down onto the loveseat with him.

"Your point, then, my dearest, if you can still remember it."

She turned so that her back rested against the side of the loveseat and she could face him. "I do."

Jeremy sighed. "I was afraid you would," he said, then grinned. "I'm sorry. Please continue then."

"My *point* is that we have clearly seen that the supplication of our assemblies, that petitions and all sorts of *polite* requests for consideration of our needs and difficulties, have fallen on the deaf ears of Parliament. From last November, when we first heard rumor of a stamp act, we have petitioned, which is one of our fundamental rights as Englishmen. Is that not so?"

"Yes it is. Remember that I was in London at that time and had friends at Westminster. Their feelings, and my own at the time, as you well know, was that Parliament was asking no more of its colonial citizens than it was of those in the mother country. For they are subject to even greater taxes—"

"But they are also *represented*—actual representation. I know, the argument goes that by the fact of being Englishmen so are we, but that is symbolic representation. It is our *right* as Englishmen to be represented *in* the bodies that tax us, those bodies being our own assemblies. It was our right to have our petitions addressed. But did Parliament even pay us the respect of rejecting the American petitions? They simply refused to consider them at all. Did they not clearly tell us in effect how little they cared for our rights or dignity, let alone liberty? Did they expect us to humbly submit to an act which violated the very *basis* of constitutional government?"

"I am in agreement with you on this point. But the Stamp Act Congress will convene in October. The Virginia Assembly has recently petitioned Parliament. The colonial cause has outspoken supporters within Parliament, like Colonel Isaac Barre, whose very words were taken by these groups across the colonies who call themselves 'The Sons of Liberty.' And the fine man, General Conway, has been just as ardent."

"But can you be sure that we will be heard? For we were ignored before the act was passed. What makes you so certain that Parliament will be moved to repeal the Stamp Act? Would they be willing to admit that they have thereby denied us our rights as Englishmen, our rights as men by a higher natural law and by common law?"

Jeremy shook his head. "I just do not believe that Parliament is trying to push tyranny down our throats as some of the more vociferous essays over there suggest," he answered and waved his hand toward the desk. "And I do not see how those who call themselves 'The Sons of Liberty' will affect any change with their childish pranks and propaganda that only succeed in alienating our supporters in the colonies and in London."

Abigail sighed. "Are you going to tell me again that Governor Bernard is as opposed to the Stamp Act in *private* as the rest of us? And Lieutenant Governor Hutchinson as well?"

"I have told you so and I will again! For the man confides in me. I do not deny that Bernard is a petty, irritating man who takes even rational arguments as a personal affront. That is why I have tried to impress on you that it is important for me to keep my position, rather than leave and go into private practice as you and Michael continually suggest. For although Bernard is quick to blow up and fly into a tantrum, he is far from an evil man, and I am able to reason with him. I have been able to prevent a half-dozen writers and printers from libel suits in the past two months, by commiserating with him until his ego is salved and then explaining how the particular essays may be in bad taste but are within the rights of the press. I *lead* him to suggest *himself*, that if we prosecuted, it would only fan the flame of the propagandizers and that he is too 'big' a man to allow some vulgar personal attacks to endanger the colony."

"This is the first time you have been so straightforward with me, Jeremy," Abigail said as she mulled over the new viewpoint he presented to her.

"I did not wish to be praising myself so immodestly." He rose quickly. "I certainly would like a brandy. And yourself?"

"Aye," she answered. "But just a wee bit, thank you."

Jeremy poured the brandy from the decanter into the goblets. "And I should add that often it is Thomas Hutchinson who enables me to bear the governor. You don't know how often I wish that Thom was the governor rather than lieutenant governor. It angers me when I read sly, nasty remarks about him, for he is Boston born and bred, and a true lover of the Massachusetts Bay Colony. He is a decent and honorable man."

Abigail accepted the brandy. She sipped the strong liquid slowly, thinking. "I appreciate much of what you say. But I still do not understand your apparently extreme suspicions of The Sons of Liberty. For the Stamp Act will directly affect the common man, the poor man and his family in ways that the Sugar and Navigation Acts did not. For it is they who will have to pay for the official stamps to be put on all papers used in business, legal papers, marriage licenses, playing cards, dice, calendars and newspapers of course. And it will be more than a few pence in many cases. Some of the taxes will amount to shillings—shillings to be paid by men and women who *already* cannot provide properly for their families."

Jeremy contemplated her words. Finally he spoke. "It is difficult for me to verbalize what is just a feeling. But following what you say, I fear that what the poorer citizen is expecting from the repeal—what they have been deceptively *promised* by the radical leaders —is a transformed society. I have heard talk of promises of suffrage for those without property, means, or the right to such." Jeremy finished his brandy. "I have heard talk of Ebenezer McIntosh, the leader of the South End Mob. His greatest contribution to our society has been his periodic street brawls with his rival North End gang. Yet suddenly he is being courted by the likes of Sam Adams. Just today, I saw McIntosh strutting down the street in a blue and gold uniform and walking cane. I have heard that when he led his mob against the North Enders and beat them last spring he used a speaking trumpet to bark forth his orders. The man is a sometime cobbler by trade, but I would call him a common brawler to his face. Is he the sort of man who will help carry a reasoned appeal to the Parliament?"

Abigail tried not to laugh, but Jeremy's description of McIntosh, whom she'd seen but once or twice, tickled her. But her smile was stillborn, for Abigail remembered Levi speaking admirably of the man a few months before. Was this the kind of man with whom her brother spent his evenings? No, Levi was too levelheaded for that. But she had no reason to doubt Jeremy's vivid description of McIntosh, for she had heard remarks of a similar nature about him before . . .

"What is it, Abigail?" Jeremy asked. "You were far off." Her green eyes had turned dark and stormy. A sure sign that she was troubled.

Abigail grasped his hands tightly. "Jeremy?" Could she really bring herself to ask him, to demand what she was about to demand? She realized that neither of them could accurately foretell the outcome of the tense political situation in Boston. Nor could they personally alter it in any direct way. But they could do so with their own lives. *That* power they held within their hands, if their hearts were truly bound to one another.

"What is it, Abigail?" Jeremy asked with growing concern as he saw her eyes fill with unspilled tears. "I do not know you to not speak your mind, or you wouldn't be the Abigail I adore—even if you do infuriate me at times," he said half in jest, hoping to make her open to him.

"I want us to be married. As soon as possible."

"Well hallelujah to that, I say! But why the furrowed brow and tear-filled eyes?"

"Because tonight is the first time I have heard a good reason for you to remain in your job. And yet, I am asking you to resign. To resign tomorrow, if you truly want to marry me."

How could one woman, a small, beautiful crimson-haired, emerald-eyed beauty, be such a paradox? Was she testing his love? Didn't she understand that he would do anything humanly possible to please her? "Why? Do you doubt my love?" he asked tensely.

"No, of course not. But as long as you remain in your position on the governor's council, Levi will never hear of our marriage. And as much as I love you, I do not wish to lose my brother's affection. Can you understand that?"

"And what if he still objects, after I have resigned?"

"Then I will marry you on whatever date you wish in any case." She attempted a smile without much success.

"Are you saying that if I resign from my job tomorrow that you will speak with Levi tomorrow as well? That we could set our wedding date this evening then?" he asked levelly, unwilling to feel his joy unless he was certain this time.

"I am saying exactly that. I will not be able to speak with him until after dinner, for Levi informed me that he had some business tomorrow that would keep him from the shop most of the day."

"What kind of business would keep him from his business?" Jeremy asked and smiled along with Abigail at the humorous phrasing of his question.

"I do not know," she answered. Why did she not tell him that she believed it had something to do with The Sons of Liberty? But of course, that was a mere suspicion and not relevant to their vital conversation. "So? What is your answer?"

"Must I gaze into your soulful, loving eyes as I answer?"

"Aye."

"Aye," he said, mimicking her speech.

"Aye what?" Sometimes he so confounded her!

"Yes. Aye: Yes! I will resign from my position tomorrow. First thing tomorrow morning! I shall find some good excuse and recommend David Pelham, a fine lawyer with many of my better sensibilities, I suspect. Now you—it is the woman's prerogative, I believe, to set her wedding date. Any day after tomorrow is *perfect* for me. When is your birthday, Abigail?" he demanded, full of energy as he brought her onto his lap.

She could not believe it. He agreed! He truly loved her. "My birthday is the first of September. I will be twenty-one."

"Then we should be married a week before, say the twenty-seventh of August?" he stated emphatically.

"Wonderful, any day is wonderful," she said as they

hugged. "But why the insistence before my birthday?"

"Because, since I am about to marry an 'old maid' I would prefer for her to be as young an old maid as possible!" he declared as he grinned from ear to ear.

"Jeremy Blackburn! Why you—" she began, but he caught the rest of her words in his mouth as he tumbled backward with her beneath him on the loveseat.

# Chapter Sixteen

## *August 14, 1765*

JEREMY ARRIVED AT THE GOVERNOR'S OFFICE AT THE State House wearing one of his finest dress suits: a braided beige waistcoat beneath a brown linen, skirted coat with matching breeches. He adjusted the sheer linen ruffle at his throat and wrists, before he knocked.

"Yes, come in, come in," the governor said so distractedly that Jeremy realized that he was not to find Bernard in one of his lighter moods this sunny, early morning. Jeremy entered, but still Bernard did not look up from whatever he was reading with an especially sour expression.

"Excuse me, Your Excellency," Jeremy began.

"Mr. Blackburn. You are just the person I wished to see!" The governor broke into a conspiratorial smile, causing Jeremy to sense that he was most definitely in for trouble. Bernard looked down again.

"Governor Bernard. There is a subject of great importance which we must discuss. It cannot wait another moment, I am afraid." Jeremy forged ahead with his resignation speech.

"Have you seen this incendiary rubbish!" The governor's face reddened as he waved a paper in the air. He hadn't heard a word Jeremy had just said. He would have to calm the man down before he would be able to talk to him, Jeremy realized with chagrin. Well, what was one more day of it?

"What rubbish is that you are reading, sir?" Jeremy asked, falling into his usual placating routine.

*"This* rubbish," Bernard tossed the paper at him as if it were a smelly dead fish, "extolling the virtues of The Sons of Liberty and their efforts to bring Parliament to its knees! Can you imagine such words? Is that not sedition, I ask you?" Bernard asked rhetorically. "You must prosecute this one, I tell you!"

Jeremy tried to fold the rumpled paper back into its original order, to see if this was another of the *Gazette*'s pieces.

"And written by a woman no less! What does she intend to do? Start a new treasonous group and call it 'The Daughters of Liberty'?"

Well, at least the governor had not entirely lost his sense of humor, Jeremy thought as he folded back the paper. He chuckled, then looked up at the governor. Bernard's fierce scowl indicated that his humor had been unintentional, Jeremy realized as he watched the governor search for something in his desk. Daughters of Liberty. He would have to remember to tell Abigail, for she would laugh heartily— Jeremy's own humor fled as he reached page one. It was the *Boston Word*. Abigail's paper!

" . . . I absolutely insist that you prosecute this woman . . . what's her name? . . . Abigail Pea . . . ah, Pea . . ."

"Peabody," Jeremy interjected as calmly as possible. "Now, Governor Bernard. It is more than rubbish," he declared as he skimmed her article which he had not seen before. "It is foolishness. A silly woman's ranting. Would you want to lower yourself to sue a woman—"

"Ah, but that is just the point!" the governor blustered. "She is merely a *front*. For what woman could write so well? What I mean is that while it is libelous, seditious, and clearly treasonous, its grammar and construction are excellent. Obviously it was written by one of 'The Loyal Nine' and that *woman* who is a mere mechanick, at best of the middling sort I would suppose, is being cleverly used. We will expose the truth! You will expose the truth!"

Jeremy had to think quickly, for he could see that the governor was deadly serious about his conspiracy theory. He was most dangerous when he was most serious. "But what if the woman claims she did write it? What if she displays other articles of similar style and cadence? Will we—*I* not look foolish? And will *I* not then, most badly reflect upon *you* and your high office and therefore the Crown itself?"

"When she is faced with *jail* we shall see if the woman does not speak the truth and admit that she was used! Perhaps all of her articles have been written by the prolific Mr. Edes of the *Gazette* himself. Or Sam Adams. Had you not thought of that? Or more likely James Otis . . . now that I mention so, it does have the ring of Otis to it. Do you not agree?"

"I would have to study it further to say, Your Excellency. In fact, I will have to study it to see if we do have a case. After the Peter Zenger trial—"

"Please. Do not speak to me of that New York printer again. I have given his case some study of late. Times were different back in '35. I don't believe he would be able to win today in any court, even the biased colonial courts."

"Governor Bernard, I fear you are making a mistake." Jeremy knew he was speaking rashly, for the governor had to be handled so very carefully. Yet he did not know how best to handle this. He was grateful that the governor continued to rave and rant at his indelicate accusation, for it gave him time to think.

If he resigned as he had planned, the governor would appoint someone to his position contingent upon that man's agreement to prosecute this case. Once the governor learned that Abigail was to become Jeremy's wife, then his wrath would be boundless, for even a suggestion of collusion or of personal betrayal meant the man would never be stopped. It was common knowledge that he'd been feuding with some of Boston's finest citizens since his appointment as governor of the Bay Colony in '61.

Nor could he and Abigail wait out the storm,

Jeremy realized. For if the case did come to trial, it could take years to be adjudicated. The Zenger case itself had taken two years and that was in days of less turmoil. He could not resign. He could only help Abigail by remaining in his position and cleverly making the governor drop the issue of his own volition. All he needed was time, and God help them, a new, more serious crisis. For the governor was known to jump from one issue to the next with no apparent memory, except in the case of a personal feud. Jeremy only hoped that Abigail's article contained no inflammatory personal remarks.

"Governor, I must speak with you," said a rich loyalist merchant, whose name Jeremy had forgotten, as he appeared at the door unannounced.

"Can it not wait, Martin?" the governor asked, annoyed.

"I'm afraid you wouldn't want it to, Your Excellency," the man stated confidently.

"Oh, all right then," the governor acceded. "Sit down, please." He turned his attention to Jeremy. "Please study the matter *at once*. I shall meet with you again within the hour, Mr. Blackburn," he pronounced, and Jeremy was dismissed.

Never had he been so glad to flee from the governor's office, he thought, as he closed the door behind him.

Levi paused with McIntosh and other patriots by Deacon Elliot's house on Newbury Street, to admire the handiwork on which they had labored long into the night. For there, near the junction of Essex,

241

Orange, and Frog Lane, stood a grove of fine elm trees. The biggest and most handsome was known as the Great Tree. But Levi knew that after today, as the aristocratic patriotic leader who had slipped in to check on their progress last night had said, it would be known forever as the Liberty Tree.

Levi tried hard not to laugh as the citizens of the southern part of Boston stopped in their tracks at the grove. The objects of their astonishing discovery were two effigies hanging from the lower limbs of the Great Tree. One of the crude figures was clearly named "The Stamp Officer." This was the effigy of Andrew Oliver, Lieutenant Governor Hutchinson's brother-in-law, who according to reports from England had been appointed the Distributor of Stamps for Massachusetts. Alongside the figure of Oliver hung an enormous boot, out of which peeked a horned devil's head. No Bostonian who passed could miss the intended insult to Lord Bute, one of the King's former ministers and the most hated man in England. The large boot was an obvious pun on the Earl of Bute. Lord Bute was said to have been directly responsible for the passage of the Stamp Act.

Within an hour, the crowd had grown manyfold. Levi and the others easily slipped within its midst. The plan was working even better than they had hoped, Levi thought proudly, as word was spread through every Boston street and the crowd became a gathering. Little work would be done in Boston today, he thought triumphantly. And this was only the *beginning* of today's adventure.

When Nathan came running into the shop, his face

flushed with laughter and excitement, telling of what they were already calling the Liberty Tree, Abigail fetched Jane. With baby Sarah the three of them walked south, among the neighbors who poured out of their homes and business establishments. Nathan had run ahead with some of his friends.

When they arrived at the grove, the crowd was larger than it had been at the Spinning Day Celebration. Abigail tried to discern the facts after viewing the hanging effigies with delight. But she could find no one who would say outright who had hung the images or who had made them. There were whispers, however, that McIntosh and his followers was responsible.

"So that's the business that occupied Levi," Abigail whispered to Jane, whose shake of her head indicated that she had already come to the same conclusion. As Abigail left Jane and the baby and forged into the center of the crowd, closer to the tree, she overheard more rumors. Abigail felt someone tap her on the shoulder. It was Polly Osborn. "Isn't it wonderful, Abigail!" Polly exclaimed. "It's so exciting! I just knew that Charles and Levi were—"

"Polly, please!" Abigail warned in a sharp whisper. "Lower your voice. You do not know who is among us!"

Polly's eyes widened at Abigail's sharp admonishment. Then Polly smiled again, just as brightly as before. "I understand," she whispered. "I have already heard rumors that it was Paul Revere, that clever craftsman, who made the figures in the night."

"Is that so?" Abigail whispered back, trying to remain the dispassionate reporter. Polly continued, but her whispers were lost as a round of spontaneous cheers broke out among the crowd. Abigail joined in the second cheer and the round after that.

She moved further toward the tree, to get a better look. From the corner of her eye, she spied Levi standing amongst a group of men. As the crowd shifted, she saw that the man who stood in the center wore a blue and gold uniform. So her brother was one of McIntosh's followers, just as she had supposed! She frowned, but then another cheer arose from the crowd of fine citizens and Abigail decided that she was needlessly worried about Levi having been engaged in this well-received, finely-spirited display of resistance. No harm was done and the point was well made. Even Jeremy would have to agree to that, she decided, wondering if she would encounter him as she made her way back to Jane and baby Sarah.

Governor Bernard waited to meet with his council. He had received news of the effigies from Martin, who had been sent by Thomas Hutchinson with the message that the lieutenant governor was calling together members of the Assembly and the sheriff, and requested the governor's attendance. Bernard had decided to leave all of that business to Thom, and had instead called for his council to convene at the Town House at midafternoon. After all, wasn't that what they were paid for?

By noon, individual members of the council began to arrive. Some told Bernard that it was only a boyish prank, for they had each gone to the scene to see for themselves. Jeremy Blackburn, whom Bernard had immediately summoned back into his office after

Martin left, had been at his side continuously, except for the half hour when Jeremy had gone to view what he reported that the people were calling the Liberty Tree.

Jeremy had spotted Abigail's long red hair and slim figure, but he did not call out to her, for this was not the time to draw unnecessary attention to any relationship between them. He had seen Abigail laughing and smiling, and found himself growing angry at her naive good humor, when he knew all the dangers they faced. But when he reached the effigies, he found it difficult to keep a smile from his own face. While crude and hurried, the effigies were nevertheless obviously done by a skilled hand. He wouldn't be shocked to learn that they had been created by Paul Revere himself, the master silversmith and engraver, and a reputed patriot.

Jeremy saw no sign of the sheriff or his men, who had been ordered by Hutchinson to cut down the effigies. Jeremy was not surprised, for he suspected that this crowd, neighborly and as happy as on a holiday, could fast turn ugly if anyone tried to remove the objects of their enthusiasm.

As Jeremy turned to return to the governor's Town House, he wondered if this was the "crisis" he had wishfully hoped for this morning. It was too soon to make such a judgment. But he knew he would return with the goal of cajoling the governor from inflammatory action. Jeremy agreed with some of the council members he'd spoken to before his arrival at the Liberty Tree; it was another childish display from The Sons of Liberty, but no more than that. Jeremy was pleased that Thom Hutchinson as lieutenant governor was also chief justice of the colony. He knew Hutchinson to be too sensible to press his sheriff, who would undoubtedly report that they could not cut down the effigies without inciting a riot.

Upon his return to the council room, Governor Bernard informed Jeremy that Sheriff Greenleaf had just left after arriving breathlessly with the news that his men could not cut down the offensive objects without endangering their lives. Therefore, the sheriff and his deputies did not even attempt to do so.

"I think that was a judicious decision on his part," Jeremy replied, trying to placate the thundering Bernard, "as I'm sure you do. You would not want to endanger lives because of such a ridiculous incident, I know."

"*Who* said I—" Bernard began to bluster. Red-faced, he turned and strode from the room. Jeremy sighed with relief. Maybe the governor could still be manipulated into rational behavior. The other members of the council, nine of the gentlemen who could be found, filed into the room. Jeremy exchanged polite words with them, for no real discussion would begin until they all had time to gauge the disposition of the governor.

"Gentlemen," Bernard said, as the men rose from the table and stood until the governor was seated. "It is incendiary rubbish such as *this*," he shouted, as he waved the too-familiar paper in full view, "this article in yesterday's *Boston Word*, that has incited this treasonous display. This rubbish, lauding the virtues of The Sons of Liberty, has definitely caused this

Liberty Tree debasement!" he proclaimed, spitting out each word. "Mr. Blackburn will begin to prosecute the publisher of this paper, who *claims* to be the writer of this so-called essay. This 'Daughter of Liberty!' We will win this case and it shall be a warning to all of these rebel printers! For the definition of sedition is . . ." The governor looked down at scribbled notes before him. "Sedition . . . conduct or language inciting to rebellion against the authority of the Crown." He turned to Jeremy. "Is that not correct, my dear barrister?"

Damn him! Jeremy composed his face. "That is a correct definition, Your Excellency, but—"

"There are no buts to it! Now on with the matter at hand."

The council debated as the afternoon sun sunk behind Beacon Hill. Some members continued to insist that it was merely a prank unworthy of further action. Others argued that it was serious, but felt that the government shouldn't push the issue since they weren't strong enough, without British troops, to risk a confrontation. However, they were unwilling to go on record as having done nothing. It was decided to throw the problem back on the sheriff, who was again instructed to have his peace officers remove the effigies. While the council was not surprised when Sheriff Greenleaf reported to them, officially this time, that his officers could not do so for danger of their very lives, his explanation was noted in the minutes. At least they had made some face-saving gesture that would become part of the official record.

Jeremy said little as the hours dwindled by, for he

247

was trying to think of how he could move Bernard from his seemingly implacable position of ordering prosecution of Abigail. How would he tell her? Should he tell her? Worst of all, how would he explain the fact that he had not resigned as promised . . . He worried that he would be stuck in the governor's Town House all night at this rate! Finally, Jeremy decided. He would explain the course of events from the moment he entered the governor's office this morning. She would understand and he would make certain to reassure her that the governor had *no* legitimate case to prosecute at all—that would only be to keep her from worrying, which would not alter the events. Except for this "optimistic" reassurance, he would be otherwise completely forthright, for hadn't their lives already been almost ruined as a result of lies and false pride? He was an excellent trial lawyer. But if worse came to worse, he would plead the poorest case in his career, probably in legal history. He would lose the case and be dismissed by the governor. As much as his ego might be bruised by public ridicule, if it assured Abigail's safety and their lives together, he would do so a dozen times over.

The debate in the governor's Town House dragged on. But by nightfall, for those gathered at the Liberty Tree, Levi among them, the real excitement was just beginning. Among the regathered group were not only McIntosh and his followers, but forty or fifty tradesmen, decently dressed, mingling among the seamen and laborers. Some dressed as tradesmen were patriotic aristocrats in disguise, Levi knew.

The effigy of Oliver was carefully cut from the tree,

and with McIntosh at the forefront, a torchlighted procession moved up Newbury Street until it arrived at the Town House. "They're in there!" someone shouted. "The bloody Tory governor and his bloody councilmen!"

Another voice rang out, "Let's show the Tory bastards what we think of them!"

"Aye!" Levi shouted with the others in joyous defiance.

As they sat wearily debating in the council chamber, Jeremy heard the rising voices outside the State House. He rose and walked to the window. Before him stood a mob with torches in hand. He couldn't make out the individual faces in the night, but he clearly saw the effigy of Andrew Oliver. As the torches moved closer, illuminating the square, Jeremy saw that the leaders were dressed as pallbearers. It was an ominous sight, which chilled Jeremy, who was relieved that the governor refused to show his face at the window.

"Let's let'um know who's runnin' the town of Boston," McIntosh barked and patted Levi on the back. Levi beamed at the man. "Hip, hip, hurrah!" Levi shouted with the others gleefully.

Jeremy watched as the crowd gave three huzzahs, which the governor appeared to pretend not to hear. Then they turned and filed back down State Street. The worst was over, Jeremy thought with relief.

Abigail sat beside Jane, who was busily knitting. Abigail tried to read but couldn't concentrate. Levi had not returned for dinner. Abigail assumed that he was celebrating in some South End tavern. But a growing fear nagged at her. Why had Levi not appeared for dinner? He was not one to waste money on the high cost of tavern food. She would have thought that Levi would have wanted to be at dinner to revel them with tales of the success of the Liberty Tree escapade. Something was wrong. Nor had she heard from Jeremy. She had been so certain that he would have sent a note telling her that he had indeed resigned from his job as he had promised. Abigail grew tired of rocking and thinking about all these threads that didn't weave themselves into a whole cloth. "I am going to go to my room and work on my report of today's events," she said to Jane.

"Good, dear. I will call you down when Levi arrives." Jane didn't attempt to disguise her own growing concern.

Not only was Abigail upset, but she was frustrated. She had awoken in the morning believing that by this time of evening she would have talked to Levi, no matter how difficult he might prove to be, and by now announced her impending marriage to Jane in a long heart-to-heart talk. Abigail started for the stairs. Abruptly, she turned. She could wait no longer. "Jane, I would like to talk to you. For there is much I have been wanting to tell you for some time. Could we speak now?" Abigail asked, suddenly shy.

"Well, Mistress Peabody," Jane said with a deadpan expression as she rose and pulled Abigail's rocking chair closer to her own. "Why are you standing there then, like a child who has been caught stealing a cake from the ledge? Sit down, sit down. For I am bored to tears by this knitting! I do hope you have

something to say that will enliven this weary body!"
Jane reclined in her rocker.

Abigail stared at Jane with wide eyes and opened
mouth. She watched as Jane looked down at her
knitting and tried to mask the twinkle in her eyes. She
already knows! Abigail didn't know whether to laugh,
cry, or rage. Her hands rose to her hips. "Mrs.
Stewart! I do believe that *you* might have a thing or
two to explain as well!"

"Humph!" Jane declared. "Mind your manners.
Just because you're going to be the wife of a fine
gentleman is no reason to suddenly get snooty with
me. You're still not too old or too big for me to put
over my knee, you know!"

Abigail ran to Jane and hugged her so hard that
they both almost fell backward except for the sturdi-
ness of the rocker that Abigail's father had built years
before.

"Are you certain that the building Oliver just
constructed on his dock on Kilby Street is meant to be
the new Stamp Office?" Charles Osborn asked Levi.
"For I heard say that he intended to divide it into
shops and rent them."

"What else would he say?" Levi answered scornful-
ly as they marched to the dock. "Would he post a
large painted sign announcing the stamp office prem-
ises?"

"No, I guess not," Charles agreed. But he was
troubled. The effigies had been a wonderful idea. But
this he was not so certain of.

In five minutes, with McIntosh giving instructions,

the brick building was leveled by the mob, which then proceeded to Oliver's house on the nearby street which bore his family name. Standing in the street, the leaders presented those inside with a pantomime show, as they beheaded and abused the effigy while the rest of the crowd threw stones, gathered from the demolished brick structure, through Oliver's windows.

"I think I'm going home," Charles whispered to Levi. Adam had already left before the bricks began to fly. "It isn't right," Charles whispered.

"You're a coward, Charles," Levi said contemptuously.

Charles studied Levi's eyes that glinted strangely in the torchlight. Levi had changed since Katie died. Charles had tried to make excuses for his friend, but the more time Levi spent with McIntosh, the less he was the Levi Charles had known all his life. Levi's wild, hotheaded streak had overtaken the softer Levi. Charles wanted no more of this. He turned away without a word, for all he would hear would be angry accusations.

Levi turned and saw Charles walk away with nary a good night. He started for his friend, then halted. Good riddance to you, too, Levi thought, as he turned and searched for McIntosh.

McIntosh was already leading the group onward down the block to Fort Hill, the pallbearers carrying what was left of the effigy. At the summit of the hill, the figure was ceremoniously "stamped" and then burned in the bonfire that had been started from the wood carried from the building on Kilby Street.

Levi was mesmerized by the bonfire that he knew

could be seen by most of the city. Eventually, he noticed that people were leaving. Was it over? he wondered disappointedly. For he saw that the gentlemen members of the crowd, disguised in trousers and jackets which marked workingmen, seemed to have grown tired of the evening's entertainment.

"Is it over?" Levi asked McIntosh as he rushed to the exuberant man's side.

"Far from it. Stick with me, son! Now's the time that separates the men from the boys. The genteel among us have had their fun. And they've been a help to us. But you stay at my side, Levi Peabody. You're my kind of man, eh?" Levi beamed as McIntosh clapped his shoulder.

So it was the real patriots that stuck through to the end, Levi thought to himself, as he followed McIntosh and the others back to Oliver's house. As Levi joined in, ripping the fence palings, beating down the doors, and smashing a looking glass he had once heard was the largest in North America, he thought of all those Tory bastards who believed they were better than he. Who believed they could do whatever they liked, whether it be raping his sister or a poor whore in an alley. Or even having him falsely arrested and therefore unable to save his own wife's life. See, Katie, he thought. I'm doing this for you. You were so kind and gentle. Too good for this world. And look what happened to you and my son because of those bastards like the two from Cambridge. And Jeremy Blackburn. If you hadn't been so worried for us, you never would have run to his house in the night—you'd be alive today, with our son. I can't bring you back, Katie. But I can do this much for you, Levi thought as he saw his green eyes filled with tears in part of the remaining looking glass, until he sent a rock hurling and the image shattered to bits.

Governor Bernard waited in his chambers for a return message from the colonel of the militia. After receiving word about the havoc being wreaked on Oliver's house, he'd ordered the colonel to beat an alarm for the colonial militia to assemble. Bernard waited with just two or three councilmen, for the others had excused themselves for various reasons. Jeremy Blackburn had gone to Hutchinson's house to apprise him of the council's action.

A boy ran in breathlessly. "The colonel's reply," he said, "Mr. Governor, sir." Bernard snatched the note from his hand. The boy watched as he read it, as did the gentlemen. Bernard turned livid.

"Can you believe this reply?" he said with genuine alarm. "He writes that any drummer he would send out to beat an alert would be knocked down and have his drum smashed before he could strike it. Moreover, he suggests that most of his drummers are probably helping to smash Oliver's house. This situation is most definitely out of control! I suggest you gentlemen flee to the safety of your country homes! I intend to take refuge in Castle William in the Harbor! Only when I am surrounded by protective British troops will I feel my family and I may sleep safely! Good evening, gentlemen."

Lieutenent Governor Hutchinson, Sheriff Greenleaf, and Jeremy hurried from the Hutchinson house. The lieutenant governor paused. "Jeremy?" he asked. "Are you certain you wish to venture to Oliver's house? The sheriff and I must go, but you— The last reports say that most of the mob has dispersed. It is almost eleven and perhaps the rest have grown weary. But it may still be a dangerous—"

"I understand, Thom. I wonder if we three are not being foolhearty, but I would like to see for myself. Perhaps the reports of the damage have been exaggerated," Jeremy added as they stepped into the governor's carriage.

"Gentlemen!" the lieutenant governor called to the men, still many in number, as stones continued to fly against the house. Inside the house, its doors smashed open, there was continuing tumult. "I order you to cease and desist! This is your Lieutenant Governor, Thomas Hutchinson, speaking!" he called out.

"Aye, and Sheriff Greenleaf. Halt at once, gentlemen!" the sheriff called with less firmness to his voice.

Jeremy, deferring to the official status of his companions, stood behind quietly, taking in the appalling scene.

"The lieutenant governor and the sheriff!" rang out a voice, probably McIntosh's, Jeremy guessed. "To your arms, my boys!" the man shouted, and a rain of stones flew at the lieutenant governor and sheriff, who ran toward the carriage as they tried to protect their faces and heads. Jeremy, already behind the reins of the carriage, watched as two or three young men with rocks in their hands chased after them. The man in the lead had red hair, and as he flung his rock at Hutchinson, missing the man's head by inches, he threw a string of curses. Jeremy recognized the voice even before the face appeared behind the lieutenant governor, just inches from the carriage—Levi Peabody.

Levi was about to haul a smaller stone—

"Levi! Don't, damn you!"

The familiar voice which he couldn't place stopped him. Levi looked up at the open carriage. It was Jeremy, who stared at him with such contempt that for a moment Levi was frozen.

"So this is how your fine patriotism shows itself?" Jeremy called out, his voice steeped in sarcasm.

Levi watched as Jeremy helped Hutchinson and then the sheriff into the carriage. He tried to think of just the right words to hurl as he stood staring at Jeremy. "What would you know of patriotism!" he shouted.

Jeremy glared at the wiry red-headed man whose green eyes gleamed with open hatred. My future wife's brother, he thought, and without a word turned away.

Levi took Jeremy's action as a sign of fear. He always knew that Jeremy was as much the coward as his brother Damon had been! "Come down here and fight like a man, Mr. Blackburn!" he shouted in an excited voice. "You are a bloody Tory coward like the rest of them!"

Jeremy was tempted to jump from the carriage and give Levi what he deserved. But what was the use? Hadn't enough harm been done tonight, he thought, as he gazed over Levi's head at the house that stood in ruins, though the men continued to assault it. Better to get Hutchinson and the sheriff to safety, Jeremy decided, as he saw another group, with stones in hand, approaching. Jeremy started down the road, the horses breaking into a fast pace at his expert direction. He heard the stones that fell behind them on the cobblestone, and the cries and curses as they rode into the darkness. "Are you all right, Sheriff Greenleaf? And you, Thom?" he asked, for Hutchinson seemed dazed.

"Why would they attack me that way? For have I not been a true Bostonian in word and deed? . . ." he pleaded.

"They're hooligans, those ones," Sheriff Greenleaf tried to reassure him. "I've seen their faces in many a brawl over the years, sir. They've had their fun, at poor Oliver's expense, I'm afraid. But I believe that the worst is over."

Jeremy wished he could agree. It was just beginning, he feared.

# Chapter Seventeen

ABIGAIL WOKE FROM A TROUBLED SLEEP IN THE ROCKer where she'd sat waiting for Levi, as she heard the back door open. "Levi!" she called out. She tried to rub the grogginess from her eyes. "Where have you been? It must be the middle of the night—"

"Hold your tongue, sister, for I am more than a bit drunk and very tired!" he said sharply. "I am going to bed. I will be glad to talk to you in the morning."

Abigail stared at her brother, who appeared even drunker than he claimed. She was horrified, for his clothing was dirty and he was so disheveled. Just where had he been and what had happened? They must talk *now,* she decided, as she ran ahead of Levi and blocked his entrance to his bedroom. "No! You must tell me—"

Levi laughed and shook his head. "I'll tell you this much. Tomorrow, Mr. Andrew Oliver will most definitely resign his position as stamp distributor," Levi said in a slur and began to laugh uproariously.

"Quiet, brother!" Abigail whispered and grabbed him by his shoulders. "You will awaken baby Sarah. She has been up half the night. Jane thinks it is another tooth, but she felt feverish to me."

"Should I look in on her?" he asked, his drunken eyes trying to focus.

"If she wakes and sees your appearance you will frighten her!" Abigail said sharply. Levi looked so contrite that her heart softened. "Go to sleep, brother. But tomorrow we must talk. Sarah will be fine." Abigail turned and wearily started for her room.

The rest of the night she lay in bed, her body exhausted, her eyes so heavy that they ached, but still her mind would not allow her to escape to the refuge of sleep as her thoughts raced till dawn broke the night.

When Abigail opened her eyes, the room was fully sunlit. She looked at the clock. It was after ten—she must have fallen asleep listening to the morning birds, she realized. She pulled herself from her bed.

"Where is Levi?" Abigail asked Jane, as she came down the steps.

"And good morning to you, too!" Jane responded as she stood stirring a pot at the hearth, her back to Abigail.

"I am sorry," Abigail said and then yawned. Jane turned to her, and Abigail saw the worry in her face.

"My, you look a sight. I was right to guess that perhaps you slept little last night. Levi left about an hour ago. He said he'd be back later. He drank some strong tea but it did little to relieve his bleary, puffy eyes, and sour disposition. I held my tongue, assuming you two had spoken last night. By the looks of your own face, may I take it you did not?"

"He was drunk. He went to sleep and we were to talk this morning. What is wrong with him?" Abigail raged.

"He lost his wife and son, for one," Jane answered gently.

"I know! But he—it's more than that! And I know you don't approve of his association with McIntosh any more than I do—" Abigail's head throbbed and she knew that venting her anger on Jane was as useless as it was rude. "I'm sorry. . . . I think I could use a strong cup of tea myself." Abigail started for the shelf that held the cups.

"Sit down and I will serve it to you," Jane said. "I understand you're upset. I do. Soon he will be home and you can talk to him."

Baby Sarah began to cry. Abigail walked to the cradle and gently rocked it. "Has her fever gone down?" Abigail asked worriedly.

"She was cool this morning," Jane answered as she smiled at the baby, who had already fallen back to sleep. "And she ate well. I believe it is just another tooth."

Nathan came running into the kitchen with a sealed note in his hand. He handed it to Abigail. "A gentleman stopped me on the street and asked me to give this to you," he said.

It must be a note from Jeremy, Abigail thought, as she smiled and felt her heart lift. She opened the wax seal and was disappointed that the handwriting was not familiar. As she began to read the note her smile left her. What was this? "Dear Daughter of Liberty." Abigail looked up. This note was probably not for her.

"Nathan," she called as the boy was almost out the door. He returned. "What gentleman gave you this?"

"I don't know him, Abigail. He asked me if I was the apprentice boy for Peabody Printers. When I said aye, he asked me to please give this to you at once. So I did."

"Did he call me by name?" She watched Nathan silently recall the conversation.

"Aye. He said, 'Please give this to Mistress Abigail Peabody at once, boy.' Those were his exact words. . . . Is something wrong?"

"No. No, it is fine. Thank you for bringing it to me, Nathan," she answered, forcing a smile.

Jane watched Abigail as she read, her face turning from puzzled to disturbed to puzzled again. "What is it, Abigail?"

"One moment, Jane," Abigail answered without looking up as she again read the note. Finally she looked up, her green eyes turbulent, her mouth tight. "I do not know if this is a bad joke or what . . . I don't understand . . ."

"Read it to me, then, if you would," Jane answered as she put Abigail's tea before her. It was at times like this that Jane wished she'd learned to read and write.

Abigail took a sip of tea and reread the note. "It cannot be so—" She looked up at Jane's impatient face. "I'm sorry, Jane . . . It is addressed to 'Dear Daughter of Liberty.'"

"What does that mean . . . Oh, I see! Like The Sons of Liberty! That's rather clever, don't you think—" Jane stopped as Abigail looked at her with an expression that suggested she found little humor in the address. "I'm sorry. Please go on."

"It says, 'We have information, from a reliable source, which we believe is *vital* for you to know. Governor Bernard intends to bring you up on charges of sedition for your fine and courageous essay which appeared in your newspaper on the thirteenth of August. His charge will claim that it was your essay that incited the destruction of the future Stamp Office and attack on Oliver's home last night. You have patriots in full support of you and our cause. We will be in touch. You are not alone and we will contact you shortly. Do not worry, for a fine lawyer shall take your case for no fee. We shall show the Royal Governor that he can not suppress freedom of speech in Boston. Your name shall appear in the annals beside that of the great Peter Zenger. We are behind you and thank you, dear sister. Signed, The Sons of Liberty.'"

Jane sat down. "Read it to me again. Slowly this time. For my mind cannot absorb as quickly as yours."

"I still do not understand—" Abigail said as her head throbbed with confusion and her hands grew cold despite the heat of the August morning. "I will read it very slowly. Perhaps I will finally comprehend it myself." She read the note aloud again, shaking her head in astonishment as she read slowly and clearly. When she finished, she and Jane stared at one another in silence.

"Oliver's house was attacked last night? By

whom?" Jane asked indignantly. "And how could such a terrible event be linked to you?"

"Jane? Abigail?" Jeremy's voice called as he knocked at the open back door. Abigail raced from the chair and flew into his arms. Unashamedly, she hugged and kissed him.

Jeremy tensed and quickly looked to Jane Stewart. His heart warmed as he saw her glowing at them. So Abigail had told Jane and Levi. Now he must tell her what had transpired, and learn—

"Would you show some propriety, Mistress Peabody, and let the gentleman enter the house before leaping at him in a most unseemly fashion that shocks poor Jane's ancient eyes," Jane called as she smiled at them and winked to Jeremy.

Abigail pulled herself from Jeremy's strong arms and turned to Jane, her face heightened in color from her impulsive display. As she turned and saw Jane's twinkling smile, she felt relieved but still a bit embarrassed. She led Jeremy to the table.

"Good morning, Mrs. Stewart," he said with a grin.

"And good morning to you, Jeremy! You are a welcome sight for more than the most obvious of reasons. For perhaps you can inform us of last night's events and make some sense out of this peculiar letter Abigail received this morning! Sit please and I shall bring you some tea and cake."

"What letter?" Jeremy asked as he turned to his beloved Abigail, whose face was as pale as it was perplexed. Had Levi told her of their encounter? No, somehow Jeremy doubted that he would have admitted to his participation in the destruction of Oliver's house. And from the framing of Jane's request, Abigail and Jane did not know the details of last night's events.

"This letter," Abigail said, as she handed him the cream-colored, fine stationery.

Abigail's face brightened as she rested her hand upon his for a moment. "But first, before you read this, please let me hear the good news from your own lips. Speak freely, for dear Jane knows all, even though I wasn't able to—but I will tell you of that after. Now tell me you resigned yesterday!"

He had practiced his speech all through the night, but suddenly his lines were lost as he looked at her smiling, lovely face. "I didn't—I mean I couldn't—not yet. Something happened yesterday. It is a long, ridiculous story that led into a worse day. I will tell you of each minute. But allow me to read this first, for this may not require the time . . ." Jeremy was prepared for Abigail's disappointed expression, but as he saw her smile eclipse and her face tighten and pale, he wished they were alone and that he could sweep her into his arms and kiss and caress her in a way that would reassure her.

He looked down distractedly at the note. But as soon as he saw the salutation, his throat tightened. Obviously someone on the governor's council had written to her; he read quickly. As he became more horrified, he sought to mask his worry so that Abigail would not know. Damn! Someone on the council was an informer for The Sons of Liberty. That explained many things, but none that mattered now. How was he to explain this growing morass to her in a way that would not alarm her? This letter had shattered his original plan—

"What are you doing in my house!" roared Levi, causing both Abigail and Jane to gasp in shock, since no one had heard him enter the kitchen. Baby Sarah began to cry. "Get out of my house, you Tory bastard!" Levi yelled as he approached Jeremy with clenched fists.

Abigail leaped up and rushed at her brother. "Stop it, Levi!" she shouted. "I've had all the bad temper and rudeness from you that I will stand! This is my house too. And Jane's. And Jeremy is soon to be my husband and your brother-in-law!"

Levi looked at his sister's blazing eyes and quivering mouth. She was such a fool! He began to laugh. He stood and roared with laughter. He placed his hands on Abigail's shoulders and stared into her shocked, pale face as he laughed. Then he began to shake her. "Are you telling me that you intend to *marry* the man who named you 'Daughter of Liberty' and intends to prosecute you for sedition! You are a fool, Abigail, a fool—"

Jeremy had stood enough. He had tried not to fall to Levi's brutish level, but this was too much. He could not stand and watch Levi shake Abigail so harshly. He crossed the room in long, steady strides, and yanked Levi's hands from Abigail's shoulders, hurling Levi backward from the force. "Say your piece, but do not lay your hands in an ungentlemanly way upon Abigail."

Levi regained his balance. "Who are you to tell me what to do, or not to do! She is my sister!"

His laughter stopped. "Oh, I think I see," he said as he watched Abigail standing before him with Jeremy's arms around her shoulder in a most familiar manner. "So you have already become his whore!"

Jeremy grabbed Levi by his shoulders and pushed him against the wall. As Levi tried to swing at him, Jeremy lifted the slighter man off his feet and pressed him against the wall so that all Levi could do was dangle. "You shall apologize to your sister this moment or it will be the last words you will say for a while, Levi," Jeremy stated in a deceptively even tone, which his darkened eyes, piercing into Levi, belied.

"I shall apologize only if Abigail can tell me that she has not become the whore of the man who has agreed with the governor's orders to prosecute her for sedition. Is it not you, her 'beloved,' who has willingly taken the case?"

Jeremy could contain himself no longer. Levi was intentionally distorting whatever he had learned to make it appear— As his clenched fist started for Levi's laughing face, Jeremy somehow stopped it in midair. If he hit Levi, Abigail would believe her brother. That was just what Levi was goading him to do. He released Levi so abruptly that Levi fell to the floor. Jeremy felt Abigail's arms pulling him away from her brother.

"Stop it, stop it! Both of you!" Abigail demanded. Sarah screamed though Jane tried to comfort her. Abigail pushed herself between the men. She stared down at her brother. "Jeremy is no longer working for the governor!" she shouted. "He resigned yester—"

266

Wait. Abigail felt herself go limp. Hadn't Jeremy said just before— She turned.

How could he make her hear, Jeremy wondered as he watched her stare at him with a tortured face. "Did you, or did you not resign from your position, Jeremy?" she asked, her eyes pleading for the answer she demanded but that he could not give to her as simply as she wanted it. Needed it! He reached out his arms to her but she stood like stone before him. "Please. Let me explain . . ." He felt his heart pound as he watched her fight back the tears that filled her eyes. She righted her slender shoulders rigidly.

"Please leave my home at once, Jeremy," she said in a voice as dead as it was steady.

"No! You've got to listen. He's twisting all of this intentionally because I saw him smashing Oliver's house last night and stopped him from almost killing Lieutenant Governor Hutchinson! Tell her the truth, Levi! For once in your life. Do it for your sister, as much as you despise me. Tell her the truth," he pleaded, never removing his eyes from Abigail's face.

"What story are you inventing now, Jeremy? You're almost as good a liar as your brother was. And we know what a liar he was, don't we, Abigail? I never saw you last night, Jeremy. That's the truth, Abigail. I'm your brother. Have I ever lied to you?"

Abigail turned and looked at her brother. He spoke with such sincerity. She turned back to Jeremy, whose words she couldn't even hear. Levi would not lie and ruin her life—but she was so sure that Jeremy had truly loved her! She turned to Jane who appeared more uncertain than Abigail had ever remembered. "Is it you who is supposed to prosecute me—"

"Let me explain!"

She couldn't listen anymore. Oh, why could you have not said no, Jeremy! The tears blurred her eyes as she turned and ran to the staircase.

"Abigail!" Jeremy shouted. "If any of the vows of love you gave me were sincere, then just let me explain!"

"He used you, Abigail. Just as Damon tried to do. Jeremy got the revenge he wanted! Enough damage has been done. Don't let him use you any longer, sister, for I can not save you from him as I did from Damon."

Abigail raced up the stairs.

Jeremy started after her but Levi blocked his way. "Move or I'll kill you," Jeremy yelled. "It would be my pleasure for what you've done to us and how you and your gang beat my brother to a bloody pulp!"

Abigail stood at the bottom of the second floor staircase, listening. As she heard Jeremy's fierce words, she folded onto the step, all hope draining her body. He had sworn that he believed that Levi had not killed Damon, that Levi was nowhere in the vicinity. And she had believed him. She had loved him and believed him when he said he would resign, and now he was going to prosecute her. Levi was right. Jeremy had cleverly reaped his revenge on them. She had openly and willingly become his whore. May God forgive her! She sat on the step with her head against her knees as the blood drained further from her head.

". . . Abigail, please." He kneeled before her. "Let me explain. You will understand everything once you listen. I love you and want to marry you and intended to fulfill my promise just as I—"

"Jeremy. Go away. I can't listen because I will just be taken in by more of your lies." She couldn't raise her head as she whispered. "You have had me and had your revenge. I was never your intended wife, just your—I am glad that my father is dead and can't see the shame I have brought to his name." Using will more than strength, Abigail rose and ran up the stairs to her bedroom, slamming the door behind her as she fell onto her bed.

Jeremy sat uncomprehendingly. Finally he raised his body and slowly climbed down the steps. She had never truly loved him. For how could she refuse to listen if she had? How could she not see Levi's twisted mind reflected in his smirking mouth and glinting eyes? Even though he was her brother?

Levi stood at the bottom of the steps, grinning. Jeremy was tempted to punch the grin from his face. But what good would that do? How would it matter now? He turned away and walked out the front door.

"Mrs. Latham," Jeremy said sharply as he sat behind his desk in the study, law books piled before him. "I thought I told you that I did not wish to be disturbed by *anyone* under *any* circumstances—"

"If you're going to behave priggishly, Jeremy, then take it out on me. For I practically had to push Mrs. Latham from the door to enter!" Michael said as he strode into the study with greater vivacity than Jeremy had seen him display in years. "And it is I who should be offended, for you were to meet me at Giles's Tavern for dinner tonight, if I am not mistaken?" Michael poured himself a brandy.

"I am sorry for snapping, Mrs. Latham. Truly," Jeremy said.

"Your apology is appreciated and accepted, Mr. Blackburn," Mrs. Latham answered with a soft smile and sympathetic nod. She did not know yet what catastrophe had occurred at the Peabody house, only that Jeremy had left for Abigail's with love brimming in his eyes and had returned looking as if the world had ended. He had gone to his room where he remained through dinner. Then he'd come downstairs and locked himself away in the study with the orders that he not be disturbed. She had worried that he intended to drink himself into a stupor, which was one of the reasons that she was so grateful when Dr. Harrington appeared at the door. Mrs. Latham was more than relieved to see Jeremy apparently sober and at work, although it grieved her how pale and grim his face remained. "I will retire for the night, for it is after eleven, sir?"

"Certainly, Mrs. Latham." She saw his attempt to smile. "Sleep well, and I am sorry for being so unpleasant to you tonight. Please send my regards to Prissy, by the way, when you write."

"I shall, sir, and thank you." Mrs. Latham closed the door and thought that perhaps she *would* write a letter to Prissy, who had gone to work as a governess for a family in Virginia. Now that Michael Harrington was with Jeremy, she could allow herself to think of something else, at least for the moment.

Michael poured another brandy for himself after

handing the first to Jeremy, who came around from behind his desk to receive it. "I'm sorry about dinner, Michael. It completely slipped my mind."

Michael studied his friend. Jeremy looked pallid and his usually clear brown eyes were reddened and bleary. He saw the tight lines formed around Jeremy's mouth and the accentuated hollow of his cheeks. "You look as if you have something more serious filling your mind at the moment," Michael said evenly, gently, trying to make the skittish Jeremy speak openly.

"I do. But I don't wish to speak of it at the moment." Jeremy raised his glass in a toast to his friend as they sat in the leather chairs facing one another. "To your health. For you have never looked better!" Jeremy said.

"And to yours," Michael added. "For you have never looked worse!"

Despite himself, Jeremy chuckled, and drank the brandy down. "So tell me what cheers you so— besides seeing me look so poorly. I know that the moment you saw me you thought to yourself, Ah ha! Another paying customer!"

It was Michael's turn to laugh. "That was exactly what I thought! Seriously, I am much cheered by yesterday's events and their results today. Did you already hear that Oliver resigned as stamp distributor this morning?"

"In fear of his life, probably," Jeremy replied sardonically. "Actually, how could he resign when he has never been officially commissioned?"

"Jeremy, what's gotten into you?" Michael's blue eyes flashed with anger. "You're sounding like the

271

narrow-minded Tory you were when you first arrived back in Boston!"

Jeremy sighed wearily. "I am not sorry that Oliver resigned. But was it necessary to destroy his warehouse and vandalize his house to get him to do so?"

"I know . . ." Michael sighed and took another swallow. "Many of us weren't in favor of that action. I for one believed the effigy and the bonfire were enough."

"Then you were not in favor of the rocks thrown at Hutchinson and Sheriff Greenleaf, I take it? One rock thrown, which I witnessed last night, that could have killed Thomas, if the man's aim had been as strong as his intentions."

"I did not hear of such. When did this happen?" a much disturbed Michael asked.

"I accompanied Hutchinson and the sheriff to Oliver's house at about eleven last night. Thom was insistent about trying to stop the vandalism. McIntosh ordered his boys to attack in response, and they did, with a rain of stones. I remained in the background and quickly readied the carriage. I suppose that I stopped Levi Peabody from throwing the second rock at the lieutenant governor after his first missed its mark. I suppose I *accomplished* that much, if that is the correct word."

"We heard nothing of this! Now I understand why McIntosh's group went to Hutchinson's house tonight, after their bonfire on Fort Hill." Michael was troubled, and Jeremy's look of alarm did little to ease him. "No, he's all right, in answer to the question in your eyes. I suppose it got quite nasty. I heard on my way here that they beat at his door and shouted for him to come out. But a neighbor convinced them that he and his family had fled, so finally they drifted away."

"These are your Sons of Liberty? Tearing down one man's property and vandalizing his house. Then the next night terrorizing a Boston-born lieutenant governor, right down the street from our own houses. If you ask me, it is the mentality of a mob! Who will they terrorize next? What will they destroy next?"

"You exaggerate otherwise justified concerns, Jeremy. For it is all over now. We have made our point. There was hardly a citizen today who didn't cheer yesterday's actions. There will be no need to make the point again."

"I hope you are right. Perhaps I am upset more by other events that seem so interconnected—"

"You told Abigail of her brother's participation last night and she doubted you? Is that it?"

Jeremy began to laugh. "Oh, how I wish it were that simple, my friend." Jeremy leaned forward. "I am ready to talk. I need to talk. Are you prepared to listen?"

"Only if you'll be finished by nine in the morning when I have an appointment at the hospital," he answered.

Jeremy rose, appreciating Michael's humorous reassurance. "A double whiskey for me. How about you, my friend?" he asked.

"A double for me too, only if you agree that we go into the kitchen and hunt down some food as well, for you. Have you eaten at all today?" He watched as

Jeremy tried to remember. "Just as I thought. Do you agree?"

Jeremy wasn't hungry, but already he could feel the brandy going to his head. What good would Michael's advice be if it fell on whiskey-deafened ears? "Agreed."

Abigail walked to her desk and unlocked the lacquered chest in which her diary laid. Perhaps if she tried to sort it out in words. But a wave of dizziness sent her back to her bed. Perhaps she should have eaten the dinner Jane brought up an hour ago. Lying on her back, Abigail stared out at the dusky sky. It was almost eight o'clock. She heard the front door slam and listened to Levi's heavy boots clomp as he strode down the cobblestoned streets. He was out for the evening again.

She had meant to go down and talk with him, for she suspected that he had not been completely truthful with her about his activities last night. Jane had told her that she had heard confirmation of the news during the afternoon that Oliver's Stamp Office had been leveled and his house pillaged. But Abigail was so tired. And there were no questions she could ask, or answers she would receive, that would change the essential facts she knew to be incontestable. Jeremy had not resigned as he had promised. She was about to be sued for sedition. Jeremy, as the barrister for the governor, would be the one to file the case against her. He had never loved her. He had wanted revenge and he had gotten it. But why then did a part of her, deep in her heart, try to deny it? Pride? Shock?

Vanity? Fear? Exhaustion? All of those, she knew.
. . . She was too tired to think anymore . . .

By the time the eight o'clock bells in the church
steeple rang, Abigail was asleep.


Jane heard an insistent, light rapping at the back
door. Had Levi forgotten his key again, she wondered, as she lit a candle and threw a shawl over her
nightdress. Slowly, she climbed down the stairs,
yawning, for it had been a most exhausting day whose
problems lingered with her in a restless light sleep.
She passed the clock and saw it was after eleven. The
light rapping continued. "Coming, coming," she whispered. "If you wouldn't lose your key so often—" she
said as she opened the door. "Jeremy!" Jane exclaimed.

"Please, Jane. May I come in? I know the hour is
indecent, but I've got to speak to Abigail!" he whispered urgently.

Jane stared at his haggard, handsome face, at his
brown eyes filled with turmoil. "Aye, come in, come
in. You'll get the death of a chill, even in the summer
night air. You look terrible! Even worse than Abigail,
and she looks as if she died but forgot to leave her
body!"

Jeremy followed her quietly into the kitchen and
watched as she tried to light the oil lamp. "Allow
me," he said and lit it quickly. He took Jane's hand.
"Please. Tell me that you believe me. It matters to me
what you think, you know."

Jane stared at Jeremy. Finally she smiled and patted
his hand. "I am still confused as to the details, but no

man accused of the caddish, calculated acts you've been found guilty of in this house could look as anguished as you do. The soul is in the eyes, Jeremy. I believe what I see in your eyes. I am sure that later I will learn the information which will support what I see so clearly. . . . Abigail is upstairs, asleep. Go to her. Make her see it too."

"Thank you, Jane," he said and bent to kiss her on her cheek. "Whatever happens, I will never forget your faith in me." He started for the staircase.

"Jeremy," she whispered urgently, and he turned to her. Never had he seen her face look more tired or old in its naked worry.

"If I believe in you, which I do, then I am frightened for what that means about Levi. I think of him as a son. I am very worried—"

"Jane, I swear to you that I would never seriously harm him. Those were just words of rage and frustration—"

"I did not mean that. I know so. I mean for him. He has become a stranger to us all. And I do not know how to keep him from a course I don't understand, yet know can only lead to doom . . ." Jane's eyes filled with tears.

"I understand. It is strange how much like Damon Levi has turned out to be, in a different manner. If I can make Abigail understand and believe me, then we shall all help him."

"And if not?"

"Then I will be of little use to anyone, I fear. For I love Abigail more than anything in life."

Jane pushed him away. "Go, go to her and make that frightened girl hear your words. Make her see what you have shown me tonight. Hurry, for it is possible that Levi may arrive home soon."

Jeremy opened the door and entered the dark room with the candle Jane had given him in hand. He crept closer and placed the candle on the table beside her bed. He stood and listened to her steady breathing as he watched her sleep, so beautiful and vulnerable that the sight of her formed a knot in his throat, making it difficult for him to swallow. He sat on the chair for a moment, realizing that he'd never been in her bedroom in this house. He watched her sleep, her full mouth opened slightly, her hair in profusion against the pillow. No matter what happened, he would have these last images of her forever.

She shifted and her lips moved. "Jeremy," she said so softly that he believed he'd imagined it. "Jeremy, my love . . ." she said again. Was she awake? No, he realized, and the knot in his throat grew tighter. She was asleep, and dreaming about him.

He crept to the bed and leaned above her. Slowly, he lowered his face until it almost touched her own. Gently, he pressed his lips onto hers. Her arms wrapped around his shoulders, pulling him to her as she kissed him languidly, her eyes still closed. He sat on the edge of the bed and pulled her into his arms as she clung to him, still on the edge of sleep.

"Oh, Jeremy," she said as she held him tightly. "I had the worst nightdream . . . it was so very horrible —Jeremy!" she cried as she pulled away in a mixture of shock and horror as consciousness hit her hard with the force of memory. "What are you doing in my bedroom? In the house? Leave, Jeremy, please—"

He shook her, for he could see that she was on the verge of hysteria. Then he held her in his arms. "If you ever loved me, then just listen to me. Do that much for us. If you don't believe me after you've heard me through, then I'll leave and never bother you again. Please."

She pulled back from him, fully awake now, and leaned against the backboard. He looked terrible! "Aye, I will listen," she said.

By the time Jeremy told her everything and answered her questions, his throat was raw despite the glass of water she'd poured for him. He looked into her green eyes that gave away no answer, in this, the most important case that he would ever plead.

He had explained and reexplained. His face so drawn and earnest. If only she could fall into his arms and make it all go away. But she had to trust him fully, believe his every word. He was so skilled a barrister . . .

She searched into every corner of her mind, for she could have *no* doubts—even he had demanded so. Something nagged at her, something neither of them had spoken. It had to do with Levi . . . but then, so much did, for it had come to Jeremy's word against Levi's. If Jeremy spoke the truth, then he was telling her that her brother was a stranger to her! That it was Levi who was the vengeful liar and bully—that was it! That was the question that had nagged at her, when she sank to the step this afternoon. Jeremy believed that Levi had killed Damon, although he had sworn otherwise. His own words in rage had spoken his true thoughts today. If he lied about that . . .

"You told me—you swore to me—that you believed, finally, that Levi did not kill your brother, that he was not even in the area. Yet you shouted at Levi that he and 'his gang' beat Damon to a bloody pulp," she said as evenly as possible.

Jeremy remembered his vow to her that night, how her question had been so worded that he could answer honestly and yet protect her from the truth about her brother's act. Now he would have to tell her the entire story, all that Michael had told him. Until now, he knew that Abigail could believe him since she could allow herself the escape of attributing Levi's despicable behavior to the shock of Katie's death. Jeremy, himself, had no doubt that the deaths of Katie and the baby had unleashed the worst in Levi, and that Abigail's unfortunate explanation as to why Katie was at his house that night had brought Levi's simmering hatred of him to a boil. But when he told her of Levi's outright lie, almost five years ago . . .

"Why are you not answering?" Abigail asked. If he was being forthright, then why did he have to think so upon it? Had he rehearsed all he intended to say, intended her to believe, after all?

"Because I love you and I wish to shield you from a truth that will be so very hurtful—"

"I do not wish to hear your excuses. Just the truth," she said. He spoke so easily and finely that it was too dangerous to listen to his verbal caresses.

"I know that Levi did not kill Damon. I didn't lie about that." He took a deep breath. "I also know—for certain now—that Levi and his friends, four or five of them, came upon Damon. They beat him, as I said, to a bloody pulp, and left him in the alley, bleeding and a waiting victim to the murderer or murderers who robbed and stabbed him."

It couldn't be! "That's a lie! You're saying that my brother attacked him, not even man to man, but like a bullying child—like a coward. And then they fled and left Damon. So in a way, Damon couldn't defend himself against another—you do believe that Levi caused Damon's death!"

He hadn't said that. He hadn't even thought that—but yes! Damn her incisive mind, for she had destroyed whatever saving grace her brother had wrongfully claimed in Jeremy's mind. "I didn't say that. They didn't mean for Damon to die. If I had been Levi I would have beaten Damon as well—"

"With a gang as you claim he did?"

"No. No! I wouldn't have done that! I would have fought like a man, and not jumped a sad drunken fellow in a dark alley in the dead of night! I wouldn't have and I won't apologize!"

"Nor would my brother!" she yelled and jumped from the bed.

"My brother was a liar and a rapist! But yours is an honorable man—is that what you have the nerve to say?"

"Aye. That is so! My brother *could not do* what you claim—"

"But Michael Harrington heard him bragging about it!"

She stared at him unbelieving. Lie upon lie! "You never mentioned Michael before. He testified at the trial. He said nothing of the sort!"

"That's because he felt sorry for Levi. He knew Levi hadn't killed Damon, for Damon spoke to him before he died—but that is another matter. He didn't want Levi convicted for a murder he didn't commit, and if he told what he knew he was afraid Levi would be found guilty—"

"So now you are saying that my brother perjured himself. He swore under oath." How could Jeremy lie so? How could he love her and lie so viciously? Suddenly, all this new information, to make his case. He was, in effect, claiming that Michael Harrington had perjured himself as well. It was because of Damon. Jeremy needed to make Levi as evil to her— "My brother is not a liar and a coward, nor vicious or evil as Damon was!"

What more could he say? She had all the facts and used them to attack him. It was hopeless. Yet he had to make her see. He rose and placed his hands on her shoulders. Violently she shook him off. He grabbed her hard. "You will listen to me," he said as he pressed so hard that he saw her wince. She tried to fight him off but he held her firmly, even as she kicked at him.

"You can hurt me, even hit me," she said with eyes crazed with anger and pain. "But never can you make me believe that Levi is any of the things you say he is! I don't believe a word you've said," she told him with such conviction that he felt a chill run up his neck.

He released her so quickly that she seemed shocked by her freedom. "Then damn both you and your brother to hell!"

He turned on his heels. The door, which he slammed behind him, thundered.

# Chapter Eighteen

## *August 26, 1765*

ABIGAIL WORKED AT SETTING THE TYPE WITH NATHAN'S help. She worked diligently and quietly. For the past week she had thrown herself into her work and helped Jane at chores when she had any remaining time. Occasionally she would fall into bed and sleep a dreamless sleep until she would wake in the morning and begin again.

"It is time for lunch," Jane announced as she entered the workroom.

"Good. I am very hungry," Levi called out. "I hope there is an extra helping of soup for me. How about you, Nathan?" he asked with a teasing smile, making the boy laugh.

"I'll be in as soon as I've finished this page," Abigail said softly, purposely keeping her eyes to her work to avoid Jane's disapproving face. Abigail just had no appetite of late. In fact, in the mornings she found herself sick to her stomach. She attributed it to her sorrow, which she held tight inside, allowing no one near it. Just when Levi was once again his old self, she was forgetting what her old self had been like.

"Abigail, leave the work. Come and eat," Levi said, patting her on the head. "You've become skin and bones these days. Starving yourself will not help," he said and cupped her chin, forcing her to meet his eyes, so like her own. "I know that, in my own way, now. And you were a help to me, the night of our talk. Won't you let me be the same for you?"

"Thank you, dear brother. I will. Just not yet."

He gave her an uncharacteristic peck on her cheek and fled into the kitchen.

Abigail thought of the talk she'd had with Levi that had gone long into the night. The same night, nine days ago, after Jeremy had cursed them both and stormed away. Levi had admitted to her that he had not behaved as well as he should have since Katie's death. He blamed it on drinking. He admitted that he had been among those who damaged Oliver's house and spoke of his guilt. But he adamantly denied that he had thrown a rock at anyone, let alone the lieutenant governor. Nor had he seen Jeremy. He openly admitted that he despised him for the very reasons that had turned out to be correct.

Levi had cried, then, and asked her forgiveness for the vile names he had called her. He told her that he knew she had always loved Jeremy, and that since her love was so honest and giving, surely the Lord would forgive her. He said that their father would have understood, for hadn't he loved their mother with the passion so rare in his day, let alone their own?

Abigail had tried to explain the difference between

patriotic action and mob violence. Levi had listened carefully and agreed that perhaps McIntosh was not the kind of man he should spend much time with. He told her how he had alienated Charles and Adam, and agreed to make amends, for he missed them. Days later, both Charles and Adam were over for dinner. Good to his word, Levi had apparently successfully mended his fences. As pleased as Abigail had been, as much as she liked both men, she had excused herself early, pleading tiredness, which was in part not an excuse.

"Excuse me, miss?" a workman called from the entrance. "I am looking for Goodman Peabody. Is he here?"

The man was not familiar to Abigail. She assumed it was a business matter. "He is not available at the moment. May I help you?"

"Oh, thank you, miss, but it's a personal matter. I have a message for him," the man said, shifting his weight awkwardly from one foot to another.

"May I take the message for him, then? I am his sister, Abigail Peabody."

"Oh, so you're the 'Daughter of Liberty' he's been bragging about to the mates!" the man said excitedly. "Pleased to make your acquaintance," he said as he walked to her and offered his hand. "Peter Clarke, ship caulker, Miss Peabody," he offered. "It's a real pleasure to meet you. Maybe I could give you the—no." The man shifted awkwardly again. "I'm afraid I can't."

He certainly was a mysterious, though amiable, man. Abigail did not remember Levi ever mentioning his name. "Mr. Clarke. Why don't you have a seat and I'll fetch Levi," she said.

"Thank you, Miss Peabody. I'd certainly appreciate that."

"Oh, so you've found your appetite after all!" Levi said when she entered the kitchen.

"Aye, but I came in to tell you that there's a man waiting to see you. His name is Peter Clarke. He's waiting in the shop." Was it her imagination or had Levi become nervous at her announcement?

"Thank you, Abigail," he said as he rose quickly, still smiling. "Did he say anything more?"

Abigail was about to repeat the peculiar conversation, but something made her hold her tongue. "No, just his name and that he wanted to see you."

"I see, then thank you," he said and quickly left the room.

It wasn't her imagination. He had been relieved at her last response and he was nervous.

"Are you going to sit down and eat or not?" Jane demanded.

"Yes, I'm quite hungry, actually," Abigail answered with a false smile that was so convincing that Jane smiled back. "Oh, dear—I left the—I'll be right back," Abigail said and hurried from the kitchen before Jane realized that she hadn't made any sense.

Abigail crept quietly to the office door. Levi and the man stood with their backs to her. She held her breath and listened hard, for they were speaking fairly softly.

". . . and the others will be ready. McIntosh doesn't know of our side trip, but I'm certain, as you said, that he will be pleased. So we'll meet at Blue's Tavern at nine, make your special visit, and join up with the others at Hutchinson's."

"And you've got the hats and masks?" Levi asked.

"Aye," Peter Clarke answered and laughed. "And a large hat it will take to cover that carrot-top head of yours."

Abigail slipped back into the kitchen, hoping that her face was composed for Jane. "I'm so hungry," she said as she sat down at the table and forced the soup into her turning stomach.

"Are my eyes seeing rightly?" Levi asked, as he entered a few minutes later. "Is Abigail actually eating?" he exclaimed with mock astonishment.

"Aye, and the soup is good. Hurry or yours will grow cold." She forced another spoonful down her throat. "What did that man want?" she asked casually.

"Oh, he's a friend of a friend. He's looking for work. He's done some printing, but I was sorry to tell him that we had no funds for assistants. I suggested he pay a visit to Ben Edes."

"That was kind of you," Abigail answered evenly, with just the right touch of a smile.

"Well, times are hard for us all. It was the least I could do, was it not?" he asked, then kept his eyes on his soup.

Abigail skipped dinner, claiming fatigue, which again was in part so. She felt weak yet heavy. She had vomited the soup she'd forced down for lunch. Now, she *was* very hungry, but needed the time alone to think. It had been trying, to compose her face into a calm countenance, since she'd overheard Levi's conversation. She had heard enough to alarm her, but not enough to be certain that she wasn't jumping to all the wrong conclusions. She dragged herself from her bed. She knew what she had to do.

"Is there any dinner left?" Abigail asked. "I had such a good sleep and woke quite hungry."

Jane looked as if she would burst with pleasure. "Is there any dinner left? Humph! Are you suggesting that I have become a stingy cook? Sit down! It is your favorite, roast chicken, child."

Levi was finishing his pudding. He smiled genuinely at her. "I am glad to see you are feeling so much better, Abigail."

"Oh, I am! I think you were right, earlier . . . and I thank you. In fact," she said, apparently so spontaneously that she was surprised at how easy this charade came to her, "what are you doing tonight, Levi?"

"I'm meeting Adam and Charles at Giles's Tavern. Why do you ask?" he said with a tinge of suspicion in his voice.

"I ask because it has been so long since I have been out among company. May I join you?" she asked brightly.

She watched his eyes widen in amazement. "Abigail. You've never gone to a tavern."

"I know. But ladies go there, do they not? Please take me along, Levi! I really would like to have some entertainment. It would be a new experience." She intentionally looked hurt. "Unless you would feel embarrassed to be seen with your sister—"

"Oh, no, Abigail," Levi quickly replied. "I think it's a fine idea and I wish that we could do it tonight . . . but you see, Adam has been most upset. He wants to propose marriage to Polly but can't find the courage. So this was to be a night of man talk . . ."

"Oh, I understand," Abigail said sympathetically. "Well, perhaps another time, then?"

Levi smiled broadly. "Let us not just *say* another time. Let us *set* a time. I shall speak with Adam and Charles. Perhaps Polly and her sister could join us. It would be a regular party! What do you say?"

"Oh, I think that sounds wonderful," Abigail said as gaily as she could. Levi smiled so happily that apparently he believed her.

Levi finished his pie quickly and went to his room to change, but the five minutes they had sat together, exchanging idle talk, had seemed an eternity to Abigail. Once she heard Levi reach the second floor, she sighed with relief, totally forgetting about Jane standing nearby. Abigail turned quickly, hoping that her sigh had escaped Jane. Jane stood, hands on broad hips, staring at her. She walked to Abigail.

"Do you want to tell me what you're up to?" Jane asked softly.

"Nothing—I can't tell you now, Jane." Abigail could not bear another lie. "Trust me."

Jane studied her. "I do. I only hope that it will end your agony." Jane looked as if she wanted to say more, but hesitated. She turned and walked toward the hearth. Then she turned back and again stood inches from Abigail, her look wordlessly daring Abigail to disagree with her. "And end Jeremy's agony as well." Abigail stared back at her. But to say she was shocked at Jane's short declaration would not have been a truth.

Once again, Jane Stewart had picked the right word. For agony was what Abigail experienced as she paced the small space of her bedroom. She had intended to follow Levi, but he had lied so completely that she didn't see the point. He had lied about everything concerning Peter Clarke—even the man's occupation. And he had lied so well! If she hadn't eavesdropped and heard with her own ears . . .

Her pain was so terrible that Abigail wished she could cry, for it would be a release. But she had shed all her tears those first days over a week ago. There were none left. All that was left now was the excruciatingly empty feeling in the core of her very soul. She had lost the most important person in the world to her and she had worked hard to do so. How Jeremy had pleaded with her; how she missed him.

But still, even now, she found herself making excuses for Levi. He was still with that McIntosh mob. That was obvious from the conversation. So was the fact that after ten days of peace in Boston, Hutchinson was to become the target again tonight. She had to take action to prevent an attack upon his house. But what could she do? She wasn't even certain she'd understood correctly. And if she did go to the lieutenant governor's home to alert him, would he believe her, now that she was known as the "Daughter of Liberty"? Michael Harrington! She could tell him all she'd overheard. He would know what to do, for he was a patriot, but not one who approved of violence and mobs. She would go to his house. Quickly, she pulled open her closet and pulled out a proper chemise and petticoat.

"I'm sorry, miss," the Harrington butler said, "but I don't know when he will return. May I give him a message?"

"No, I don't think so, thank you." Abigail turned and fled down the path. "May I tell him who called?" the butler called after her. Abigail didn't answer. It was after seven already. She didn't know what to do. Jeremy. She had to go to Jeremy. Perhaps he was not at home either, but she had to try. Jeremy was a friend of Hutchinson. If there was to be violence and she allowed herself to do nothing, she would never forgive herself. She wondered if Jeremy would even see her. She was afraid, as she remembered his final fury and curse. But she had to make him listen.

So the shoe is on the other foot, she thought. And it pinches terribly. She finally understood the real meaning of that expression.

Jeremy poured himself another whiskey and paced the study. Even getting drunk seemed to have lost some of its curative powers, he thought, and laughed aloud as he drank down the whiskey. He walked to the shelves of books and ran his hand across the leather-bound volumes. Then he punched at them. Two books fell from a shelf. He picked them up. One was a history volume, the other a book of poems. He put the history book back onto the shelf. He started to do the same with the poetry volume, but it slipped from his hands. He bent to pick it up as it lay on its leather cover, and noticed that a marker was inserted between the two open pages. Ah, so his father was a secret sentimentalist, Jeremy thought to himself as he carried the book to the sofa and sunk into it.

Anne Bradstreet. A strange choice for Sir Bentley . . . No! He remembered now, somehow, through the fog. Abigail had borrowed this volume from him a month or more ago. He had to concentrate to focus his eyes. "If ever two were one, then surely we, If every man were loved by wife then thee—" What did Abigail ever know of love, he thought as the fury rose within him. He took the book and flung it across the room. It hit the mantel and landed by the fireplace. If it were winter he'd burn the damn book, he thought.

"Mr. Blackburn. Please open this door!" Mrs. Latham called.

What did that infernal woman want *now*, he wondered. He felt guilty, for he knew she was genuinely concerned, but he was too drunk to care. He staggered to the door. It was easier to do her bidding and thus rid himself of her. Otherwise she might stand there pleading half the night. He fumbled with the keys until he finally found the right one that unlocked the door. He slid it back. "What is it *this* time, Mrs.—" He was drunker than he thought. Drunker than he'd ever been. He stood open-mouthed, for Mrs. Latham stood before him, but he was seeing a vision of Abigail . . .

"Oh, dear Lord," Abigail cried as she saw him standing before her. He was unshaven and his hair was disheveled. His eyes were almost slits in his hollow-cheeked, ravaged face. She had done this to him! "Jeremy . . . I am so sorry," she said, and suddenly she could say no more because all the tears that had hardened in the pit of her stomach gave way.

It was Abigail! But why was she crying? Had he said something to hurt her feelings? He hated it when she cried. He let her lead him to the couch. When he woke, he was lying in her lap, and she was applying cold compresses to his head. He lifted his head but the pain that shocked his brain made him lie back. Was he dreaming? Perhaps he had died and gone to heaven. The thought made him laugh, but it hurt to laugh so he stopped.

"Drink this, dearest," she said to him, holding the cup of strongly brewed tea to his mouth. Please, Jeremy, wake up enough to help me, but not enough to turn me away. She looked at the grandfather clock. It was almost eight. Levi had said he would meet the man at nine and that they would do something and then meet up with McIntosh at Hutchinson's house. So that meant that by no later than ten . . .

"Jeremy, please. Drink more tea, as much as you can."

By nine, with Mrs. Latham's help, Jeremy was sober enough to start becoming angry. He pulled away from her. "I know I'm asking of you what you pleaded for from me. And I denied you. But you've got to listen to me! For it may mean the safety of Thomas Hutchinson."

"What are you speaking of? The mobs have stopped, or haven't you heard, 'Daughter of Liberty.' There is no danger. I know why you've really come . . ." Suddenly he grinned and rose unsteadily. "Mrs. Latham, some more tea and a banquet for the lady, if you please. We shall be down to dine in a short while. But I must show Abigail something upstairs." He bowed gracelessly. "Will you do me the honor of accompanying me, my lady?"

Abigail didn't know why he was leading her upstairs, but then she decided he didn't either. The walk up the flight of steps to his bedroom would do him good.

He closed the bedroom door behind them. Abigail gazed about, remembering all the lovely times, remembering the love, the passion that had flowed from them and filled this room until even this large bedroom, larger than two bedrooms together in her house, seemed too small to contain it. Love lingered in the room . . . even now, weeks later, she could feel its presence.

"Jeremy, what are you doing?" Abigail asked as she felt him grab her from behind and lift her into the air. "You'll fall!" she called out as they tumbled onto the bed. She began to laugh, but the glint in his eyes stopped her. He began to pull at her clothes. "Stop it, Jeremy." She wanted him desperately, but not this way. He kissed her drunkenly as she fought him.

"I know what you've come for. Isn't this it, Abigail? You didn't want to be my wife. Perhaps you *would* prefer to be my whore." Her slap stunned him. He let her go. He rose from the bed and walked to the dresser. He stared at himself in the looking glass. You are disgusting, Jeremy, he thought and picked up a china pitcher from the dresser top. He hurled it at the looking glass. He turned to Abigail, who cowered against the bedpost. "Why didn't you love me enough to trust me?" he yelled in a broken voice.

"I did love you. I don't expect you to ever forgive me," she answered quietly. "I don't even know why, Jeremy. I don't. He's my brother . . . I couldn't help myself. If I had to do it all over again I would have chosen to believe him, although I loved you more than any words can ever say. . . . Just help Thom Hutchinson. He doesn't deserve to be harmed. I'll stay out of your life forever, I swear to you. For I *still* cannot believe that Levi did what you said to Damon. There is no hope for us, Jeremy."

Jeremy walked to her. He kneeled before her and placed his head on her lap. "Maybe it is God's way of punishing me for what I did to you. Please. I love you. I have never wanted another woman and never will. Let us just forget this," he pleaded.

"Oh, but if only we could . . ." Abigail whispered, as she stroked his head.

There was a thunderous clamor at the front door. Jeremy rose and a rock sailed through the window, narrowly missing his head. The window glass shattered into the room. Abigail started up, but he pushed her back down on the bed. As his heart pumped, his head began to clear. "Stay down. Do not move, whatever you do, *unless* I call your name. Then flee through the back door and hide in the carriage house. Do you understand me?" Abigail nodded but couldn't speak.

Jeremy blew out the candle, then ran down the stairs. Abigail heard him yell orders at Mrs. Latham but couldn't understand his words. As the bedroom door flew open, Abigail's heart seemed to stop beating. She shook with relief to see Mrs. Latham, who crouched across the room to the bed.

"Jeremy told me to make sure that you stay away from the window," the frightened woman said. "There are four or five men out there dressed as sailors. They are cursing and tried to beat the door down. One keeps calling Jeremy's name! I pleaded with Jeremy not to open the door—Tom is off for the night— Oh Lord, Abigail! What do you think those men will do?" Mrs. Latham began to cry.

"I don't know, but I intend to do more than cower on this bed!" Abigail declared as she crawled off and over to the window.

"Abigail, don't," Mrs. Latham pleaded.

"We're safe. The room is dark now, so they can't see in, but I can watch until I can think more clearly." She saw four men dressed as sailors. Three held torches in their hands. The leader—she assumed it was he—stepped back from the door, but she couldn't make out his features and Mrs. Latham's crying made it hard for her to hear their individual voices. They all wore hats, the leader a large one. She watched as he hurled a large stone at the door, she shuddered reflexively as it thudded.

"Come out, you Tory bastard!" one of the men with a torch yelled. Then all three yelled. The leader was silent. "Come out or we'll burn the house down!" one of the men demanded.

"Oh, please no, God," Abigail whispered aloud. Fire. You couldn't breathe and everything was black and hot, even in the frigid night air. And Father rushing back into the house . . .

"You will have to kill me first!" Jeremy shouted as he appeared in view. "I may not be able to take all of you, but I will take one or two. That I promise you,"

Jeremy said as he drew his sword. Abigail watched as one of the men with a torch in hand began to shift awkwardly from foot to foot. Oh, no!

"Get him!" the leader spoke. But Abigail felt no shock when she heard Levi's voice. She felt nothing at all. "Mrs. Latham, in a minute I want you to race as fast as you can through the back of the house and go to the nearest neighbor. Bring help. Do you hear me?" The woman sat frozen. Abigail shook her. "Mrs. Latham. You must get help. Do you hear me?" Finally, the woman nodded.

Abigail raced from the room and flew down the steps. As Abigail reached the front door, already flung open, she trembled at what she saw. Jeremy had been dragged onto the grass. One of the men was lying off to the side, clutching his stomach. The other two men held Jeremy down as her brother stood with Jeremy's sword pointed at his heart. "Put it down, Levi," she said evenly as her whole body quaked. "Put down the sword, brother."

Levi, his red hair showing beneath the wig that sat askew under the large hat, stared up at her. Wordlessly, he dropped the sword. "Abigail . . ." he said. He lowered his head. Then he looked up at her as he lifted the torch. His eyes burned as brightly.

Why had she not seen before? "Abigail . . . I'm sorry . . ." He turned and fled down the road. The others followed him.

Abigail ran the few feet to Jeremy. He lay so still, oh, please, no . . . Blood poured from his face. She raised his head onto her lap. "Jeremy, oh please, don't die." Her tears fell, mingling with his blood.

"Oh, please. For if you do it will be I who killed you. I love you, Jeremy. I don't care if you never speak to me again . . . all I want is for you to live . . ." Oh, why didn't he stir? She lowered her head to his chest. His heart beat . . . "Oh, please, Jeremy, wake up . . . help is coming," she said as she ripped at her petticoat and used the pieces to wipe the blood that dripped down his face from a deep cut on the side of his head. "Please wake up and live!" she said and sobbed.

"I will . . . under . . . under one condition . . . that you set the damned wedding date . . . before I'm too old to care . . ."

"Oh, Jeremy!" she laughed and cried as he groaned and then closed his eyes again. Abigail heard a carriage coming. It rode up to the house. "Help! Please!" she called in the darkness.

"I'm here, Abigail! Mrs. Latham and I!" It was Michael Harrington. How did Mrs. Latham get to his house so quickly? But she had no time to ask as Michael jumped from the carriage and kneeled beside her. She watched as Michael ministered to Jeremy.

"His pulse is a little weak, but he'll be all right. Has he stirred at all?"

"He spoke to me, just before you arrived."

"Good. Then it's probably that nasty cut on his forehead and the pain that makes him faint."

A man dressed in nightclothes came running up the lane. "I heard the commotion. Is he all right? What happened?"

"Can you help me carry him upstairs?" Michael asked the man.

They lifted Jeremy from her lap. Abigail sat for a

moment, trying to catch her breath. Mrs. Latham came to her side. "How did you get to Michael so fast?"

"I didn't. I was just up the road when he came riding toward the house. I didn't know it was he but called out. He told me that when his butler told him a red-haired girl had been frantic to find him, he knew to come here, somehow." Mrs. Latham hugged her. "Come inside, Abigail."

Abigail rose, but suddenly the ground swirled and everything went black.

Abigail woke to find herself in Sir Bentley's bedroom once again. Michael sat beside her. She tried to rise, but the dizziness caught her again. "How is he?" she asked weakly.

"He'll be fine, though he'll ache for a time," Michael answered. "His ankle will heal in a few weeks, and I stitched the cut, which looked worse than it was. The question is, How are you? This is not your first episode of dizziness, is it?"

"No . . ." She hadn't thought of it in any pattern . . .

"Tell me. Have you been sick to your stomach? Especially in the mornings? Sometimes at night?"

"Yes . . ."

"No appetite, then ravenously hungry?"

"Yes, but I thought it was—" Abigail stopped and thought. She had been so miserable that she hadn't even thought that her monthly flow had not come on— "Am I . . ."

Michael began to laugh as he watched her face and neck turn almost as red as her hair.

"Michael . . . how can you laugh when I'm . . ."

"I can laugh because there's a man *screaming* one thing *over* and *over* in the next room." Michael laughed so hard that he couldn't speak and Abigail watched as he wiped the tears from his eyes. "Even when I was stitching him, he kept saying between moans of pain, 'Michael, if you're my friend, get her to set the damn wedding date!'"

Abigail herself began to laugh, for she remembered he'd said the same thing outside when he was barely conscious.

A gale of laughter swept through Michael again. "Now, my dear Abigail, I think you'll have to . . . and quickly, for propriety's sake, of course."

"May I see him?" Abigail asked as she slowly rose. The dizziness had subsided.

"Can I stop you, is a better question."

Abigail lay beside Jeremy, who was bandaged, stitched, and wrapped. "Jeremy," she said as she stroked his head, "what will they do when they find Levi?"

"I don't know. But I don't think he'll be found."

"Why do you say that? You don't mean that he harmed himself—"

"No, no dearest," he said and tried to swing his arm around her. "Ouch . . . I think that he's probably on a ship ready to go out to sea."

"Aye . . . he always wanted to sail. . . . Are you going to tell the sheriff that?"

"Tell him what?"

"Oh, Jeremy." She hugged him gently, but still he winced. Tears filled her eyes. "How can you find it in your heart to forgive him? He was going to kill you . . ."

"I've finally decided that forgiving is not up to me. Not for Levi, or Damon. I think we have enough to worry about with just the *three* of us, don't you? To say nothing of Jane, Nathan, Baby Sarah, Mrs. Latham . . . it wearies me to go on!"

"Are you really happy about the baby?" she asked again.

"More than happy. I'm elated. Couldn't have been a better time!"

"Why? Oh, the wedding date."

He grinned then grimaced with pain. "That too," he sighed. "But I think, with my condition, and yours, we might as well be accomplishing *something* constructive!"

"What? . . . Oh!" Abigail realized what he meant. She blushed despite herself. "Michael told me I'd be feeling very well as soon as the morning sickness passed. Do you think we may hope the same for you?"

"I think you may count on it."

"Jeremy. You still haven't quit your job!"

"Ah, but I did. Last week. Lucky for you that you're marrying into a family of the 'better sort.' That means you may sell the shop and close down the paper—"

Abigail darted upright, accidently poking Jeremy in his ribs. He cried out in pain. "I'm sorry—I mean for hurting your side. But I have no intention of not publishing my paper—"

Jeremy bit his lip to keep from laughing. "That settles it, then."

Abigail stared at him with alarm. She couldn't stand the thought of another battle. Perhaps they were never meant to marry—

"Oh, do stop frowning. It makes you look—"

"Unattractive?"

"No. Far too enticing for my condition. Do you want to know what I meant before by 'that settles it'?"

"Yes, of course. I will not give up my paper, Jeremy! I thought you understood that."

"I do. And the way you write those seditious, libelous, and slanderous essays, I shall devote my entire law career to trying to keep you, and the likes of you, out of jail!" He began to laugh again. His wince made Abigail laugh despite herself. She leaned toward him carefully and kissed the tip of his fine nose.

"Agreed?" he asked.

"Agreed!"

He frowned. "Well then. When are you going to set the damn date?!"

"Oh, let me see . . . how about day after tomorrow?"

"Are you serious? Where will we be married?" She didn't answer. Was she teasing? "In my bedroom?" he asked seriously.

"Why not?" Abigail asked. "If we wait until you are healed enough to stand before a minister, your worst fear will be realized."

"And what is that?" he asked quite seriously.

"You will be marrying a *genuine* old maid!" she laughed. "Remember?"

"Yes, I do. And what would be even worse is a

genuine old maid with a stomach out to here," he gestured. "Day after tomorrow. What a relief. I think I'll sleep until then! Good night, my lovely Abigail."

Abigail leaned back against the pillow. She knew he was pretending, but she needed to think. They had been making light after such a frightening time, but she knew that neither of them would ever forget the horror their brothers had brought to their lives. Damon was long dead. Abigail asked God to watch over her brother, Levi, and to help him heal himself. She touched her stomach, knowing that she would soon feel the life inside her. If the Lord could create miracles like that, perhaps he could heal a soul or two along the way. She was lying next to Jeremy and they would be married the day after tomorrow. If that were so, then *anything* was possible!

"Jeremy," she whispered, wanting to share her thought. "Jeremy?" She turned to him. He was fast asleep. Abigail carefully curled against him. He didn't stir or wince. She rested her head on his shoulder and closed her eyes . . . she had so much to think about . . . she yawned and felt her eyes grow heavy . . .

When Jane opened the door to look in on them, she saw them sleeping like two babies. She turned to Mrs. Latham and patted her hand. "Well. At least they're not fighting . . . we'll see how long *that* lasts!" she whispered and closed the door again.

# AUTHOR'S NOTE

On the night of August 26, 1765, when Abigail and Jeremy were happily reunited in *Daughter of Liberty*, history tells us that Lieutenant Governor Thomas Hutchinson did not meet an equally happy fate. For that night, twelve days after the attack upon Andrew Oliver's building and home, McIntosh and his mob descended upon Hutchinson's house. McIntosh and his mob made the destruction on the night of August 14 look like child's play by the time they completed their obliteration of Hutchinson's home. They destroyed anything they could and stole cash, clothing, and silverware. All of Hutchinson's papers were lost in this ravage as well. It was only the ensuing daylight that ended their zealous night of ruin.

There are historians who claim that the "Loyal Nine" had instigated the attack. Others claim that McIntosh and his mob acted independently in this mission. There is no conclusive evidence to support either claim, but my readings led me to believe that while the "Loyal Nine" may not have intended the pillage of Hutchinson's home, they had most probably known of the impending attack and had given orders for it or at least tacit approval.

Whatever the case, the rage and destruction of that night alarmed the "better sort" of Boston's citizens.

For regardless of initial intent, all agreed that the mob had gotten out of control and that rather than being actors in the rebellion against the Stamp Act, McIntosh and his followers had become its directors. A town meeting was held and the action was condemned and disavowed, although it is probable that many who participated in the devastation were at the town meeting.

McIntosh was arrested, and the militia was called to patrol the streets. It was rumored that unless McIntosh was released, militia or not, the custom-house would be destroyed. McIntosh was released. No one was ever tried or punished for the ruin of Hutchinson's property. *But* from that night onward, the leaders of the Rebellion firmly reestablished their control. Furthermore, their message had been made clear to Governor Bernard and to Parliament.

On February 22, 1766, Parliament repealed the Stamp Act. The riots in Boston were but *one* of the many significant moments that led to this repeal. For those who wish to learn the full story I suggest that they refer to some fine sources listed under *Acknowledgments*. As we all know, this was not the *end*, but the *beginning*, which would culminate in the Declaration of Independence ten years later. But the events in Boston in the summer of 1765 altered the minds and hearts of those who were and would be known as the great Patriots. For the night of August 26, 1765, had taught all of the colonial leaders a lesson they were not soon to forget.

## Author's Biography

Johanna Hill is a former history teacher. She lives and writes in Manhattan and travels extensively.

# HISTORICAL ROMANCES

## Next Month From Tapestry Romances

MASQUERADE
by Catherine Lyndell
BANNER O'BRIEN
by Linda Lael Miller

POCKET BOOKS

# Home delivery from Pocket Books

Here's your opportunity to have fabulous bestsellers delivered right to you. Our free catalog is filled to the brim with the newest titles plus the finest in mysteries, science fiction, westerns, cookbooks, romances, biographies, health, psychology, humor—every subject under the sun. Order this today and a world of pleasure will arrive at your door.

**POCKET BOOKS, Department ORD**
1230 Avenue of the Americas, New York, N.Y. 10020

---

Please send me a free Pocket Books catalog for home delivery

NAME _____

ADDRESS _____

CITY _____ STATE/ZIP _____

If you have friends who would like to order books at home, we'll send them a catalog too—

NAME _____

ADDRESS _____

CITY _____ STATE/ZIP _____

NAME _____

ADDRESS _____

CITY _____ STATE/ZIP _____

366

Printed in the United States
By Bookmasters